Her world ... *his rough* ... *better access.*

She swam in the mounting fire of his mouth caressing hers, teasing her, asking her to participate and join the scorching heat growing rapidly between them. Sarah trembled violently as his tongue moved slowly across her lower lip and then invited her to respond. It was almost as if he were teaching her how a man could pleasure his woman. Her arms tightened around his shoulders, her breath becoming ragged. Ethan pulled her tightly to him, no space left between their straining bodies. She arched fully against him, wanting more, much more. His fingers trailed tiny fires down across her cheek, framing her face so that he could take her deeper. The last vestiges of her fear dissolved.

Dear Reader,

Risk Taker is about Chief Warrant Officer 4 Sarah Benson, U.S. Army. She pilots a Medevac Black Hawk helicopter and rescues wounded military men on the ground in Afghanistan. She is fierce in her commitment to these men, yet stands apart from them. When U.S. Navy SEAL Ethan Quinn steps onto the scene, Sarah's life changes. Ethan sees beneath her mask.

Creating this two-book series (*Degree of Risk* to follow in March 2014 in the Harlequin Romantic Suspense line) has been a special joy. I couldn't have done it without three men who were in my life almost constantly on these two books. For all things SEAL, I'm indebted to Chief Michael Jaco, U.S. Navy SEAL, retired, who helped make the heroic warriors you find in these pages as factual and real as possible.

For all things helicopter-flight related, I turned to my U.S. Air Force helicopter pilot consultant, Bill Marcontell, Captain, USAF, retired, who helped make the helo scenes accurate and breathtaking. Bill, your kindness, sense of humor and heart make it a joy to work with you.

The beautiful poetry you find in this book was written by Darius Gottlieb, poet extraordinaire. Without his generous contribution, *Risk Taker* wouldn't be what it is right now—a powerfully moving love story.

I hope you enjoy reading *Risk Taker* as much as I did creating it. Love always finds a way....

Connect with me at www.lindsaymckenna.com.

Lindsay McKenna

RISK
TAKER

—

Lindsay McKenna

H HARLEQUIN® ROMANTIC SUSPENSE

Recycling programs
for this product may
not exist in your area.

ISBN-13: 978-0-373-27857-2

RISK TAKER

Printed in U.S.A.

HARLEQUIN®
www.Harlequin.com

Books by Lindsay McKenna

Harlequin Romantic Suspense

ΩHis Duty to Protect #1691
ΩBeyond Valor #1739
Course of Action #1775
   "Out of Harm's Way"
‡Risk Taker #1787

Silhouette Romantic Suspense

Love Me Before Dawn #44
^Protecting His Own #1184
Mission: Christmas #1535
   "The Christmas Wild Bunch"
ΩHis Woman in Command #1599
ΩOperation: Forbidden #1647

Silhouette Nocturne

*Unforgiven #1
*Dark Truth #20
*The Quest #33
Time Raiders: The Seeker #69
*Reunion #85
*The Adversary #87
*Guardian #89

^Morgan's Mercenaries
ΩBlack Jaguar Squadron
*Warriors for the Light
‡Shadow Warriors

Harlequin HQN

Enemy Mine
Silent Witness
Beyond the Limit
Heart of the Storm
Dangerous Prey
Shadows from the Past
Deadly Identity
Deadly Silence
The Last Cowboy
The Wrangler
The Defender

Other titles by this author
available in ebook format.

LINDSAY MCKENNA

is proud to have served her country in the U.S. Navy as an aerographer's mate third class—also known as a weather forecaster. She was a pioneer in the military romance sub-genre and loves to combine heart-pounding action with soulful and poignant romance. True to her military roots, she is the originator of the long-running and reader-favorite Morgan's Mercenaries series. She does extensive hands-on research, including flying in aircraft such as a P3-B Orion sub-hunter and a B-52 bomber. She was the first romance writer to sign her books in the Pentagon bookstore. Today, she has created a new military romantic suspense series, Shadow Warriors, which features romantic and action-packed tales about U.S. Navy SEALs. Visit her online at

www.lindsaymckenna.com
www.twitter.com/lindsaymckenna
www.facebook.com/eileen.nauman

Chief Michael Jaco, U.S. Navy SEAL, retired, thank you for all unclassified SEAL info you've imparted to me. *The Intuitive Warrior* by Michael Jaco, www.michaeljaco.com

Bill Marcontell, Captain, USAF, retired, who flew Search and Rescue helicopters for the 38th ARRS in Southeast Asia in 1966-67. Thank you for information involving anything and everything that has to do with helicopters, their flight and their issues.

Darius Gottlieb, poet extraordinaire, who was kind enough to allow me permission to use "As Long As I Breathe, I Will Seek the Diamond of Your Heart" and "A Love Poem to Sarah by Ethan" in this novel. "Love Poems and Other Elixirs" by Darius Gottlieb, www.poetphotos.com

Chapter 1

They called her Blue Eyes.

Ethan Quinn, a Navy SEAL, turned the ice-cold beer around in his hands as he sat diagonally across the canteen from her. The place was noisy, filled with laughter and with mostly military black ops types. Some were Special Forces, Marine Force Recons, Rangers, CIA spooks, Delta Force or SEALs. There were a couple of tables of Night Stalker pilots in one corner, guzzling beer down like it was their last day on earth. A group of women Apache pilots from the Black Jaguar Squadron at FOB Bravo had a table off in another dark corner. They were drinking beer and chatting among themselves, ignoring the testosterone at the bar looking longingly in their direction.

Ethan had been warned by his SEAL buddies from

the platoon stationed at the forward operating base that Blue Eyes shot down every red-blooded American male who tried to sit at her table. Hell, he couldn't blame any of them for trying. She wasn't what Ethan would call model beautiful. No, but she had a square face with wide cheekbones, a sinner's mouth that would beckon to any man and those incredibly beautiful, large blue eyes. He liked the way her shining black hair lay around her shoulders, somewhat mussed, not perfect, but perfect for her.

It didn't hurt that Blue Eyes was about five feet nine inches tall and curvy as hell. They said she was always in her Army flight uniform, a drab green, when she came in off a medevac mission and ordered a beer. She always sat at the same small wooden table near a wall, where the light wasn't so bright. Where she could hide? Ethan wondered.

Someone else had told him over at the SEALs HQ that Blue Eyes was single. How they knew that, Ethan couldn't fathom. No one in the military wore rings on their fingers since it was against the rules. A ring could cause you to lose a finger under the right circumstances. He snorted softly to himself as he lifted the beer to his lips and drank deeply of the cold, bubbling liquid.

Some sex-starved jerk must have spread the word that she was single because he'd wanted her to be single. Not that Ethan knew anything one way or another about her. Base gossip had buzzed among the competitive Delta Force operators. They were betting which one of them would get to her first. Ethan had declined to join the bet. Women weren't pieces of meat to be sold to the highest bidder.

He felt sorry for her, being the center of so much male attention and curiosity. How would he feel under a constant spotlight like that? Blue Eyes often sat with the Black Jaguar Squadron women pilots, but not today. The women, he'd found, usually stuck together, such a small percentage versus the thousand men who worked at Camp Bravo. Talk had spread that when Blue Eyes had bad missions, she sat by herself, wanting to be left alone.

He tipped his head slightly forward so he could watch her without her seeing him stare blatantly at her. What was it about Blue Eyes that set fire to the male imagination? She did look sad. Her full mouth was slightly pursed, the corners drawn in, as if she was experiencing pain of some kind. Even in the poor light of the naked bulbs strung overhead in the canteen, he could see the breath-stealing color of her eyes.

The color reminded Ethan of the calved glaciers up in Alaska where he was born. When a glacier split and fell into a bay, the light pierced through the newly created sections, revealing a translucent turquoise blue. It was the most unearthly color he'd ever seen in his life. And now, through his short lashes, he was staring at eyes that were the same remarkable color. They were absolutely mesmerizing. No wonder guys hit on her. What would he do if he really saw her, up close and personal? Judging from the stories circulating among the SEAL platoon, guys were rendered speechless and stood like stunned, hormone-ridden teenagers before her.

Her gaze looked far-off as her slender hands held the can of beer. Sometimes she'd move her thumb, pushing beads of condensation away. What was she thinking about? Where was she? Ethan could see she was completely oblivious to the milling group of men surrounding the bar. They all watched her like hungry predatory animals on the hunt. Every last damn one of 'em. The flight suit didn't exactly spell out her lush body. Though Ethan figured he'd have to be dead not to see the way the green folds curved here and there, giving hints to her hidden assets.

She seemed lonely to him. He found himself holding his breath for a moment as she tipped the beer up and her full lips touched the edge of the can. Two things made him go hot. First, that full mouth of hers, the lower lip slightly pouty. Second, her grace as she tipped her head back, revealing the long, slender column of her throat. His juices were definitely going—and he wasn't alone.

Ethan laughed to himself. Women in combat were okay with him. They'd more than earned their stripes in battles across the Middle East, long ago proving they could get the job done. But there was just a damned demarcation line drawn between males and females. And he couldn't fully explain the pleasure of simply watching a woman move. It was magic. It was hypnotic. It was…well, hell, there were way too many lonely men, married or otherwise, at this FOB. Women were a dif-

ferent energy, different anatomy, different in the best of
ways that just hooked a man's full, undivided attention.

Ethan couldn't sit there and admit he wasn't attracted
to her. He was. But so was his heart. This wasn't just
about sex. Sex would be great. But there were deeper
layers to Blue Eyes that he wanted to explore, ones that
had nothing directly to do with sex. Maybe he was curious. Or infatuated like every other dude on the FOB.

He'd arrived at Camp Bravo last week as a strap-
hanger, a SEAL from another platoon who replaced a
man who had been badly injured. Charlie Platoon lost
their radio comms guy. Ethan's specialty was just that.
Patrols always wanted someone who knew how to work
the radios, the laptop, the connections with Apaches.
He was JTAC trained and able to talk to the loitering
F-18 Hornets and B-52s on racetracks that circled forty
thousand feet above them. Because when a crisis happened, it was the comms SEAL that saved the collective ass of the team out on a mission.

"Hey, Ethan. How's it goin', bro?"

Ethan looked up to see his LPO, lead petty officer,
Derek Tolleson. He walked over and pulled a chair up
at his table, a beer in hand.

"Okay. Just trying to get this damn sand out of my
throat."

Tall, blond-haired and blue-eyed Tolleson chuckled. "Yeah, man, I know what you mean," he said as
he sat down. He tipped his beer back and drank half of
it. Tolleson wiped his hand across his mouth and then
rubbed his unruly beard. "Thank God they let us have

beer out here." He shook his head. "Don't know what I'd do if they didn't."

SEALs were beer drinkers, pure and simple. Ethan smiled a little and took another sip.

"You just got here a few days ago—did you meet Blue Eyes yet?"

"I heard some of the guys talkin' about her last week," Ethan admitted. He turned and looked over at Tolleson, who was in his SEAL cammies, wearing a SIG pistol in a drop holster on his right thigh.

"I'd say you picked the perfect place to look without touching." He chuckled. "Nice stealth move."

"She's good-lookin'. You've got to admit that."

"I've been here three months, and that's the table she always sits at when she's not over at the Apache women pilot's table. Probably had a bad mission today and not up for chatting. Or at least that's the scuttle-butt I hear about why she sits alone." He ruffled his fingers through his short, sweaty hair. "What gets me is she looks so damned sad. Like she's going to cry or something."

"Who knows her around here?"

Shrugging, Tolleson moved the can around and around in his large hand. "She's attached to the mede-vac squadron. Flies a Black Hawk helicopter."

"Pilot or copilot?"

"I heard she's a chief warrant officer and a pilot in command. Why?"

Ethan drawled, "Well, I'm single, and if scuttlebutt is true, she's single. I'd like to meet her, warrant or not." Ethan was a first-class petty officer and warrants were out of his pay grade. They weren't supposed to fraternize per military law, but that had never stopped him before. He took a sip of beer and wiped his mouth. He needed to trim his beard because it was getting too long.

Snorting, Tolleson said, "You and the thousand other dudes here. I'm married, so I'm not interested."

"I was thinking of going over to her squadron at Ops and snooping around, getting some dope on her. Find out if she's really single or not."

"She'd see you comin' a mile away, bro. A SEAL snooping around Ops? You don't fly—you hitch rides. And she'd know in a heartbeat if you were scheduled out there on a patrol with a banana or not."

A banana was the odd-looking CH-47 Chinook helicopter, their main air transportation around Afghanistan. Ethan finished off his beer. "You're right. I'll probably just keep a tab on her here and see what gels over time. I have a lot of patience."

"Uh-oh," Tolleson muttered, gesturing toward Blue Eyes's table. "There goes a Delta dude thinkin' she's gonna swoon when he walks over to her table to dazzle her with his one-liners."

Ethan watched as a tall, muscular red-haired Delta operator strutted toward Blue Eyes's table. He had on all his gear, probably just came off an op like they had. It was the arrogance in his walk, which was typical for a Delta type, meant to impress her. Ethan had a hunch it wasn't going to do anything except piss her off.

Ethan leaned toward Tolleson. "What does she do when this happens? Shoot the dude in the balls?"

Tolleson laughed. "No, but close. She has a black

belt in karate. I heard one time a CIA case agent invited himself to her table. He sat down, and she told him to leave. He didn't. She warned him that if he didn't go on his own accord, she was going to throw him out of the chair he was sitting in."

Ethan grinned. "And?"

"She threw his sorry ass about five feet away and he landed on the floor, his pride hurt." He grinned. "Blue Eyes might look sweet and sad, but she packs a punch, so be warned."

Ethan didn't think he'd try that ploy on her. The whole bar quieted as the Delta dude swaggered to a halt in front of her. He gave her a big grin and put his hands on his hips. Ethan was amazed at how everything went silent in the canteen; all eyes were riveted on the confrontation.

"Sweet cheeks, what do you say I buy you a beer? You look like you need another round."

Ethan rolled his eyes. Women hated lines. Not that he hadn't thrown a few at them, too, but it almost always backfired. Judging from the narrowing of Blue Eyes's gaze, Delta's line was about as popular as a fart in a sleeping bag.

"No, thank you."

Delta shook his head. "Come on, honey. Just one for the road? I'll buy." He gave her a leering grin.

"Here it comes," Tolleson warned him in a whisper.

Blue Eyes's relaxed face went hard. Military hard. And those wide, gorgeous eyes of hers narrowed even more and became laser intense on Delta. Her luscious mouth curled into a slight sneer, and Ethan knew she wasn't going to sit still for this kind of macho nonsense.

"I really don't want to embarrass you in front of your guys, Captain, so why don't you leave while you can? That way, your pride will remain intact."

Delta jerked his head, mouth opening and then snapping shut. His eyes rounded, as if stunned by her response. His cheeks colored, and he started breathing hard, angry. "Who the hell do you think you are, bitch? I was being nice was all."

She gave him a cool, cutting smile. "Get over yourself. You black ops types are all alike. You think you're God's direct gift to women. I got news for you—you aren't."

Her voice was low and controlled. Ethan looked up toward the bar to see three other Delta operators watching and frowning. Would they be as stupid as he thought they were going to be? Jump into this little tempest in a teapot? And then, sure enough, all three of them started toward her table, as if on cue.

"Dammit," Ethan breathed, standing. All he'd wanted was an ice-cold beer and to sit and recharge after a fourteen-hour ball-busting patrol in the more than one-hundred-degree heat in that furnace of a desert. Not get into a fight with other operators.

"Yeah," Tolleson growled, following him. "Good odds for SEALs…"

They walked across the plywood floor and met the three Delta operators, stopping them before they could reach Blue Eyes's table.

Ethan confronted them. "Hey, guys, let's ramp this down, shall we?"

"Get the hell outta our way, tadpole," the tallest operator snarled.

Tolleson held up his hand. "Hey, come on. Name callin' isn't gonna help resolve this situation."

The big blond Delta operator sneered. "Why don't you two frogs go back to your friggin' lily pad and sit this one out? You weren't invited to this party."

Ethan glared at them. SEALs were a pretty laid-back group, generally speaking. They didn't strut around like roosters in a hen yard. They were night shadows, kept a low profile. They didn't start fights, but they sure as hell finished them. "Since when," he asked, raising his voice so everyone in the canteen could hear him, "does it take four Delta guys to pick on one Black Hawk pilot who just happens to be a woman?"

All three Delta operators colored with embarrassment as jeers, hoots and insults erupted from the rest of the men and women in the crowded canteen. They threw their middle fingers up in the air in response. The catcalls increased in volume.

Tolleson tried to calm them down. "Look, take a time-out, okay? The lady doesn't want company, so leave her alone."

Ethan looked like he was casually standing in front of the three Delta guys, who were now angry. But looks were deceiving. There was a commotion behind him. He turned to see if Blue Eyes was in distress.

"Why don't all you boys grow up?" Blue Eyes

snarled as she halted and glared at them. "You're an embarrassment to the human race!"

With that, Blue Eyes spun around on her booted heel and marched angrily out the door.

More hoots, hollers and laughter broke out. The Delta dude who'd tried to pick up Blue Eyes brushed by them and went back to the bar with his buddies. Ethan looked sheepishly over at Tolleson and shrugged his shoulders.

Ethan ambled back to their table. Tolleson was grinning.

"A little excitement," he said, sitting down.

"We get enough excitement out on patrols without this," Ethan muttered. He pulled his black baseball cap out of his pocket and settled it on his head. "Later. I'm off to the showers to get this grit off my skin."

Tolleson tipped the chair back, still smiling. "I'm right behind you. I'll bet Blue Eyes thinks you're a knight in shining armor, coming to her rescue. You were the first dude to stand up to stop those Delta guys."

Snorting, Ethan shook his head. "Doubtful. She lumped all of us into that comment. Or did you not get that?" Judging from her demeanor and coolness under fire with the Delta guys, she didn't need any hero to protect her. Nope, she was a Black Hawk driver and she risked her life, day in and day out, landing in hot landing zones, RPGs being thrown at her helo, to rescue wounded men or women who desperately needed medical help or would die in the battlefield. If anyone was a hero…it was her. "Later," he murmured to Tolleson.

"We got mission planning at 0800 tomorrow," the LPO reminded him.

"I'll be there with bells on," Ethan growled, sauntering out into the bright sunlight. The canteen was in the center of Camp Bravo. To his left, Ops and the runway. He heard a C-130's whistling engines as it came in for a landing. The smell of kerosene aviation fuel used by the helicopters was everywhere; the wind carried it in his direction. Overhead, the June Afghan sun bore down on him like a heat lamp out of control. Already Ethan was starting to sweat again. The eight-thousand-foot mountain where the FOB was located was dry and freakin' burning up under the heat. He was from Anchorage, Alaska—he loved the cold and hated desert infernos.

Ethan quickly walked down the avenues of camouflage tents sitting on concrete blocks with plywood floors. The dirt was fine and dusty and got into every crack, pore and crevice that a human being owned, not to mention his M4 rifle and the SIG pistol he always wore.

The sky was a light blue as he walked alertly down several other avenues, heading for the showers. There were only forty SEALs on this black ops FOB. They were a small but mighty contingent on this 24/7 base.

He turned down toward the main supply building, an area clear of tents and a shortcut to the men's showers.

"You sonofabitch! Get *off* me!"

Ethan wheeled around toward the woman's angry voice. His eyes widened when he saw Blue Eyes down in the dirt with an enlisted Army sergeant on top of her, groping at her flight suit. The sergeant's big hand reached down and ripped open the front of her uniform. He held her down with his other hand, fingers closing around her throat.

Blue Eyes weighed a good hundred pounds less than the guy, but, as Ethan ran swiftly and silently up behind him, she was giving a damned good account of herself. The man's nose was broken and bleeding, and he sported a black eye. SEALs made a living out of being shadows. With one swift movement of his fist, he coldcocked the unknown assailant in his left temple. The man went flying off her, knocked unconscious.

Ethan turned. "You okay?" he asked, kneeling down. She had blood on her cheek, and her nose was bleeding heavily.

"That stupid bastard," she breathed angrily, trying to pull her torn uniform closed at her neck.

Her eyes were blue fury. Ethan glanced over his shoulder—the stranger was out cold. "He won't bother you again," he murmured, giving her a concerned look. Her hair was dirty, and blood ran down her lips and dripped off her chin. Digging out the dark green bandanna he always wore when out on patrol, he said apologetically, "It's dirty, but maybe you can use it to stop your nose from bleeding?"

She gave him a mutinous look, grabbed it and pressed it against her nose. "Thanks," she mumbled, rolling over to her hand and knees.

"Are you hurt? Can I get you over to the dispensary?" Ethan held out his hand, but she refused it.

"I'm all right!" She tried to rise, but her knees buckled beneath her.

Ethan moved swiftly, catching her before she hit the ground again. "Okay, look," he coaxed in a low, even voice. "You aren't in any shape to be going anywhere just yet. Did he hit you?" Dumb question: he could see she'd been struck. He was trying to talk her down so she'd become reasonable.

"Hell, yes, he hit me!" She glared up at him, breathing hard, gripping her uniform closed so he couldn't see her bra beneath it.

"Where?" Ethan asked quietly, as if he were talking to a fractious horse he was trying to settle down. He knelt near but kept his hands off her. He didn't want a broken nose.

"The head. He jumped me from behind, the sonofabitch!" She glared over at his unmoving body.

Ethan looked at her dust-covered brow and noticed swelling on her right temple. "He tried to knock you out."

"Ya think?"

Ethan nodded, knowing Blue Eyes was in shock. Her hand trembled, and there were tears in her eyes. "Well, he won't do it again," he promised her. Assaulting any officer was a major offense, and the man would be going up for court-martial.

"I hope you killed him. I wonder how many other military women he's stalked and jumped and then raped?" Her lower lip quivered with fury as she looked accusingly up at him.

Ethan saw Tolleson coming with a set of towels, a washcloth and soap in hand. He gestured sharply for him to get his ass over there pronto.

Tolleson skidded to a stop, his eyes widening as he looked down at them and then at the unconscious man. "What the hell happened?"

"The guy jumped Blue Eyes—I mean…" Ethan gave her an apologetic look, making a point of looking at the last name embroidered in black across the top of the left pocket of her flight uniform, "Chief Warrant Officer Benson."

Tolleson nodded, stepped back and pulled a radio out of his cammie pocket. He called the military police and gave them their location. He looked down. "Do you need medical help, Chief Benson?"

"Hell, no! I just want to get out of here and get back to my tent." She looked down at her dusty uniform.

Ethan felt sorry for her. She was angry and upset. He could see her tremble as adrenaline raced through her bloodstream. "I can walk you to your tent, Chief Benson. Tell me what you need?" She seemed to calm a little beneath his quiet tone. Tears splattered down her cheeks, making trails through the dust.

"Just help me up, will you? I need to get to my tent and get cleaned up." She reluctantly held her hand out toward him.

Ethan stood up and wrapped his fingers around hers, gently pulling her to her feet. She wobbled on unsteady knees. Her attacker had nearly knocked her out. A dark fury moved through Ethan. Delta Dude and his team had remained in the canteen. Had this Army sergeant been waiting for the first woman who walked by to attack her? Had Blue Eyes been at the wrong place at the wrong time?

Ethan cupped her left elbow. "Come on," he urged her quietly. "I'll take you to your tent. Just give me directions." He felt a shift, as if his whole life was about to change.

Chapter 2

Sarah felt her knees going. Again. God, why couldn't she just tough this one out? The SEAL who had intervened and saved her hide swiftly reacted. In seconds, he'd picked her up and brought her into his arms.

"Put me down," she ordered angrily.

"Can't do it, ma'am. I'm taking you to the medical dispensary."

Ethan's voice was low and firm. His arms were strong. Sarah closed her eyes, fighting the urge to simply surrender to him. The rage she felt over the attack was dissolving as the adrenaline slowly left her system. She was exhausted and, worse, weak. A feeling she hated more than anything.

"You can relax," Ethan told her, his lips near her hair.

"There's a time to fight and a time to take a step back and reassess the situation."

Sarah also felt needy, which was so unlike her. His voice was soothing, and the anxiety rushing through her abated. He carried her easily, as if she were a feather, and yet Sarah knew she was no lightweight. As she held his green bandanna over her nose, the blood continued to leak out of her nostrils. Her nose burned like fire and her head throbbed.

She looked up at him. He glanced down at her. His beard, although well trimmed, made him look even more dangerous to her. His eyes were a light gray with large black pupils, like those of a raptor.

"Doing okay?" Ethan asked her in a conversational tone.

"I've had better days," Sarah muttered. She saw the corners of his mouth lift slightly. There was such tightly held tension in him. She'd seen him move so damn swiftly when he saw what was happening to her; it left her stunned. He was grace, tension and power all in one decisive action. "You're a SEAL?"

"Yeah." Ethan laughed to himself. He hid a part of himself from his SEAL brethren; he journaled and, sometimes, wrote poetry to express what he saw or experienced. It was a way to get his emotions out instead of always putting them in his kill box, which was what all his brothers did.

She saw his focus. He was carrying her through rows of tents, alert and missing nothing. Intense. That was the word she'd use for this SEAL. Slowly, Sarah reluctantly relaxed into his arms. He had a powerful chest and a broad set of shoulders that looked like he could carry the world on them. Even though his face was hard and nearly unreadable, she sensed kindness in him. Maybe it was his full mouth, now pursed, holding back feelings she couldn't even begin to decipher.

"You can put me down now. I'm okay."

Ethan smiled at her. "Not a chance."

"The pilots in my squadron will make fun of me. I really need to walk." And she hated pleading, but she added, "Please?"

His straight black brows dipped a little at her request. There was hesitation in his gray eyes. Sarah touched her aching throat where the bastard had gripped her and held her down.

"Tell you what," Ethan murmured. "If *any* of those Black Hawk drivers give you grief because I'm carrying you over to the dispensary, you let me know." He gave her a slight grin. "I'll settle it out with them privately and personally. Okay?"

Sarah sighed. "Are all SEALs stubborn?" She heard and felt him laugh.

"We're a hardheaded bunch, I suppose. I'd like to think we're focused and intense about our objective." And right now, he couldn't believe he was carrying Blue Eyes in his arms. He was in another kind of shock. A good kind, but he wasn't about to share his euphoria with her.

Ethan turned a corner and up ahead was the two-story dispensary that had been built out of cinder blocks. It wasn't very large, with only two Navy doctors and a small staff of two nurses and several combat medics manning it. When any serious medical issues came up, the person was flown directly to Bagram Air Base near Kabul.

"How are you feeling?" he asked, glancing down at her. She was very pale. Those beautiful blue eyes of hers were shadowed and frightened-looking.

"Whipped," Sarah admitted, feeling safe enough in his arms. She would never admit that to the male pilots she flew with. They'd call her weak once they found out what had just happened to her. And then they'd brutally tease her or tell her it was her fault, that she'd invited the attack. She hated that.

"I'm Ethan Quinn. What's your first name?"

She looked up and drowned in his soft gray eyes. Opening her lips and then closing them, Sarah felt an incredible sense of protection surrounding her. It was him. Reeling from the attack, she didn't have her normal defensive walls in place. "Sarah Benson."

He nodded. "My teammates call me Hawk." And then he smiled a little. "You have a beautiful name." *To go with your incredible blue eyes.* But he didn't add that, seeing her eyes widen as if in wonder for a moment. There was a definite connection between them. He could feel it. The sensation, whatever it was, was palpable and it felt damn good.

Ethan knew where the E.R. was located; he'd been there the other day with Tolleson, escorting another SEAL because he'd twisted the hell out of his ankle.

He walked up to the sliding doors, then waited as they opened. Inside, there were a number of military guys waiting for medical attention at the clinic. They looked up in unison at him as he entered the air-conditioned dispensary.

Moving through another entrance, Ethan carried Sarah directly into the E.R. area.

It contained four curtained cubicles. A Navy nurse at the nurse's station in the corner saw him arrive. She was older and had peppered hair of black and silver.

"Chief Benson needs medical attention right now," Ethan told the nurse. "Which cubicle can I put her in?"

Sarah felt his authority even though he spoke quietly to the nurse. The older woman quickly looked her over.

"Cubicle one, Petty Officer."

"One it is," Ethan said.

The nurse called for an orderly—a young man—and by the time Ethan had gently deposited Sarah onto the gurney, a woman doctor had arrived. He stood back, letting the medical team help Sarah.

"What happened?" Dr. Johnson asked Sarah.

Sarah told her, mumbling through the bandanna. The doctor scowled, then glanced over at the SEAL and asked, "Who is he?"

"Petty Officer Quinn. He broke up the attack," Sarah told her. "And he brought me over here. I'm not walking very well right now."

"I see." The doctor stared at Ethan. "You need to leave, Petty Officer. Thank you for your help."

"Yes, ma'am," Ethan murmured, starting for the opening in the curtain.

"Wait," Sarah called, gripping his arm as he passed her. She looked at him. "There's going to be an investigation. Can you tell the MPs where I am? I know they'll want my statement."

Seeing the exhaustion settling into her blue eyes, Ethan nodded. "Don't worry about anything. I'll tell them and get things in order so you don't get overwhelmed by the paper chase." He gave her a brief smile and felt her hand drop from his arm. His flesh tingled where her long fingers had curved around his biceps. Ethan saw something else in her eyes, something he couldn't translate. Her lower lip trembled as she took the bandanna away for a moment. He wanted to say to hell with it, slide his arms gently around her shoulders and just hold her. She needed that right now, and they both knew it. But it wasn't going to happen.

"I'll check in on you later," he promised.

Sarah nodded, pressing the bandanna back to her nose, which continued to bleed.

As he stepped out into the E.R., Ethan noticed two medics carrying in the Army guy he'd punched. The man was semiconscious, muttering and cursing. Ethan stopped and watched where they put the bastard. Lucky for him it was cubicle four, as far away from Sarah as he could get. Flexing his fist, his knuckles swelling and bruised, Ethan wondered if he should stay. Just in case the Army jerk started to make more trouble for everyone. He was sure the assailant didn't know he'd just brought Sarah in. The guy was ballistic in his opinion and not to be trusted.

Two Army MPs entered the E.R. Both had grim looks on their faces. They went directly to where the Army guy was being taken. Breathing a sigh of relief,

Ethan knew the MPs would stand guard over him. He felt better about leaving Sarah alone now. Tolleson had done his job and gotten security in motion.

To say that security was in chaos was a mild understatement when Ethan arrived at the single-story building. Four Army guys, probably friends of the assailant, argued heatedly with a Army lieutenant, with an MP armband on his left arm, outside the office. They didn't know he was the one who had decked their friend. He moved past them and went into the MP office. He spotted a young woman with red hair behind the desk. Ethan told her who he was and what had happened.

"You're the guy we want to see," she said, gesturing to an office on her right. "Lieutenant Taylor will want to take your statement. Can you tell me where Chief Benson is?"

"The E.R.," he told her. "She's pretty shaken up and she's been injured."

"I'm sorry to hear that," she said, leading him to the office and opening the door. "I'll go over in a while and interview her. I'm sure she's feeling pretty ragged at this point."

Ethan nodded. "Yeah, but the bastard that attacked her is feeling even worse." And he smiled a wolf smile.

"Well," Dr. Johnson told Sarah an hour later after examining her. "No permanent damage done, Chief Benson."

Sarah was sitting on the gurney. "That's good news. I have to fly tomorrow."

"No way," Johnson said. "I think you've suffered a

mild concussion even though the X-ray came back normal. I'm giving you a sick chit for four days without flight duty. Then you will come back and see me on the fourth day. The nurse will give you an appointment."

Stricken, Sarah slid off the gurney, her legs none too steady. Too fast a movement—her head began to throb. She touched the area where the man had struck her. "But…we're short-handed in our squadron, Dr. Johnson. I *can't* be put on flight waivers." She gave the Navy officer a pleading look.

"No can do, Chief Benson." Johnson handed her the chit, which would be given to her CO, Major Donaldson. "Rest," she ordered. "Go over and spend some time with the Apache gals. I know you women are tight with one another. Catch up on gossip. Write some emails home. Things that won't stress you out. Okay?"

Disheartened, Sarah glumly took the chit. *Dammit!* Angry at the Army sergeant who attacked her, she pursed her lips.

"Hop back up on that gurney. I want you to stay here for another half hour, and then we'll see how steady you are on your legs at that time. You're still not stable."

"Okay," Sarah muttered tiredly. Hell, she needed this like a hole in the head. They were already short two pilots, and medevacs were literally a lifeline to all the men out there hunting down the enemy.

Dr. Johnson gently patted the shoulder of her dusty uniform. "That SEAL was at the right place, right time." She smiled a little. "He really did some damage to the guy who attacked you."

"Yes," she whispered. "He came out of nowhere."

"Hope you get to thank him."

Nodding, Sarah said, "I will."

By the time Ethan got done with the process of the interview with the lieutenant, it was 1800, 6:00 p.m. He was starving, but he swung by the E.R. to see if Sarah was still there. She was gone, and no one would give him any information on her condition because he wasn't married to her or a family member. Undeterred, Ethan decided to walk over to Ops to see if he could find her.

The thunking noise of Apache helicopters warred with the shriek of the twin-rotor Chinooks as they all slowly trundled down the helo strip to take off, one after another. Ethan popped into the main Ops building and headed for the desk. There was an Air Force tech sergeant manning it.

"Hey, I'm looking for Chief Warrant Officer Sarah Benson. Can you tell me where I can find her?"

The man nodded. "The medevac squadron office is right over there, to your left. Major Donaldson is in charge. He can probably answer your question."

"Thanks," Ethan said. The door to the medevac office was open, and he stepped in. An Army major in his mid-forties with gold wings on his chest looked up. His gaze narrowed speculatively as Ethan came to a halt in front of him.

"I'm looking for Chief Warrant Officer Benson."

The man scowled, looking Ethan up and down. "Is it official business?" he demanded.

"No, sir, it isn't." Ethan could just about read the officer's mind, thinking he was chasing Sarah.

"She's not available," he snapped.

Okay, so plan B. "Thank you, sir." Ethan turned on his heel and left. Heading out of Ops, he found an Army driver standing near a Humvee. Drivers on the base knew the area like the backs of their hands. Ethan went over and asked what tent section the Black Hawk pilots were located in. The guy gave him specific directions, and Ethan took off, on the hunt.

The tents were all lined up on one dusty avenue, each one looking like the next. There were no names on any of them, and Ethan slowly walked down the road. A male pilot—a warrant officer—emerged from his tent. Ethan stopped him and asked about Sarah. Instantly, the pilot frowned. What was it about these Black Hawk drivers? They were all damned suspicious.

"I haven't seen her," he said abruptly.

"Look, she was in E.R. two hours ago. I'm just trying to find out how she's doing."

He squinted. "You the SEAL that saved her?"

Ethan nodded.

The pilot pointed to a tent down on the left. "That's her tent. But you know the regulations—no man is allowed inside a woman's tent."

"I know the regs," Ethan said.

"She's sleeping right now. I'd leave her alone." Ethan watched the pilot push by him, in a hurry, heading toward Ops with his helmet bag and kneeboard in hand. He was probably going on duty.

Ethan stared at Sarah's tent. Okay, it was a dead end. His stomach growled. Rubbing his belly, he decided to call it a day and head to the chow hall. He glanced down at his Rolex watch, knowing he'd already screwed the pooch by missing the 1700 hours mission briefing for the op they would go on later tonight.

Ethan decided to swing by SEAL HQ. Tolleson understood why he couldn't make the briefing, so there should be no recourse. Master Chief Gil Hunter wouldn't bust his ass, either.

As he walked, he couldn't stop thinking about Sarah. She'd felt good in his arms, and he'd thrilled at having her firm, soft body against his. Dragging in a deep breath, Ethan shook his head. He sure as hell had wanted to meet Blue Eyes, but not this way. Now she probably would lump all guys into one bin labeled "would-be rapists." And then she wouldn't allow him within ten feet of her.

Grimacing, Ethan flexed his right hand as pain drifted up from his swollen knuckles. He couldn't deny his satisfaction over decking the bastard. It was worth bruised knuckles for a week. More than anything, he wanted to connect once more with the mysterious, exotic Blue Eyes. But how to make it happen? SEALs were creative if nothing else. They were good at thinking outside the box. Work-arounds. Ethan grinned and took off for his tent in SEAL territory.

Chapter 3

When Sarah sat up on her cot the next morning, her head aching, she saw someone open the tent flap just enough for a crisp white envelope to slide beneath the fabric of the closed flaps. She recognized the back of Ethan Quinn's head. What was he doing there? What was the envelope? Did he go get her mail for her? The feelings over his act flooded her with warmth and confusion.

She needed coffee first. It would help tame her headache. She sat in a pair of long gray cotton gym pants and a red tank top. In case Bravo got hammered by Taliban, her flight boots, her .45 pistol in the holster, her Kevlar vest and her helmet bag were all stowed below her cot.

She was stiff and bruised. In fact, her knuckles were

black and blue where she'd struck her attacker in the nose. She moved her long fingers gingerly, and they felt stiff, too. Sighing, she went over to her hot plate and set a copper kettle on it to boil. Coffee consisted of a terrible instant variety, but it was better than nothing.

The envelope sitting on the plywood deck called to her. It resembled a greeting card more than a business letter. Once the teakettle whistled, she took it off the hot plate and poured the steamy water into a bright red mug twice the size of a normal coffee cup.

After stirring her coffee, Sarah pulled out a couple of old cinnamon rolls she'd taken from the chow hall yesterday morning. This would be breakfast. Outside, she could hear helos, both Apaches and Chinooks, spooling up, their engines sounding very different and distinct. She glanced at the watch on her wrist. Her lower arm, she noticed to her chagrin, was purple with bruising. It was 0600.

Scowling, she set the two dried-out cinnamon rolls on the small TV tray that doubled as her table. There wasn't much room in these tents and everything had to be squeezed in to fit. Leaning down, her back protesting, she scooped up the envelope. On it, in beautiful black ink calligraphy, was her name.

Ethan Quinn had delivered it. Was it from him? There was no return address. *Nothing.* After ambling back over to her table, she sat down in a camp chair and picked up her black coffee, sipping it gratefully. She then slipped her finger beneath the envelope, and it opened. Inside was thick papyrus paper that almost matched the color of her eyes. Something good flowed through her.

Sitting back, she opened up the folded paper. Inside was a poem written in beautiful calligraphy.

Sarah,

> *As Long as I Breathe, I Will Seek the*
> *Diamond of Your Heart*

It isn't enough for a poet to entertain;
I want also to connect—
There are precious few who ever get to view
Both the wildflowers and ornate lawns of your
garden...
(to be continued as poet gets time)

She smiled and felt her heart flutter. The letters were crisp and lovely to look at. Ethan had written this? Someone at this forward operating base was a *poet,* of all things? Ethan? He had delivered it. Or was this a sick joke by her squadron mates? Her mind revolved back to her medevac squadron, wondering if one of the guys was pulling a trick on her. For all she knew, someone could have stolen this from a real poet to make it look like he'd written it. Her heart told her Ethan had not only delivered but had written it.

Still, her fingertips tingled as she held the rich paper. The words, if she were honest, touched her deeply. She loved symbolism and saw it in just about everything in her life. Growing up, she'd found solace reading poetry.

Although she couldn't write a line of iambic pentameter to save her life. Intuitively, Sarah knew Ethan had written it even if he hadn't signed it.

She looked at the green metal locker in the corner of her tent. In it was her favorite book of poems, a small leather-bound volume by a Jewish American poet who wrote lush, drenching prose that made her heart sigh just as it did with this stanza of a poem Ethan had written for her.

Sarah felt oddly comforted by the words. Did Ethan see her as a garden filled with beautiful flowers? Was that his message? An invisible balm eased through her heart. Here she was, out in a war zone, getting shot at almost daily, and this beautiful poem arrived at the door of her tent. The title...well, that held her heart captive, too. Wouldn't any woman want the man of her dreams to whisper those words to her? That she was seen as a diamond, multifaceted, complex, having depth? Of course. Well, she would. Her experience with men had left her wary. To them, she was something to be lusted after. Something to be chased and caught and used.

Her lips drew into a soft smile as she reread the lines of the stanza. They made her feel good. An invisible touch from a potential lover? Snorting softly, she laid the envelope aside and picked at a cinnamon roll. She was such a sucker for stuff like this. A romantic idealist, which was not a good way to be. Her love life resembled the chaos of a bull hooking its horns around in a china shop, not the reverent beauty of the words contained in this poem.

As she sipped her coffee, Sarah felt a kind of mellowness invading her stiff limbs. Ethan's words *were* beautiful. And profound. And sensitive.

Shaking her head, she thought of the other sensitive guy at the FOB, Pascal, one of her medics who flew with her. She liked all the medics, truth be told. The rest of the pilots were thick as bricks, for the most part. All they saw when they looked at her was a body. Sarah was sick of being hit on by those Neanderthal types. She yearned for a deep conversation, flights of fantasy, someone who could join her on the magical carpet ride of her imagination and fly with her.

"Hey, Sarah? Are you in there?"

She started. "Aylin? Come on in. I'm home." Sarah grinned as the nearly six-foot Apache combat helicopter pilot pushed open the flaps.

"Hey, I'm checking up on you. We just got word over at Jaguar you got attacked yesterday afternoon. Are you all right?"

Sarah gestured for the Turkish pilot to sit down on the cot. "He got the worst of it," she said, glad to see her friend.

Aylin was in her flight suit and had her helmet bag and kneeboard in hand, which meant she was going to be flying soon. Her black hair was captured in a ponytail. Her golden eyes were slightly tilted, giving her an exotic look.

"Hmph," Aylin said, sitting down. "You look beat-up. What the hell happened?" Her friend sat down, placing her helmet bag next to her flight boots.

Sarah told her and saw anger leap into Aylin's eyes. She was a deadly woman in the air as well as on the ground. They were sisters in that they both carried a black belt in karate. But Aylin also knew Krav Maga, the Israeli Defense Forces self-defense system, which was especially deadly.

"Where's the bastard now?" Aylin gritted out, flexing her fists.

"They took him to Bagram. He's going to be held there for court-martial. Eventually, I'll have to fly in and testify."

"Too bad he isn't still here."

Sarah knew Aylin was good for her word. "I'm glad he's gone."

"You look tired."

"Very," she admitted.

"And you said a SEAL saved you?"

"Yes. God, did he ever move fast."

Aylin chuckled. "Black ops. Those boys haul ass."

"Where are you off to?" Sarah asked.

"Going to go with my wingwoman up toward the border," Aylin said in a bored tone. "The Pakistanis are throwing 105s across into Afghanistan and at some of our Army forward operating bases. We're supposed to fly in as a show of force." Her eyes narrowed, predator-like. "Frankly, I'd love to throw some Hellfire missiles into those sites that are sitting just a few meters inside the Pakistan border. It would only have to happen once and those cowards would stop. Of course, that would be an act of war. No one said war made sense, right?"

Laughing softly, Sarah agreed.

"Is there anything I can do for you, Sarah?"

"No. I've got four days to rest up."

Aylin's arched black brows rose. "Oh, good. You can join us tomorrow then. We've got a poker tournament starting up." She rubbed her hands together and grinned. "Going to be a big pot. Come and join us?"

"I'll come as your cheerleader. How's that? I'm not a very lucky person." She snorted and pointed to her face.

Aylin looked at her watch and stood up. "Okay, drop by if you feel like it and be my good luck charm, then. It starts at 1900 in the ready room. Gotta go, girlfriend." She picked up her bag and left.

The tent diminished in energy as The Turk, as they referred to Aylin, left. Sarah felt better having had some company. The Jaguar women pilots had embraced her wholeheartedly. Sarah finished the first cinnamon roll and picked up the second one.

It felt rather lovely to just sit and not have to be on the flight roster. She felt a little guilty about it since she knew some of the pilots were going to max out their flight hours every day because she was sidelined. They were missing two pilots who had been killed three weeks ago. A Taliban RPG had rocketed into their Black Hawk just as it had landed to pick up some wounded Special Forces operators. Everyone on board had died, the two pilots, an aircrew chief and a medic. It had been a huge and devastating loss to the squadron.

Sadness moved through Sarah. She'd lost her only male friend at Bravo on that ill-fated flight. Chief Warrant Officer Ted Bateman had been her age, twenty-nine, with three kids and a wife he loved very much. He was sensitive, someone she could confide in. There was never a time he wasn't respectful of her. Most important, he'd treated her as an equal.

Sarah quickly closed her eyes. Ted had been an incredible pilot—so damned passionate about his job—and she'd seen him fly into a firefight many times to rescue wounded men. Many of the pilots would not. Major Donaldson, who ran the squadron, never wanted to lose a multimillion-dollar Black Hawk. It would risk his yearly budget's bottom line. He would rant and rave during planning sessions about never risking the helo. The man or woman who was bleeding on the ground could wait until the firefight was over, and then they could fly in to safely pick them up.

Wiping her eyes, Sarah sniffed. She ached to have Ted around right now. If he'd found out she'd been assaulted and nearly raped, he'd be right there at her side. He had been a fierce advocate for her to be in the squadron. When Ted came into the squadron, the rest of the pilots didn't heckle her or play mean jokes on her as much. She wasn't a man, so in those pilots' eyes, she was defective. Ted always wanted to fly with her because, as he'd told her once, she had a set of invisible titanium balls. She'd laughed with him, shaking her head. He had always lifted her spirits and had been a role model of what a medevac pilot should be.

"Oh, Ted," she whispered. "I miss you so damned much...." Sarah had felt terribly vulnerable since his death. Three weeks ago, she'd penned a long letter to Ted's wife, Allison. He'd always called her Ali. Sarah had written between her tears, the words blurring as she poured out heartfelt words for Ali. She'd included a CD with the letter of all the photos she'd taken of Ted over the past three months they had flown together. Sarah closed her eyes and hoped that Ali would treasure the photos and that her words would help her bear her grief in some small way.

Making a grumpy sound, Sarah finished off her breakfast. She hated going to the chow hall precisely because she was usually the only female. Ted wasn't there anymore to escort her and keep the men from hitting on her. And all the Jaguar pilots were done eating and in the air. Sarah tried to eat with the Apache pilots every time she could.

After she pulled on a pair of tennis shoes, she put a towel and her weight lifting gloves into a small bag and got ready to go work out. It was 0700, and most of the guys would be out of the gym by now. Maybe some of the off-duty Apache women pilots would be over there. It would be nice to have some female company. Sarah worked out with them as often as she could.

Of late, she'd been pulling eight hours of flight time every day or night, the max any pilot could fly in a given twenty-four-hour period. There had been no downtime since the loss of the two pilots, and she knew she needed to work out. Sarah pulled on a loose T-shirt that had a black dragon snarling on the front of it. She always wore it in the hopes it would scare off any guy who thought about giving her a line and trying to pick her up. She put on her red cotton gym pants, pulled on her green baseball cap with the medevac squadron symbol on it and left her tent.

The morning was cold for June. She pressed the Velcro shut on her tent flaps and turned, appreciating the white clouds over the camp. Sarah hurried down the dusty street, heading for the gym, which was next to the medical dispensary. Her heart turned back to the poem given to her. It soothed the anxiety she always got when going someplace where there were more men than women.

Ethan was bench-pressing two hundred and fifty pounds at the end of his ten repetitions when he spotted Sarah Benson walking into the gym. He damn near lost his concentration. He'd never seen her in there before.

"Hey," Tolleson called. He was standing nearby as his spotter.

"I see her," Ethan breathed through his teeth, slowly lowering the huge barbell back into its metal cradle. Sweat was rolling off his face, his shoulders were strained and the muscles in his upper arms trembled. Ethan watched Sarah move like a shadow along the wall. There were about fifteen other men in the gym.

"Okay, rest," Tolleson told him, handing him a towel.

Ethan ducked out from beneath the barbell, sat up and wiped his sweaty face. He rested his elbows on his hard thighs. Like most of the men working out, they were naked except for a pair of gym shorts. There was a lot of grunting and straining going on. The gym smelled of male sweat and testosterone.

His heart beat a little faster as he saw Sarah walk over to the other side of the room, where dumbbells and the lighter weights were kept along the wall. Something a woman would probably want to work out with, he supposed. Damn, she was so graceful. He noticed the purple-and-blue bruises around her wrists. Anger stirred in him.

A number of the other men watched her, too. She probably felt like a piece of meat, all those eyes on her. He wouldn't like it, either.

"I'm taking five," Ethan told his LPO, wiping his face again, then throwing the towel over his shoulder.

Sarah felt Ethan's presence even though she never heard him approach. She'd just sat down on a bench with a ten-pound weight when Ethan appeared before her. He gave her a slight smile of hello and crouched down a few feet in front of her.

"Hey, how are you feeling today?"

Sarah felt heat race up her throat and into her face. The man had hardly any clothes on. Her eyes widened momentarily. "I didn't see you when I came in," she said, stiff and on guard. He was incredibly well built with powerful shoulders, dark hair across his chest and a line going down across his hard abs and disappearing beneath the waist of his dark blue gym shorts. Lean. He was built like a swimmer, and then she realized he was a frogman. So, yes, he did indeed have a swimmer's amazing body. Finding her voice, she said, "I woke up this morning stiff and figured an hour of working out will help me loosen up."

Ethan nodded, his heart contracting. "You have a helluva bruise on your temple. That's enough to give me a headache just looking at it." One corner of his mouth lifted. Her right eye was bruised and slightly swollen from the strike the bastard had given her. The bridge of her nose was also swollen. She had pulled her shining black hair into a ponytail, and he appreciated the clean, classic lines of her face, still beautiful even with her injuries.

"I took some aspirin and I've only got a mild headache now." She started repetitions with the weights, counting how many times for each arm. Panic seized her. He was a man. And he was so masculine that it triggered old memories. She almost asked him about the poem. If he had written it.

"What did the doc have to say? Are you all right?"

Sarah heard the care in his low, husky tone. She swore those gray eyes were looking straight through her. She felt off balance with him, yet she felt his protection, too. It was a crazy feeling, not one she had ever experienced before. Maybe SEALs exuded that kind of protectiveness toward others? She'd never met a SEAL before except to pick up wounded ones on the battlefield. Black ops tended to keep to themselves. It left her confused and wary.

"Just a lot of pretty bruises." She pointed to her wrist. "And my nose isn't broken, thank God. The doctor forced me off the flight roster for four days."

"Mmm," Ethan said, nodding. Sarah rarely met his eyes. She seemed shy, unlike the tigerlike demeanor he'd seen in action yesterday. He could see only fear in her eyes. *Why?* Ethan also wondered how she'd become a medevac pilot. They took risks every day out in the field and were considered aggressive pilots. "Did she think you might have a concussion?"

Sarah sat on the anxiety that bubbled just beneath

the surface and started counting again as she lifted the weight in her other hand. "Yes." She tilted her head and met his warm gray eyes. "How did you know? Are you a combat medic?"

Shaking his head, Ethan murmured, "This is my fourth rotation out here and you get used to seeing certain kinds of injuries. My specialty is comms—communication—not medicine." He hooked a thumb over his shoulder toward Tolleson, who was doing some bench-pressing in his absence. "He's my LPO. Tolleson is one of the combat medics in our platoon."

"I see." Sarah watched him for a moment. "I'm really ignorant about SEALs," she confided. Ethan was easy to talk to, and she didn't see lust in his eyes as he observed her. For whatever reason, she found herself tense, unused to a man treating her like this.

"How long you been here at Bravo?"

"Three months. Got six more to go before I get rotated stateside." Sarah wrinkled her nose. "I'll probably get four to six months home and then they're going to send me right back over here."

"How long you been flying?"

She frowned. "Joined the Army at twenty. I had two years of college under my belt and they wanted me to shoot for warrant officer status. My foster father, Hank, was an Army Black Hawk pilot during the Gulf War. I was lucky and got into their family when I was twelve years old. He'd take me flying in his helicopter duster. By the time I went into the Army, I had about five hundred hours of flight time, so the Army pushed me in that direction. I chose to become a medevac pilot."

"The Army doesn't like to waste talent," Ethan agreed. He had a tough time seeing her in the cockpit of a medevac. Those pilots were ballsy risk takers. Why was she looking at him like he was going to hit her? "You seem pretty laid-back for a medevac pilot."

Sarah shrugged and switched hands with the dumbbell. "I think the word you're looking for is *shy*. I'm a terrified introvert living in a world of in-your-face extroverts."

He chuckled, liking her dry sense of humor. "Nothing wrong with being an introvert." He shrugged. "I'm one, too."

"Could have fooled me." Sarah wiped the gathering perspiration off her brow with her towel. "You were the first guy to stand up to stop those three Delta dudes from coming over to my table. The look on your face scared the hell out of me."

Ethan absorbed her praise. He wanted to know what she thought of the poem he'd slipped beneath the flap of her tent that morning. The expression on her face kept him from asking. "No one said an introvert can't be a mean mother when they need to be," he said in defense, liking her hesitant smile. That mouth of hers was sending his body a damned heated message.

"That's true." Sarah rolled her eyes. "Every time we get a new copilot in our squadron, the major sends him to be trained by me. I think he does it just to screw around with the newbie. They take one look at my face and I guess I don't look like a warrior. Then they get hyper because I don't fit their idea of a medevac pilot. I'm a woman and—" she sighed "—I have to prove my abilities every day in the right seat. It takes a new copilot a couple of weeks to settle down in the left-hand seat with me at the helm. Like a woman can't fly a damned helo? Give me a break."

"I like your feistiness."

"More than one pilot has seen me under fire coming in for a rescue, and I'm as cool as ice when I need to be."

Ethan believed it. He held up his hands. "Hey, I'm on the receiving end of you medevac pilots. I couldn't care less what your gender is. If I'm bleeding out, all I want to know is you're going to get to me as fast as you can and save my sorry ass."

Sarah laughed for the first time. "That's what it's all about, isn't it?" She *wanted* to like him. That shocked her. And instantly another kind of cold fear settled in her stomach.

Ethan saw the happiness shining in her eyes for just a moment. Her laughter was husky, and his flesh rifled beneath it. His body had a mind of its own, reacting to her sweet smile and shy demeanor. That's great, all he needed was an erection in a pair of gym shorts. *Not good.* He remained where he was, controlling his body. Above all, he didn't want to scare Sarah off. Providence had given him an opening with her, and he damn well wasn't going to squander it away like a teenager run by his hormones. "Listen, can I buy you a beer over at the canteen without you going into your black belt routine?"

Her lips curved. "Ah, I see my karate abilities have gotten around the base?" Thanks to the pilots in her squadron, who were gossip queens that put women to shame.

"I think you could have saved yourself yesterday with that bastard because you knew how to fight back," Ethan said solemnly. He saw her eyes narrow a bit, her soft mouth become pursed.

"I busted his nose and blackened his eye. I was hoping to kick him in the crotch, but he took me down and started dragging me around the corner of the building." Sarah pushed some strands of hair off her damp brow. Giving him an earnest look, her voice low with emotion, she said, "If you hadn't come along, Ethan, he'd probably have been able to rape me. He tried to knock me out. No one would have seen him do it behind that building and he would have gotten away with it. I wondered this morning if he had, would he have killed me afterward? You didn't give him a second shot at me."

The fear banked in her eyes grew. Sarah's emotions were right there on the surface, and damned if he didn't want to straighten up, walk over and haul her into his arms. Ethan found himself wanting to protect her. But this woman was clearly able to fight a two-hundred-and-forty-pound hulk. "You sell yourself short, Sarah. I think, all things being equal, if I hadn't come along, you'd have found a way to knock the hell out of him and escape."

The look in the SEAL's eyes went along with the deadly sound in his hard voice. Sarah shrugged. "We'll never know." She set the dumbbell down on the bench. After picking up the towel and wiping her brow, she said, "Actually, I was trying to figure out a way to find you and then ask if I could buy *you* a beer to thank you.

It's the least I could do for you coming to my aid." She owed him that, scared or not.

Ethan slowly rose, making sure his towel was strategically in place over his gym shorts. This woman turned him on in a heartbeat. "Name the place and time."

"Noon? I'll buy you lunch, too." Ethan gave her a very male look, and this time, Sarah felt her heart flutter. This SEAL was incredibly confident, easygoing as if he didn't have a care in the world. And she liked his mouth because it was expressive and he wasn't acting like he was going to slobber all over her.

He grinned. "Yes, sounds good. I'll see you over at the canteen."

Chapter 4

Sarah was nervous as she sat at her favorite table in the noisy canteen. Lunchtime brought everyone out, and those who wanted American food like pizza and hamburgers came here instead of eating over at the chow hall. She'd decided to wear civilian clothes instead of her flight uniform because she wasn't on duty. After changing into a pair of loose jeans, sneakers and a pink tee with a long-sleeved white blouse to hide her curves, she nervously waited for Ethan. Sarah wanted to get up and leave. He was an unknown. And the unknown scared the living hell out of her.

She glanced at her watch; she was five minutes early. The men at the bar were looking her up and down. Sarah wished she could stop being so sensitive about male stares. Maybe it had to do with her childhood.

Who knew? She was drinking beer from a sweaty glass, a pitcher in the center of the table, when she felt Ethan's presence.

She found him smiling down at her.

"I never heard you coming."

"You won't," Ethan said by way of greeting, pulling a chair out next to her and sitting down.

"Thanks for coming. I've already ordered us hamburgers and French fries." Sarah tried not to be affected by Ethan, but that was impossible. He was wearing a red T-shirt that showed off his incredibly fit body. The jeans he wore made her lower body stir, and that shocked her. She'd now seen two sides of him, the poet and the SEAL. She noticed a number of scars, white and more recent pink ones on his lower and upper arms as well as on his large hands. When he moved to pick up the pitcher of beer, she watched his biceps flex. Every move he made was graceful, and Sarah knew only someone in very good shape could have that boneless kind of grace.

"There's that risk-taker attitude of yours," Ethan teased, grinning as he poured himself some cold beer.

She rolled her eyes. "Don't tell me you don't like hamburgers and French fries." Sarah wanted to ask him if he'd really written that poem. She didn't have the courage.

Ethan pushed the chair back on two legs. "I'm a red-blooded American male. Relax, it's fine. I can never get enough hamburgers." He grinned, seeing relief come to her eyes. Damn but he wanted to know everything about Sarah. He was afraid that if he fired off too many questions it would scare her away. All morning after coming back from the gym, Ethan had tried to figure out the best way to gain Sarah's trust. Given that a man had just beat the hell out of her, she probably wasn't too trusting toward any guy. Not even him.

"The workout go okay?" she asked, trying to get herself to relax. Sarah liked looking into his amused gray eyes, the way his chiseled mouth drew up into a hint of a smile. Heat flashed through her, stronger this time than at the gym. There was no question Ethan was sexy. Sensuality oozed out of his pores and it sure had a giddy effect on her. Actually, he could have been a cover model for a fitness magazine with his athletic body and rugged good looks. Why would she suddenly be interested in this man? Sarah quietly tucked her question away.

This guy had saved her from being raped. She should focus on him, not her own scarred past. "You aren't like a lot of these other guys."

Ethan shrugged, sipping the beer, holding her blue gaze. "If you haven't had much experience around SEALs, I'd say that's why."

Tilting her head, Sarah said, "Educate me."

It was easy to talk about his own kind. "We have an ethos, a way of living and conducting ourselves in the world. We're a band of brothers and a family. We're professionals, Sarah. We don't have to swagger around, boast or tell the world about ourselves. We let our work speak for us."

She felt the coolness of the frosty glass between her fingers as she listened to his low voice. "When I saw you coming up to hit that guy, I thought you were a shadow. I didn't even hear you coming."

Ethan's eyes dropped to her parted mouth. He struggled to keep his body in line, but damn, it was tough. "SEALs take the fight to the enemy, and they'll never hear us coming until it's too late."

The bartender brought over two huge platters of food and set them down in front of them. Sarah thanked him and put her beer to one side. "I don't know about you, but I'm starved." After the assault, she'd had no appetite. Now she did, and she wondered if it was because of Ethan.

"I don't get over here too often, but when I do, this is my order."

Sarah placed the pickles, onions, tomatoes and lettuce on the huge half-pound hamburger. "I don't get over here too often, either. Heavy flight demands."

Picking up his burger in both hands, Ethan grunted. "I must have gotten lucky seeing you the other day then."

They ate in companionable silence. Ethan was always aware of the space around him. More than a few dudes looked longingly toward Blue Eyes and then scowled, jealousy written on their faces because she was allowing him to sit with her. He had to keep himself in tight check; he had a hundred questions for her.

"I imagine being back home on such a short rotation plays hell on your family demands?" he asked. Another way to find out if she was married, engaged or single.

Shrugging, Sarah said, "My foster parents love to have me at home. They live in Dallas, Texas, and I'm always sent to an Army base elsewhere. I do take my thirty days of leave to be with them."

"No other family?" he wondered.

Sarah hesitated. Should she get personal with Ethan? There was something about him that inspired her confidence. Stiffly, she said, "No. I was given up at birth. I'm sure I have family, but I don't know who they are. My foster parents, Hank and Mary Benson, adopted me when I was twelve years old. They're my life. They took me in and I'll always be grateful."

Ethan heard the tension and emotions behind her husky voice and saw pain as well as fondness in her eyes as she spoke. "That had to be tough. I mean, being given up at birth." Ethan couldn't wrap his head around that one. There was momentary anguish in her eyes, and then she quickly hid it from him.

"I'm okay with it. Hank and Mary made up for it. They gave me love and stability and supported me."

"What happened the first twelve years of your life?"

Her mouth crooked, as if to avoid answering his question. "It wasn't pretty," was all she said, her voice clipped and growing hard. "I am who I am today because of Mary and Hank. That's all that counts."

Ethan tried to translate what he saw in her dark glance, but he couldn't. There were a lot of layers to Sarah, a complexity, and he wanted to figure it out. His nature was to delve, understand and see the larger picture. It certainly served him well as a SEAL in black ops.

She finished her hamburger and picked at her fries. "Are you an officer?"

Ethan knew where this conversation was going. Warrant officers in the Army lived in a netherworld between officers and enlisted people. The Army considered them officers, higher in rank than any enlisted person. And he was enlisted. What was Sarah thinking? Was she interested in him personally? Checking out his rank or rate status to ensure the fraternization order wasn't broken? Officers and warrants were not allowed by UCMJ law to fraternize with enlisted people. There was to be no affair, no personal relationship between the two parties.

He squirmed. "I'm a petty officer first class."

"I see," she murmured. In a way, Sarah was relieved he was enlisted. It would make it easier to stop the burning connection between them. Sarah wasn't going to risk her career on an affair with an enlisted man. And yet, as she studied Ethan's somber expression, that was exactly what she wanted to do. He had a kindness to him, a curiosity and intelligence. They all appealed strongly to her, but she couldn't get beyond that wall of distrust she had toward all men.

Ethan continued eating his French fries, no longer tasting them. He could see Sarah had already made her decision about him. She was single; that much he knew. Was she available, though? In his SEAL world, which blurred the lines between enlisted men and their officers, he didn't see this as a deal killer even if Sarah did.

Over the years, Ethan had seen plenty of officer-and-enlisted romances. If the two people involved were discreet, no one said anything. Only those stupid enough to flaunt their affair brazenly out in front of their commanding officers got the order to stop it or else. He'd seen, in some instances, the woman renouncing her military career in order to marry the officer she'd fallen in love with. And sometimes not. He understood what Sarah was thinking about. Weighing and measuring him because she was attracted to him or she wouldn't have asked the question at all. He could sense her considering the costs to her career and to herself if she allowed their attraction to grow.

"Do you have a wife and kids?" Sarah asked him.

Ethan felt himself smile. "No, I'm not married." He pushed the empty plate away and picked up his beer.

"Do SEALs replace the need for a woman in their life with their team family instead?"

He chuckled. "No way. About half the guys in our platoon are married and have kids. The rest of us are alpha male wolves without a partner yet."

She smiled at his description, pushing a few of the last French fries around with her index finger. "Maybe your job, the black ops part of it, stops you from having a serious relationship?" she wondered.

Ethan could feel her trying to grasp the world he lived in. Was this a personal question? Or just a more generalized question about the SEAL community because Sarah knew little about them? He wished it was personal, but he didn't think it was. "I don't think most women can take the nature of our business," he told her seriously. "There's a ninety percent divorce rate among SEALs. Most marriages last only ten years. It's like a disease."

Her brows flew up. "Ninety? My God, that's high!"

"Can't disagree with you." Ethan opened his hands. "Put yourself in a wife's place, one who is married to a

SEAL operator. She will never know where he's sent, the danger he's in, whether he's coming back or not. She has to take care of everything stateside, the house, the kids, and he's not there to support or help her do it. It's a pretty daunting task when a husband is sent overseas for six months and you, as the wife, only get emails and maybe a Skype call monthly, if that."

Nodding, Sarah whispered, "That would be really rough." And then she looked at him. "Is that why you never married?" Because Ethan struck her as a man any woman would stumble all over herself to be with. He wasn't like those ego-busting Delta operators. He was settled, mature, intelligent, and all those things appealed strongly to her whether she wanted them to or not.

"Just haven't run into the right woman yet, I guess," Ethan said, giving her a good-humored look. "Have you run into the right man?"

Sarah frowned. Her voice grew terse. "No." Sarah rubbed her brow, and he could see her weighing whether or not she wanted to reveal any more of herself to him. Desperate, Ethan waited, wanting to know.

She shook her head and gave Ethan a confused look. "I'll bet a lot of people confide in you…."

"I'm trustworthy," he assured her. And he was. Ethan didn't spread gossip around, and he held every relationship as sacred. Sarah was staring at him, unsure. His mouth pursed as he waited. This was a key to Sarah.

"I don't have a very good track record, so let's leave it at that."

Ethan felt sadness blanketing her. "I'm sorry. It's

none of my business," he rasped. And he was sorry because he saw moisture come to her eyes and it tore at
his heavily guarded heart. A woman's or child's tears
ripped him wide-open and he had absolutely no defense
against them. Ethan wanted to touch her but stopped
himself.

God help him, he wanted to gather Sarah into his
arms and hold her. She needed that right now, judging
by the stark look in her eyes. He could feel how alone
she was in this male world. In one aspect, Sarah looked
fragile and too vulnerable to be a Black Hawk pilot. In
other ways, Ethan sensed her steel backbone. She was
complex. And that is what drove him to know her on a
personal level. What moved her? What passion directed
her life? Why was she in the military? There was so
much more to Blue Eyes.

Sarah seemed to force a brittle smile. "It's life. Everyone gets kicked around by it sooner or later." She
finished off her beer and pulled out some bills from
the pocket of her jeans. "Thanks for letting me buy you
lunch," she told him. "I've got some stuff I gotta do over
at my squadron whether I'm on the flight roster or not."

It was a lie, but Sarah knew if she stayed there
one more minute with this SEAL, she was going to
give him her trust. And that just couldn't happen. She
owed Ethan for protecting her, but she didn't owe him
personal access into her wounded heart. That, Sarah
guarded, because she couldn't stand to have her life
ever shattered again.

Rising, Ethan nodded. "Thank you."

Sarah lifted her hand. "Stay safe out there, okay?"

Ethan knew a brush-off when he got one. He nodded and held her blue gaze, feeling the warmth and gentleness that was an intrinsic part of her despite the walls she erected. He also saw she was frightened. Of him? Why? Need for Sarah wrapped around his heart, and Ethan wanted to groan over his loss. "You, too," Ethan told her, meaning it. "There's only one of you, Sarah, and we need you here on this planet. Okay?"

Struck by his parting words, she blinked, assimilating his statement. There was a hidden depth to Ethan, and she saw it in his genuine care for her. That protective energy of his embraced her even more powerfully than before. "Yes...of course."

Well that went swimmingly, didn't it? Ethan was angry with himself as he walked toward SEAL HQ. He had to be at a mission-planning session at 1400. He'd blown it with Sarah. She was wounded, grieving, and he'd just romped into her life like a sledgehammer shattering crystal. *Damn.* Running his fingers distractedly through his hair, he wondered how to repair the damage he'd done through his ignorance and impatience.

He heard a Black Hawk spooling up at Ops. The sun, hot and burning, fried and dried out everything in its path. Ethan hated it, preferring the cool, damp and humid Alaskan wilderness. That or jumping into the ocean, where he truly felt at home.

What was he going to do to win back Sarah's attention? Should he continue his other black ops strategy with her? Continue to place an envelope with a stanza of a poem he'd written about her every morning before she woke up? Ethan felt driven to do it by some invisible, unnamed source. His drive to know Sarah to her soul was intense, almost dire. And he'd never felt this before with a woman.

Chapter 5

The next morning when Sarah awoke, she found another envelope waiting for her beneath her tent opening. Rubbing the sleep from her drowsy eyes, she sat up in her cot and looked at her watch. 0700. She was sleeping long and deep. Moving her fingers through her loose, tangled hair, she pushed to her feet. She leaned down and slid the pristine white envelope between her fingertips. Everything was so dirty and dusty here, and it looked so clean and untouched in comparison. Her heart beat a little harder as she sat down on the cot, holding it with anticipation between her hands.

Why did this matter so much to her? Did it contain another stanza to Ethan's poem? She slid her finger beneath the opening. The same blue-colored parchment was folded inside it. The paper felt rich as she slowly moved her fingers across it. What had he written this time? A part of her was eager to know. After opening it, she read.

> *And I am truly honored and humbled*
> *In this brief respite of life*
> *To be given an invitation, however slight,*
> *To take in the scope of your sacred blooms...*
> *(to be continued when poet has time)*

Sarah sighed softly, grazing the beautiful calligraphy. The black ink was bold against the blue paper it was written on. Touched, she absorbed his words, those pictures he painted in her mind with them. Ethan had written this. Even though she'd only seen him do it one time, she knew. Looking up, Sarah frowned. To think even one man at Bravo had this kind of sensitivity in his soul surprised the hell out of her.

Her mind and, if she was honest, her heart, quietly revolved back to Ethan Quinn. Frowning, Sarah didn't dare be drawn to him. But she couldn't help herself. His quietness, his insights into her, startled and scared her. Sarah couldn't get his rugged good looks out of her mind, either. His gray eyes... God, his eyes just felt like they had X-ray abilities and he saw straight through her, wounds and all. Equally important, Ethan wasn't the type to judge others from what she'd seen so far. Sarah was constantly being judged in the medevac squadron, especially by Major Tom Donaldson. He had it in for her and was being very careful as to how he put the screws to her, always covering his ass so he couldn't be officially challenged by her. *The bastard.*

Folding up the envelope, Sarah rose. Day two of her enforced healing. She decided to go over to the gym after making her instant coffee. And then to the chow hall for a late breakfast.

As she picked up a clean dark green T-shirt and a pair of clean trousers, she wondered if she'd accidentally meet Ethan. A part of her wanted to. A larger part of her didn't. He was enlisted. She was a warrant. The two could never legally mix. Mouth quirking, Sarah figured if her commanding officer ever found out, he'd take great pleasure in getting her into plenty of trouble. He was a lousy leader, interested only in protecting his career and making colonel. He didn't care what he had to do to get it, either. She'd seen him step on too many other pilots to make himself look good. Him and that damn yearly budget he kept holding in her face. Keep costs down....

Sarah swore Donaldson was an accountant wearing Army green. He felt his path to the next rank was achieved by cutting costs. And by doing that, he was willing to order a medevac flight to wait instead of flying into the fray to save a man's or woman's life. Sarah clenched her teeth, all her warm, fuzzy feelings about the poem dissolving in the reality of her life. Every day for her was getting harder and harder to work under the major's command. And today she had to go over to the office and see Donaldson.

Sarah's stomach automatically tightened when she saw Major Donaldson, his red hair close-cropped, working at his desk. She quietly entered the office, quelling her anxiety. Donaldson's thin face snapped up. His eyes were small and close together, and he rapidly raked her with an angry glance.

Coming to attention in front of his desk, Sarah reported in.

"At ease, Chief Benson," he growled, jerking out a sheaf of papers from another stack on his neat, organized desk. He threw the sheaf, and it slid to her side of his desk. "You know what this is?"

Swallowing hard, Sarah tucked her hands behind her back. "Yes, sir. It's a budget, sir." She wanted to roll her eyes, but if she did, he'd gig her on it and probably write her up on insubordination. Any little excuse would send her CO into a fit of glee as he caught her in some infraction. It would then go into her service jacket, her personnel file, and it would always be there. Such things could stop her from getting her next rank. She had to play it cool and remain detached even though she was breaking out in a sweat, feeling like she was flying into a firefight to rescue wounded men.

"Damn straight it is." He glared up at her. Jabbing an index finger down at the thick group of papers, he said, "This squadron is very close to hitting its maximum number of repairs, Chief Benson. You, of all people, need to know that."

Sarah kept her face neutral. There was no way she was going to blow back on her CO. "Yes, sir. Thank you, sir."

Donaldson lifted his lip in a sneer.

"We're probably damned lucky you got set out for

four days. That's four days I know I'm not going to have to have our mechanics section repair one of our birds you flew."

"Yes, sir."

Tapping the papers, Donaldson hissed, "When you get back on the flight roster, you damn well better stop your stupid risk taking. You hear me? I will *not* lose my colonel's leaves because of you. Dismissed!"

"Yes, sir!" Sarah snapped to attention, turned on her heel and headed out the HQ door and into the main area of Operations.

Her heart was pounding. Donaldson reminded her of the past—of a horror she didn't want to revisit. She wiped her mouth, walking straight, shoulders squared and chin up. Sarah had learned a long time ago never to show anyone she was scared. It just brought more crap raining down on her.

As she headed out the main doors to go back to her tent area to rest, she thought of Ethan. God, she couldn't get involved with him. She had to keep her head in the game. Donaldson was just aching to bring her down. Nail her ass to the deck. Embarrass her. No, she had to focus.

On the third morning, Sarah slept until nearly 0900, which shocked her. The trauma she'd endured was far deeper than she'd initially realized. And as she opened her eyes, she automatically looked toward the tent opening. Her heart raced as she noticed a third white, pristine envelope on the floor. Sarah didn't even try to fool herself about the quiet joy running through her. It was another poem from Ethan. She sat up, pushed the hair off her face and walked over and picked it up.

Sarah wanted to believe Ethan truly liked her—beyond her appearance. The chances of that, however, were slim to none. Men saw her in sexual terms only for the most part. Not romance or love—both yearnings she had but didn't feel were possible in her life. Still, as she picked up the envelope, the idealistic part of her swooned with excitement.

Sitting back on her cot, Sarah opened it up, her hand trembling slightly. She pulled it out and opened it up.

Who could guess that beneath the pastiche of outer appearances
You would be imbued with lush streams, blooming banks of gladiolas
And cypress trees? Everyone agreed
That yours is a colorful personality,
But until you recently whispered to my psyche,
Who knew you retained a range and hue of vivid colors
Streaming to the periphery of awareness, then back again?
(to be continued as poet gets a chance)

Sarah closed her eyes, pressing the envelope to her breast. She *felt* this man, his energy and his heart. How could this be happening to her? She hoped with all her heart this wasn't a mean trick being played on her, that his poem was truly as it appeared: a man courting a woman. Ethan could be doing this to manipulate her.

Her hand fell into her lap, the envelope still in her fingertips. Sarah had been hurt so often by men who professed to like her, wanted to get to know her, and it always ended up the same: they wanted to use her body and that was it. Did Ethan want the same thing, even with such an elaborate plan? She hoped not, but her years of experience in the military overrode her idealistic wish.

Slowly rising, Sarah stretched, hands above her head. The gym workouts were helping, and she was feeling a bit stronger, more together. She had tried to swallow her disappointment when she didn't see Ethan at the gym or chow hall yesterday. Maybe today? It was something she looked forward to without questioning too closely why.

On the last day of her enforced medical rest, Sarah awoke much earlier. She looked toward the tent door and saw a fourth envelope from Ethan sitting there. Her watch read 0600. This time, she let happiness flow through her as she retrieved the card. Her heart squeezed with anticipation as she sat down on the cot and eagerly opened it. The envelope awoke the part of her life that had been set aside due to her military career. War was harsh and took no prisoners. The weight of the envelope, its perfect cleanliness against the dirtiness of daily combat, transported her to another time and place. A place where civility, romance and social graces all lived. Holding her breath, Sarah pulled out the creamy papyrus and opened it up.

A lush and virtual wilderness is encamped
Next to your orderly hymns, and it is a telling,
glowing omen
That a symphony of melodies is vibrating and
humming
Beneath your outer carapace.

We thought we had glimpses of your depth, and
our own
In truth, we had barely scratched the surface of
being.
(to be continued as poet gets time)

Sarah sighed softly, allowing the words to vibrate through her. This felt so real. As if this man were reaching out and invisibly sliding his finger down the slope of her cheek, softly touching her lower lip with his grazing thumb. Her heart opened, and heat pooled in her lower body.

Sarah wondered again when Ethan was placing the envelope beneath the tent. She never heard his footsteps again after that first day. Was this whole thing a game for him? Intuitively, she didn't think so. If nothing else, Sarah thought, as she slowly read each luscious, juicy word Ethan had written, his poem gave her hope and solace. His words, how he saw her and himself, were far removed from the daily violence surrounding their lives here at this forward operating base. His words fed her starving soul in a way she couldn't describe but could only feel on a deep, visceral level. His words were healing and gave her hope.

* * *

Ethan sat with three other SEALs on the end of the runway in a QRF, quick reaction force, Black Hawk helicopter piloted by Night Stalker pilots. He had Beau, Teddy and Mac in his team. The noontime sun was beating down on them as the Black Hawk idled on the runway, awaiting orders to lift off. He had his helmet and an earpiece on, listening to all the communications between their helo and a Marine squad that was pinned down by a Taliban ambush near the Pakistan border. His heart beat slowly as he listened to the gunfire, the cursing and orders between the Marines. They were in the thick of it, having triggered a Taliban attack that had cut off their only route of escape on a hill above a valley thirty minutes east of Bravo.

Ethan shifted, one leg hanging out the open door of the Black Hawk, the other pulled up against his body as he leaned back on the airframe, listening intently. SEALs often provided QRF to Special Forces, Delta, the Army and the Marine recons in the area. It was his turn today to take his team into the fray if they were given orders to launch. A QRF was exactly that: reacting swiftly, decisively, to any enemy force that was trying to overwhelm another U.S. force out there in the badlands.

Master Chief Gil Hunter's voice came over his radio headset. "Avalanche Actual, this is Avalanche Main. You are authorized to engage."

That was what Ethan wanted to hear. He threw a thumbs-up to his eager team, who were more than ready to enter the fight. "Roger, Avalanche Main. Out." He quickly switched channels to speak to the Night Stalker pilots who would take them into the firefight. Sweat trickled down his temples. Adrenaline started leaking through Ethan, but his heart rate remained slow and steady. The Black Hawk's powerful engines engaged, and the gravity pushed him downward as it rose into the air. The wind felt damn good against his sweaty body; all the gear he wore held in the heat.

Normally, QRFs took place at night, the Taliban's time to be on the move. A day patrol being attacked, in Ethan's experience, meant it was a much larger force that had been waiting to ambush the Marines. Wiping his mouth, he pushed his wraparound sunglasses snugly against his face. The sun was blindingly bright and it was over a hundred degrees midday. It was going to be a sonofabitch of a battle because men dehydrated so damned fast under these types of brutal conditions. He'd made sure his shooters had eight quarts of water in their rucks as well as the CamelBak they carried on their backs.

The wind whipped around him, tearing at his body as he rode on the lip of the helo, his M4 rifle nose down and hanging off the nylon harness across his right shoulder and chest. It was safed to make sure no bullet accidentally got fired off into the helicopter, potentially causing a crash or accidentally killing someone. Ethan's mind churned over the intel and he closed his eyes, visualizing where the Marines were trapped. The hill was a small one, and there were Taliban coming up two sides of it, the north and east. Rocks sat on the top of the hill, where the ten-man Marine force had taken cover and were fighting for their lives.

He picked up a CIA transmission, alerting him to the fact a drone was now overhead, streaming back real-time video of the firefight. Ethan set his rifle inside on the deck, pulled his ruck over and opened it up. Quickly, he pulled out his Toughbook laptop, opened the lid and fired it up. In a minute, he was looking through the drone's orbiting eyes. *Dammit.* These Marines were in real trouble. He saw at least forty Taliban on one side of the north side of the hill, fighting and firing RPGs at the Marines on top. On the eastern flank of the hill, at least sixty Taliban attacked.

Ethan called SEAL HQ and talked to Master Chief Gil Hunter. He relayed the streaming video intel, telling him the four of them weren't going to make a huge difference in this fight. The master chief agreed and switched over to the Black Jaguar Squadron, requesting immediate Apache support.

Ethan watched the dry, yellowed and rocky earth far below skim by; the helo was at max speed. The Night Stalker pilots were skilled at making insertions and exfil for black ops groups. They flew at a high enough altitude so that the RPGs carried by the Taliban couldn't reach them.

Ethan studied the laptop, trying to decide where to insert. If they didn't get those Apaches, it was going to be a brutal, long, drawn-out fight. Marines were exactly that: steady, reliable fighters. They didn't know the words *quit* or *surrender*. Ethan liked working with the Marines because they had the hearts of SEALs.

He'd never tell them that, but those men were damned good in combat.

The Black Hawk swung down, banking sharply. Ethan was tethered to the frame with a harness, so he wouldn't fall out. He ordered his men to unsafe their weapons and get ready to bail as he stowed his laptop in his ruck. For the insert, Ethan chose the south side of the hill, which was rocky and nearly impossible for the Taliban to climb quickly. And then it would mean a swift climb over hot, burning rocks in order to reach the pinned-down Marines.

He was already in touch with Lieutenant Porter, the Marine officer leading the squad, letting him know their ETA and where they were coming in. Ethan didn't want his team to be seen as a Taliban force coming over the hill and get fired on by the Marines.

He heard a lot of other communications in his earpiece. The bad news was no Apaches were available; they were all out on other missions, raining hell down on enemies elsewhere. As the Black Hawk thunked and shuddered, drawing closer to the parched earth and rocks at the base of the hill, Ethan called the master chief and asked for other means of support.

They landed and leaped off the Black Hawk, the rotor wash nearly knocking them over as they crouched and scuttled swiftly away from the helo. Ethan used hand signals, getting his men into the rocks. Behind him, the Night Stalker pilots lifted the bird off, getting the hell out of Dodge. He called Porter and let him know they were on the ground. The officer sounded relieved.

Moving up swiftly through and between the rocks,

the SEALs spread out in a diamond formation. That way, their flanks were protected and covered. Ethan took the lead, breathing hard at the nine-thousand-foot altitude, his lungs burning with exertion. Sweat poured off him, and he constantly wiped his face with the back of his glove as he leaped and moved upward. He heard the gunfire, the screams and curses of the Taliban.

Crouched and running, eyes moving left to right, Ethan led his team higher into the rocks. The snap and pop of bullets sizzled around them while they moved over the top of the hill. Ethan spotted the young Marine officer firing at the enemy starting to come over the hill. He gave a hand signal to his shooters to spread out and help the beleaguered Marines.

"Causalities?" he shouted above the gunfire at the officer.

"Two wounded," he yelled back. "I need medevac! Two nine-liners!"

Ethan nodded and quickly made the call into Camp Bravo squadron for the Marine officer. Nine-line meant the wounded were critical. Fresh blood would be brought in a cooler to give to the men when on board. He switched radio channels, calling into the medevac HQ, apprising them of the situation and that the wounded were critical. The male dispatcher told him a medevac would arrive at the hill in twenty minutes.

For a brief second, he wondered if Sarah would be flying today. She had to be back on the flight roster after her enforced four-day rest. His gut tightened. He didn't want her flying into this hell. All Marines were on their bellies, firing systematically, not wildly. They were trained and disciplined, not wasting any more ammo than necessary to kill the enemy.

He leaned over and told the officer there was a split Taliban force of ninety men. The red-haired officer paled. Ethan could tell this was a young lieutenant, not battle hardened with experience. He then heard the throaty roar of the M4s going online from the SEAL contingent. They joined in with the Marines' M16 rifles, laying down fire and halting the Taliban attempt to overrun their position.

Ethan's job was to get the overview, assess their position and then, because he was comms, get these Marines the help they needed in order to repulse the Taliban. The screams of raging Taliban soldiers, gunfire, the explosion of RPGs and the curses of the Marines were deafening. Crouching down behind a rock, near Porter, Ethan worked the radios, seeing what he could get in the way of support.

He grinned, finding an A-10 warthog pilot loitering in the area with a load of bombs and a Gatling gun that could repulse the Taliban. Ethan quickly gave the pilot their GPS location. The pilot, who called himself Wolverine, said he'd redline to their position and get there in about twenty minutes.

Feeling better, Ethan turned, told the officer and then moved between two towering rocks. He went prone and began to pick off the Taliban as they crawled over the top of the hill. In his mind, he worried about the medevac coming in. Where should it land? He needed to know where the two wounded Marines were located. Pushing to his knees, Ethan crawled between the rocks and spotted a Navy combat corpsman some hundred feet away, tending to the Marines who were in critical condition. They didn't look good. *Damn.*

He saw the grimness in the corpsman's face as he tightened up a tourniquet on one Marine's bleeding thigh. The other Marine had a head injury. No way could he ask the medevac to wait. The Marines were critical and would die soon if they didn't get immediate transport.

Ethan wondered if it would be too late. As he turned to keep Porter updated, he couldn't help but think of Sarah. Something told him she would be piloting that Black Hawk into this fiery hell. *Dammit!*

Chapter 6

The moment Sarah heard Ethan's voice over her radio channel, her heart did a triple beat in her chest. She'd gotten the intel and GPS location of the Marines pinned down on a hill at the ready room from her flight commander. She held the cyclic and collective, pushing her Black Hawk to maximum, the blades thumping heavily, making the craft shake and shudder. Her copilot, Eddy Tait, a twenty-two-year-old warrant officer from the bayous of Louisiana recently out of training, was busy with the radio frequencies. She watched her next waypoint coming up on her HUD, heads-up display, banking to the left. In the rear was her aircrew chief, Hubbard. She had two medics on the flight, Carew and Pascal, because this was a nine-line call and both Marines were critical. Her medics were solid players, especially Pascal because he was an 18 Delta corpsman, the most highly trained combat medics in the world. Tait was questionable because this was his first rotation and he wasn't aggressive when it came down to flying into bullets and RPGs exploding around them. She'd seen the fear in his face before they lifted off. He'd gain a set of cojones over time.

The heat rising off the earth hurled the Black Hawk up and down like a yo-yo as it hit big air pockets. As she kept them as steady as possible, Sarah constantly moved her gaze between the cockpit panel and the land five thousand feet below them. Her dark helmet visor was drawn down across the upper half of her face, the mic near her lips. She felt the urgency, knowing two Marines were critical. While forcing herself not to think about Ethan being down there, she milked every bit of speed out of her Black Hawk. Tait was working the overhead throttles to get every ounce of speed from those two engines.

Within five miles of the hill, Sarah heard Major Donaldson's pedantic voice come over her radio.

"Black Dog One, this is Black Dog. Over."

Twisting her lips, she thumbed the mic. "Black Dog One. Over." What the hell was he on the radio for? She'd already gotten approval from the Marines and SEAL HQ at Bagram to fly in and pick up the wounded men. She felt dread. There was no way he was going to tell her to back off this run now.

"Loiter at five miles, Black Dog One. Over."

Tait's mouth fell open, and he quickly looked to his right where she sat, confusion in his eyes.

"That's a negative, Black Dog," she growled back. "We have a nine-liner, two critical, and I have approval from Bagram." Would Donaldson back off now? Sarah swore under her breath after she turned off the channel so her crew couldn't hear her conversation with her boss.

"This is an order, Black Dog One. Loiter at five miles until I give you permission to fly in. Over."

Not a chance. Sarah keyed the mic. "You're breaking up," she said as she played with the mic, making it sound like she was. "Can you repeat? Did not receive. Over."

Sarah heard the major angrily repeat the order. She continued to key the mic, causing static disruption. *Go to hell, Donaldson. If it were you on that hill, you'd sure as hell be screaming like a baby wanting a medevac to come and rescue your sorry ass.*

Tait appeared uncertain after hearing Donaldson's order.

"Just fly," Sarah said. He was so damn green he didn't understand that she followed Bagram's orders, not her CO's belated, secondary order. Bagram trumped Donaldson. Two men's lives were on the line. They had family who loved them, maybe wives and children. Sarah was damned if she was going to let a few bullets and the threat of RPGs stop her from landing and taking them on board.

"Hey, Chief Benson," Pascal drawled, humor in his tone as he spoke to her on the ICS, intercabin system. "Having a little trouble with our radio, are we?"

Sarah grinned sourly. "Yeah, it's messing up. Gotta have it looked at, Pascal, once we get back."

"It's been on the fritz before," Pascal said, chuckling. "I'll look at it and see what I can do."

In his early thirties, Pascal was an experienced medic and knew the dance. Then there was Tait, who scowled, his mouth set. He had yet to understand politics versus orders. She'd set him straight once they returned to Bravo.

As she banked the Black Hawk, the helo thunking and the vibrations rippling through her entire body, Sarah heard Ethan's voice on the radio.

"Black Dog One, this is Avalanche Actual. Over."

"You got me, Avalanche Actual. Where do you want me to drop in? Over."

Sarah smiled to herself, knowing Ethan would instantly recognize her voice. If he did, it didn't come through in his low, steady tone. He was speaking to her as if all were calm, but she could hear the fierce firefight going on around him.

Ahead, she noted the hill and several RPGs exploding near the rocks where the Marines were pinned. Her heart rate went up. Taliban lurked on two sides of the hill, trying to come over the top like ants and overrun the Marines. Where to land? Did Ethan have a spot chosen?

"Black Dog One, I'm putting out green smoke to mark your landing site. You're going to have to come in on the south side of the hill and land downslope, just below the top of it. Over," Ethan said.

No doubt he was trying to land her helo downslope

from the firefight. Bullets couldn't bend, and it would mean they'd take less fire as a result.

"Copy that, Avalanche Actual. Coming in hot. Out," she answered, bringing the helo in swiftly. Sarah knew from experience that the Taliban would see them coming in and throw everything, including the kitchen sink, at them. Never mind Geneva Conventions clearly spelled out that a red cross on the nose of a helo meant no one could fire at it or try and destroy it. The Taliban went by its own rules.

Ethan stood crouched behind some boulders, watching Sarah guide the Black Hawk helicopter into the fray. He'd gotten two other Marines to bring their wounded comrades up to this point. There was no way he could afford men to carry them down to the base of the hill, where it would have been much safer. The trip probably would have killed them anyway. He swiftly looked around and called Porter on the radio.

"Lieutenant, when I give the order, lay down suppression fire so this bird can land. She's coming in hot and we have to protect it."

"Roger," Porter said.

Ethan then switched channels, connecting the Marines and SEALs. "Suppression fire. Lay it down now," he ordered. SEALs knew how to lay down lead in a curtain that would keep the enemies' heads down.

He wiped his mouth, watching the Black Hawk scream in. Damn, Sarah was a hellion in the air! She flared the Black Hawk, nose up at the last moment, bleeding off forward air speed and then thunking that helo down hard on its tricycle landing gear. She would keep the speed at eighty miles per hour—takeoff speed—so she could get out of there if things turned sideways.

"Now!" Ethan ordered the Marines behind him. He got up, slinging his M4 across his back, and helped pick up the first Marine. Simultaneously, both medics from the Black Hawk leaped out and ran at top speed toward them to help, a litter between them.

Bullets started snapping around the Black Hawk. Sarah sat tensely, watching Ethan, the Marines and her medics haul the two unconscious Marines on board. Several bullets smashed into the Plexiglas on her side of the cockpit. A shower of sparkling fragments slammed through the cockpit area. She flinched but kept her hands steady on the cyclic and collective, her boots on the rudders. *Hurry! Dammit, hurry!*

Suddenly, Tait screamed. Whipping her head around, she saw he'd been hit in the arm from a fusillade of bullets shattering his side of the cockpit Plexiglas.

The medics got the Marines on board. She heard Pascal yell, "Lift off!"

Sarah didn't need any more than that. Tait lifted his gloved hand, pushing the throttles overhead to the wall, punching the fuel into her bird. She cranked up the cyclic, getting the hell off the hill. As she guided the Black Hawk down the slope, avoiding the hail of gunfire, she could hear the pinging sounds of bullets ripping into the skin of her bird. Some blew through the cabin, opening holes between the inner and outer skin going between those two layers of insulation. She prayed none of them hit the Jesus nut, the rotor assembly, or they were screwed. Tait was moaning and crying in pain, holding his shoulder, blood leaking between his fingers.

"Pascal!" she snapped into the mic. "Tait's been wounded in the left shoulder. Can you get up here?"

"On my way in a second…."

Pascal's cool, calm voice was a godsend in the chaos for Sarah. She wanted to yell at Tait to suck it up. But the copilot was crying like a baby. Hell, the two Marines in the back were wounded and neither of them was screaming like he was. Sarah guided the Black Hawk up as fast as she could to five thousand feet altitude while pushing it forward in an effort to get back to Camp Bravo as quickly as possible.

Tait handled the throttles overhead in the cockpit between their seats. Sarah had to keep both her hands on the collective and cyclic. With Tait out of the fight, she was doing both. Not a good scenario.

Pascal examined Tait's bloody arm. He said to her, "This turned into a casevac, Chief Benson. Both those Marines… Head directly for Bagram."

Heart sinking, Sarah nodded. "Roger," she said, heading west toward Bagram Air Base. It would be a fifty-minute flight. "How bad?" she demanded.

"Past critical," Pascal said, leaning over Tait, trying to size up his wound. He pulled out a pair of scissors from his trouser pocket, telling the panicked copilot to turn and sit still so he could cut into the upper sleeve of his flight suit to examine the wound.

Sarah's mind leaped ahead. Tait was too green to be of much help. She switched channels and made a call into E.R. at Bagram, alerting them to their location and the status of their two Marine patients. By the time she was done, Pascal had cut Tait's sleeve to examine the injury.

"You'll live, Mr. Tait," Pascal drawled. "Just a flesh wound. You'll be fine. I'll put a bandage on it and when we land at Bravo, you can go over to the dispensary and they'll patch you up. Congratulations on getting your first Purple Heart."

Pascal eased out of the cockpit, then turned and shared a private smile with Sarah.

Sarah got it. "Tait, get on the horn and apprise Major Donaldson we're heading for Bagram." She wasn't going to let him sit there crying and acting helpless. It was time he sucked it up and became a team member. She needed his focus on those damn overhead throttles.

"Hey, Chief Benson," Tait said. "You got blood on your right arm."

Snorting, Sarah said, "Make the call to the major, will you? I'm fine."

Tait gawked at her.

She glared over at him, daring him to say one more word.

He quickly went back to making the call to Donaldson.

Ethan wearily climbed out of the Night Stalker helicopter that had just landed at Camp Bravo. The sun was low on the western horizon. His men followed him, all of them walking a little slower, exhausted by the long firefight. The good news was the A-10 Warthog had made the defining difference. The Marines finally owned the firefight after the Hog spewed its load of bullets and bombs all over the lower slopes of that hill.

The concrete revetment area radiated heat, increasing the temperature. As they walked toward Ops, Ethan watched as a Black Hawk with a red cross on its nose landed. The cockpit area was shot up, some of the Plexiglas destroyed. Halting, he knew it had to be Sarah's helo. Why was she landing just now? She'd left the hill hours ago. He wanted to wait and talk to her.

Turning, he told his men to get cleaned up, get some chow and ramp down. He'd be over at SEAL HQ later to write up a report on the mission. As beaten up as he felt right now, Ethan *had* to see her.

Sarah was the last crew member off the bird. She felt tiredness creeping through her limbs. Pascal checked out the radio before he left for Ops. Major Donaldson wasn't going to like what he saw. Her Black Hawk was pretty well shot up and a new Plexiglas would have to be installed. Not good for his bottom line. She shrugged, climbing out, pushing up her visor. As she did, she noticed Ethan coming her way. Instantly, her heartbeat sped up. He was dirty and sweaty, his cammies soaked. His M4 was in a sling harness across his chest. He looked damned good to her, and she felt suddenly lighter.

Ethan met her with a smile, seeing the exhaustion in her eyes. There was blood on the right side of her face. The shards of Plexiglas had exploded in on her. His eyes missed nothing as he rapidly examined her standing there, one boot resting, her hip at an angle while pulling off her Nomex flight gloves.

Damn, but she was a warrior. Ballsy as hell. It was the first time he'd seen her in action, and she took no prisoners. The smile that came to her face drove heat straight down through him.

"You must have flown straight to Bagram. How are the two Marines?" he asked, drawing to a halt about six feet away from her. She removed her helmet; her black hair was in a loose ponytail.

"I don't know," Sarah said, meeting his glittering eyes, feeling Ethan's touch without ever being touched. "They were alive when we transferred them over to Bagram E.R. Pascal, my medic, is an 18 Delta guy. He works miracles." She put her helmet into the canvas bag, pushed her kneeboard into it and picked it up.

"I hope they make it," he said, slowly walking with her toward Ops. Around them, other helicopters were taking off. The air filled with the smell of kerosene aviation fuel. He was worried, looking at her upper right arm. "You take a hit?" Ethan asked, gesturing to her arm, concerned.

"Yeah," Sarah muttered. "Nothing to write home about. Pascal looked at it earlier and said it was a piece of Plexiglas in my arm. I'm going over to E.R. and have them pull it out, stitch me up and I'll be good as new."

"Probably not the first time this has happened?"

"Not the first time," she said, gazing up at him. "How are you and your guys doing? Helluva firefight you walked into." Sarah drowned in his dark look, her eyes dropping to his mouth. God, what a mouth Ethan had! It was driving her crazy. She wanted to feel his mouth beneath hers, tasting him, feeling his power, his maleness. Whatever was happening between them, it hadn't gone away. On the contrary, it had grown stronger. Sarah felt that familiar tug-of-war between wanting to trust him and wanting to pull away.

"I'm good and so are my men," he murmured, checking his stride for hers. "Bitch of a firefight."

"No kidding," she said drily.

"You're hell on wheels. You know that?" Ethan caught and held Sarah's startled glance. "You brought that bird in so damned fast, I thought you were going to overshoot the landing site." He grinned.

She shrugged. Sarah liked his smile. His eyes burned with intense interest—she hoped for her—and it felt good. It felt scary. She didn't know what to do with Ethan's attention. "Two Marines were critical," she told him. "I don't stand on much protocol when I know that. It has to be a fast infil and exfil."

"Even though lead was flying?"

"Nothing fazes me when I'm saving lives. I've got my priorities straight."

Shaking his head, Ethan smiled. "You're amazing."

Sarah took the compliment and allowed it to sink in. "Thanks. Funny, I was thinking the same about you. You were orchestrating and commanding the entire firefight." She met his hooded stare. "You're a hero in my eyes."

Her words melted through him like sweet, warm honey. "Oh," Ethan teased, "I think this is a situation of the pot calling the teakettle black. Don't you?" He watched as her lips lifted into a wry smile.

"Maybe," Sarah admitted.

"I'm going to get a shower and change of clothes. Want to meet me at the chow hall in an hour?"

Her heart lurched. She hesitated. The chow hall was in public. No one could accuse her of fraternizing there. "I'm not sure, Ethan."

He briefly touched her uninjured shoulder. "Okay, see you in a few...."

Sarah watched him peel off and quicken his stride toward Ops. Ethan wasn't taking no for an answer. He was *that* confident. He had led the QRF force and would have a ton of paperwork to plough through tonight.

Grimacing, Sarah took a look back at her helo. Donaldson was going to raise holy hell with her. But not right now. She was going to E.R., get a shower, clean off the sweat and smell of battle and climb into a clean flight suit. And then she'd meet Ethan at the chow hall. She was still on duty until tomorrow at 0800. Anxiety thrummed through Sarah, dissolving the weariness that always came after flying into a hot landing zone. As she pushed through the doors of Ops, Sarah knew Major Donaldson would have her on the carpet, wanting to chew her ass for disobeying his direct order. Tonight, she thought, she wanted to simply be in Ethan's company because he was the safest male other than her now-deceased pilot friend Chief Warrant Officer Ted Bateman, in her life. Her curiosity was eating her alive because she wanted to know a lot more about the SEAL.

Chapter 7

Ethan spotted Sarah as she walked into the chow hall an hour later. She was in a fresh uniform that hid her lush body. Her hair was clean, shining and in a ponytail. He rose and walked over to her as she stood in the chow line. All the blood on the lower right side of her face was gone, but he could see tiny red spots where fractured Plexiglas had cut into her soft, beautiful skin. He smiled when she spotted him. Her cheeks flushed, making her blue eyes even more intense in color. His entire body flooded with want. Forcing control over himself, he came and stood next to her in line.

"The doc give you a clean bill of health on your arm?"

Sarah nodded, slowing her steps, still unsure of eating with Ethan. "I'm good to go." She wrinkled her nose and added, "I told them not to send the medical report over to my CO. I didn't want him grounding me for a scratch, so they're delaying sending it over until later tomorrow morning after I'm done with my shift."

She looked up into those warm gray eyes of his. She could feel Ethan's male interest and, for whatever reason, didn't react negatively to it. There was a softening at the corners of his well-shaped mouth, and Sarah sensed kindness in him. It wasn't that obvious. Hell, he was a SEAL, and no one could ignore that. She noticed a number of men watching them. "You know the system," Ethan said, smiling a little.

"I've been at this for a long time," Sarah agreed, picking up an orange and placing it on her tray. The Navy cook behind the line put a dollop of potatoes and gravy along with several thick slices of rare beef. She asked for some corn and then was ready to leave the line.

"This way," Ethan urged, gesturing toward the rear of the chow hall.

Sarah felt her back prickle with so many damned eyes of men following her progress. She hated it. And, as if Ethan sensed her discomfort, he moved behind her, providing a barrier between her and them. She wished mightily she could get over being stared at in this military fishbowl. Right now, she felt safe and protected with Ethan shadowing her movement. And just that alone made her decide to eat with him. He was safer than the rest of the men. That's what it boiled down to.

Ethan sat down at the table, his back to the wall. Sarah settled opposite him, her back to the doors. She noticed he was casually looking around. Cutting into her beef, she asked, "What is it about you SEALs? I haven't had that much interface with them."

Ethan folded his hands, elbows resting on the table. He had a cup of coffee to the right of him, having already eaten. "What have you heard?" He watched her eat. Sarah was delicate in all her movements. Who could have ever guessed she was the kamikaze medevac pilot roaring into that firefight earlier today? Even the bulky green flight suit couldn't hide her curves from him. Heat shimmered through him, and Ethan felt himself going hard. Not exactly a good thing in a chow hall, and he was glad he was in bulky cammies where it wouldn't be seen.

Shrugging, Sarah said between bites, "Well, you guys are the blackest of the black ops groups around here from what everyone says."

"We're shadows. We don't want to be seen unless we want you to see us." He smiled, drowning in her blue eyes; her pupils were large and black, framed by long dark lashes. Did Sarah realize how incredibly beautiful she was? Ethan didn't think so. He'd never seen her with makeup on. Of course, the Black Jaguar Squadron— which was composed of only women flying the Apache combat helicopter—didn't exactly dress up, either. Still, Sarah seemed disconnected to her natural beauty. It wasn't anything that pointed to it, but Ethan could sense it. And his finely honed intuition was never wrong.

"Are you top secret and can't say anything about yourself?" she asked, partly teasing.

"Ask me anything. I'll try to answer it."

She saw the challenge in his eyes and grinned. She was fine talking about him. "Okay, how old are you?"

"Twenty-nine."

"Same age as me."

"See? We have something in common."

Sarah felt elated with that info. Good to know, but she cautioned herself. "How many tours have you had over here?"

"Fourth one. My team is on a two-year rotation schedule. We remain stateside refreshing all our skills for eighteen months, picking up new training techniques along the way, and then we redeploy to the Middle East for six to twelve months of combat duty."

"God, I know more in five minutes about the SEALs than I have in all the years I've been over here. You're an open book, Ethan."

He liked the way his name fell from Sarah's lips. "With you, I'll always try to be," he responded. "My turn?"

Sarah suddenly felt wary, but her heart pushed her to open up to him. She finished off her food, then pushed the tray to one side. "I'm *not* an open book."

Ethan hesitated because he was going to get very personal. It was his nature to dig into a person's background. It wasn't a SEAL attribute necessarily; it was just him. He liked to understand what made a person tick. He'd come to understand over the years, a person's childhood held the key to who they were today. And he was fascinated with Sarah's courage under fire. What made her that way? Most women wouldn't do what she did, but maybe that was a prejudice on his part. "Your call on this, but I remember you saying the first twelve years of your life weren't happy?"

Sarah's heart snapped shut over his softly asked question. She hesitated and stared into his half-closed eyes. Her woman's instincts were wide-open and she could feel Ethan probing her, wanting to know more than what any man had ever asked of her before.

"Why do you want to know?" Sarah muttered, swallowing hard.

Ethan sensed Sarah's immediate withdrawal; fear lodged in her narrowing eyes. That caught him off guard. "I want to know more about you. The person, not the medevac pilot." He added a slight, coaxing look, holding her guarded gaze. Ethan could sense her sizing him up as a potential enemy, just because he was curious about her.

Sarah picked up the orange and began to slowly peel it. Ethan was throwing her off balance. His face was as sincere as his question. God, did she really want to open up this can of worms to him? To a man? His gray eyes held hers, and she felt a deep emotional connection building between them. It wasn't visible, but, damn, it touched every part of her being. She kept peeling the orange, thinking, and dropped the rind into the tray. The scent of the orange enveloped her nostrils, something clean and sweet juxtaposed with her world of combat. Sarah glanced up at him and scowled. Ethan was relaxed, as if he were the most patient person in the world, waiting for her to make a decision. Her stomach tightened.

"I don't want to talk about it." The words came out

roughened, charged with a lot of barely held-in emotion. Ethan opened his hands.

"Why do I threaten you, Sarah?"

She stared bluntly at him. "Because *most* men want to take a piece of my soul from me. It happened when I was young. I'll be damned if I'm giving any other part of myself away to one." She saw him sit back, digesting her growling words. And she had growled, almost a wolf warning to back off or it would bite.

"All I want," Ethan began after the silence strung for a long minute between them, "is to get to know you better. You're an incredible pilot and woman, and, maybe it's my SEAL curiosity at work here, but I do care about you, Sarah."

Wincing inwardly, Sarah stared down at the orange in her hands, weighing and evaluating. She was so tired of hiding. So tired of trying not to be noticed because she was a woman in a male world of combat. Lifting her chin, she met his eyes again.

"When my mother, who I still don't know to this day, gave me up, a couple of winos found me tossed into a garbage Dumpster. They called nine-one-one, and I was taken to a hospital." Ethan's brows immediately drew down into a scowl. And there was actual sympathy in his eyes for her. "And please don't feel sorry for me, okay?"

Ethan nodded. "No pity," he promised, his voice strained. His heart ached over her statement. He tried to imagine how he would feel in her shoes. "Did you get placed into the children's protective services, then?"

"Yes, but I don't remember much until I was about

six," she muttered. Another peel dropped from the orange; her eyes were on it, not him. Sarah did not want Ethan to feel sorry for her. "I guess I was a sick baby and went through a series of foster homes until I landed in the one at six." Sarah shrugged. "I was a pain in the ass for families that took me in. Who wanted a kid that was always sick? Always crying?"

Drawing in a deep breath, Ethan could see the injury in her right now from that time in her life. "Well," he murmured, "you couldn't help being sick or needing attention. Even as a baby, you knew you'd been abandoned by your mother. Tears of grief…"

Sarah peeled off more skin of the orange. The scent helped steady her slowly unwrapping emotions. The memories from her past made her feel vulnerable. Somehow, the tenor of Ethan's voice, that sincere concern in his eyes, allowed her to go on. "At six I landed in a snake pit. The foster parents, Marge and Bill Caldwell, were both alcoholics." Her voice turned derisive. "The social workers did not thoroughly vet them. The state child protective services didn't do their job." Anger rose in her. Her voice became colder. "I learned not to cry, not to want anything from them. I didn't speak a word until I was five years old, so the state said I was mentally challenged. When I lived in their home, I became very scared. I tried to run away all the time, which got me into a whole lot more hot water. Marge and Bill wanted me because I was money in the bank for them every month so they could buy their bottles of whiskey."

Ethan saw how she averted her gaze. Sarah was staring at the orange in her hands as if it could some-

how take away the pain he heard in her low voice. He
wanted to reach out to comfort her, but he didn't dare.
The gesture would be misinterpreted by those around
him. And even worse, she would misinterpret it. He
watched Sarah fighting back tears, her lashes lowered so he couldn't look into her blue eyes. His heart
wrenched in his chest. Mouth quirking, he said softly,
"I can't imagine how you felt as a little girl."

His words had a calming effect on her roiling feelings. Sarah lost her appetite and placed the orange on
the tray. Clasping her hands in front of her, she lifted
her gaze and met his. Ethan's face was utterly open to
her. The man and the SEAL were two entirely different
creatures. His gray eyes burned with compassion, not
pity, for her. Every line in his sun-darkened face was
readable. Sarah saw no judgment in his eyes.

"I was too young to understand anything," she went
on, her voice hoarse. "I hated them. And they hated me.
I knew if I ran away, the social worker would come.
And every time I wanted her to take me out of there, but
she was blind, deaf and dumb to what was going on."

Ethan wanted to protect Sarah as he saw moisture
in her eyes. "Did you have to stay with them until you
got to Hank and Mary Benson?"

Sarah straightened, rolling her shoulders, wanting to
throw off the weight and haunting memories from the
past she still carried. "I don't want to say much more,
Ethan. I— It's just too personal and…" Her voice trailed
off. She was ashamed to say it. No one came to the rescue of a terrified six-year-old girl. Maybe that's why
she was so passionate about rescuing wounded men and

women who were in a wartime situation. And she was damn well not going to abandon them as she had been abandoned. No one had come to rescue her.

"That's okay," Ethan rasped, giving her a tender look. "I didn't mean to open up a can of worms."

"Some people just have sad lives and that's the end of it, Ethan." Sarah frowned and gave him a hard look. "But that doesn't mean we let our past define us, either."

"You're a damn good medevac pilot," Ethan said, meaning it.

"I know I am. I'll fight to save a life no matter how hot the LZ gets."

Ethan believed her. "So, you mentioned your CO? Major Donaldson? He sounds more conservative about how he's running your squadron than you'd like."

Sarah pulled a wedge of orange free and said, "He's a bean counter. Afraid to have his conservative budget he made up a year ago get destroyed by our helos being shot up or lost in combat," she said, chuckling.

Ethan watched her pop the wedge of orange into her mouth. He couldn't help but be turned on by it, by those lips glistening with the juice, wondering what it would be like to kiss this courageous woman. His body hardened, and he groaned inwardly. Ethan was discovering he had absolutely no defense against Sarah. "Do you think he's going to be upset with today's mission?"

"Count on it. I'm sure I'll get called in on his infamous red carpet tomorrow morning and he's going to try and take me apart, piece by piece." In some ways, Donaldson, rightly or wrongly, reminded her of Bill Caldwell. He had the same close-set small eyes, and it

sent off a vibration of terror through her every time her
CO looked at her. She hated being around the major. It
just dragged up so many feelings of being trapped, unable to escape Bill's hands, his mouth on hers, touching
her private parts, that she wanted to vomit. Though she
knew Donaldson wasn't Bill, her body and her memory didn't make that same delineation. Only her mind
did, and she had no control of how her body violently
reacted when the major was pissed off at her. Which
was often.

Sarah was always standing up to the nitpicky major
when the other pilots wouldn't. And in that snake pit
foster home of hers, Sarah had fought Bill and Marge
just as much as she fought Donaldson. Here, she didn't
run away as she had as a frightened, terrorized child.
She was twenty-nine, mature far beyond her years, and
Sarah ran toward any fight she considered worthy of
her passion. And her heart, her wounded but fiercely
ardent heart, would easily enter the fray on the behalf
of a wounded man or woman on the battlefield in a
heartbeat.

Donaldson was frustrated with her, didn't understand her commitment as a medevac pilot to go through
literal hell to save a wounded person's life. All he saw
was his budget being ripped to shreds because a helicopter required maintenance, a new Plexiglas cockpit
window installed, a new engine or whatever. He lived
in a cold world of numbers, not human values and lives.
She lived in the world of the heart, making damn sure
rescue would come for those men and women when she
was given the mission. No one was going to be left be-

hind. No one, like herself, was going to be left sitting in a closet after Bill sexually molested her, crying and wishing for a rescue that would never come.

"Do you ever get some time off?" Ethan wondered, seeing the anger and frustration in her blue eyes. He felt bad, knowing his curiosity had dredged up a very unhappy childhood for Sarah.

"We're two pilots short. We're all working every day."

"At least you got four days of rest," he murmured, searching her closed expression.

"Yeah, I should thank that bastard for that. At least I got four days of solid, deep sleep."

Hearing the derision in her husky tone, he said, "I was wondering because I work with an NGO run by an Afghan Apache pilot. Captain Khalid Shaheen is the first Afghan to be trained to fly an Apache for the Army. His wife, Emma, an American who used to be an Apache pilot, helps him with their charity along the border villages. They bring in educational supplies, desks, books and teachers. Plus, they bring in donated American clothing to the children. I work with them off and on, when I can. We're always on patrols or missions in a lot of these border village areas, and I see the poverty. In one village the kids were barefoot. Every one of them. I contacted Khalid, and he has gathered about a hundred pair of children's shoes at his villa outside Kabul and he's waiting for me to arrange a pickup and distribution for them."

Deeply touched, Sarah said, "That's very nice of you to do that."

"I hate to see these kids suffer so much," Ethan admitted. "I grew up in a happy family with two other brothers and a sister. After my dad retired from the Navy, he bought a small ranch in Texas. Looking back on my childhood, I never wanted for anything."

"You were lucky," Sarah said. She could see it in the strength of his face, his calm demeanor. Ethan wasn't like her: reactive, getting angry very quickly over situations where weaker human beings were being taken advantage of by higher ups. Or disempowered, as she had been. "Listen, I'll see what I can do. We've got extra Black Hawks here, just no pilots to fly them. Maybe my CO will let me fly a humanitarian mission for you. I can try. No guarantees."

He smiled a little. "Somehow, Sarah, I think you get your way when you want it."

"I don't take the word *no* very well, Ethan. But maybe you've noticed that already."

Chapter 8

Sarah felt her heart beat a little more strongly when she saw the white envelope waiting for her when she woke up at 0500. No longer did she try and tell herself it was a trick. Soon, she would ask Ethan and confront him about being the poet. She opened it, anxious to read what he'd penned to her this time.

*And it is yet possible that even you could not
glimpse the full spectrum of your mellifluous self,*

Since you are a multilayered being

*Of unrestrained rapture and passion.
(to be continued as poet can find time)*

Warmth flowed through her, opening her heart once more. Sarah felt the words reverberate sweetly through her. Ethan saw deeply into her. She sighed. His words were beautiful. Accurate. She was a passionate person on a mission. Her whole existence was predicated on saving lives. It was almost an obsession, driving her. Sarah felt she had survived her past to turn around and rescue those who were vulnerable and unable to defend themselves.

The words this morning felt so right to Sarah. She knew she was going into the lion's den when ordered over to Major Donaldson's office at 0800 when her shift ended. Her passion to protect and defend life was her armor. Her reason for being. And she was damned if this man, her CO, was going to strip her of it.

"At ease, Chief Benson," Major Donaldson said. He scowled up at her.

Sarah was in a clean flight uniform; she took an at-ease position in front of his desk, keeping her face unreadable. He drummed his fingers on the desk, staring hard at her. Her gaze settled on something above his head, looking at the wall behind him. Sarah knew that infuriated him. He preferred eye contact.

"I gave you a direct order yesterday on the way to that medevac mission to stop and wait."

"I didn't hear your order, sir." Sarah kept her voice even, noncombative, although every cell in her body was on guard and ready to go into battle with this officer. Her heart rate picked up because she saw the anger in Donaldson's close-set eyes. It turned her stomach. She saw Bill Caldwell's thin, unshaven face instead.

"You said there was faulty communication? It was fine on my end, Chief Benson."

"Wasn't on mine, sir. I don't know if you heard me request for you to repeat your message?" She refused to look into his eyes, feeling her entire body begin to shrink inside her flight uniform. It always happened when she felt a predatory male presence.

"Dammit, I ordered you to stand down on that flight!"

Coolly, Sarah lowered her gaze and stared hard at him. "Sir, I had authorization from the Marine lieutenant on the ground. Marine Corps HQ at Bagram. I had authorization from SEAL HQ here at Camp Bravo, and you gave me authorization. I followed procedures. All military branches involved in the medevac mission were contacted, brought up to speed on the nature of the mission and I received the order to proceed." She lowered her voice. "It was the call of the men on that hill to make and it was left up to me, as the pilot commander on that mission, to make the decision to go or no go." Her nostrils flared. "I decided to go."

"Yes," Donaldson growled. "And now I have to spend budget money I don't have in order to replace the Plexiglas cockpit windshield on your helicopter. Not to mention the four bullet holes that have torn up the fuselage cabin of that helicopter. That costs money, Chief Benson, in case you forgot."

Her anger spiraled, and she glared across the desk at the hard-set major's face. "Sir, with all due respect,

I had authorization. I did not disobey any direct order. I can't help it if our digital radio went on the fritz. It's computers and software. We were in a lot of turbulence flying to that rescue. Everything was being bounced around. You know yourself that computers can't always take a beating."

He studied her in the silence.

Sarah knew she was right. She'd been in the military too long not to know how to play the game. He could play games, too.

"You're a risk taker, Chief Benson. And that's a problem. You're like a pit bull when it comes to a mission, never using common sense when it's required. That hill was being overrun. You should have backed off and waited until it was secured."

Eyes blazing, Sarah bit out, "Sir, I'm a medevac pilot for a reason. Men's lives depend upon me and my crew getting there as fast as possible. I couldn't care less how much lead is coming our way. As long as I judge the situation as safe enough, that my crew isn't in jeopardy, I'm going in." Her voice turned steely. "I won't *ever* leave a person to bleed out when me and my crew can make the difference, *sir*."

Sarah understood that Donaldson couldn't bring her up on charges. He had given her initial authorization to fly into that hill situation. And if he tried to hang her on the second order to stand down and wait, she'd get a lawyer, go to trial against him and have Bagram's authorization to trump the major's second order that she'd disobeyed. And then his ass would be on the line and he could kiss his colonel's leaves goodbye.

"Well, Chief Benson, besides being on the flight rotation, your day off that was coming due tomorrow is
canceled. You are going to be available as a free-floating
pilot that someone else here on base might need tomorrow. You're on standby."

Sarah almost smiled. She had just such a flight in
mind. "Yes, sir."

"Dismissed."

Ethan was surprised when he saw Sarah show up at
SEAL HQ at 0900. She'd wandered into the compound
and asked for him. Beau, one of the SEAL shooters,
had brought her to where he was, inside working on
another mission in the big room.

"Hey," he said, standing when he saw Sarah, obvi-
ously distressed. Ethan pulled out a stool from beneath
the planning desk and gestured for her to sit down. He
noticed Beau grinning. Let him think what he wanted.

"Hi," Sarah said. She took off her green baseball
cap and stuffed it in her large thigh pocket. "I didn't
know how to call you guys, so I hope it's okay that I
just ambled over here for a face-to-face?"

"Sure, no problem. Would you like some coffee?"
He gestured to the small table in the corner with a pot
on a hot plate.

"No, thanks." Sarah pushed her fingers through the
loose hair that fell around her shoulders. "Never been
in SEALdom," she said, looking around the huge room.
Sarah saw an older man come out of his office and give
her a quick perusal. And then he turned and went back
into his office.

"Yeah, this is Grand Central Station," Ethan joked, sitting down and facing her. "How did the talk with the major go this morning?" Ethan had been concerned for her sake, having seen her in action. He was sure some COs would tear their hair out over Sarah's boldness.

"Well." She sighed, resting her hands on her thighs. "It's good news for you."

"Oh?"

"My CO is pissed off at me, so he's taking my day off tomorrow and assigning me to standby flight status. That means as a pilot, me and my Black Hawk are at anyone's disposal." That same tug-of-war went on inside her. She wanted to be with Ethan. And yet Donaldson had just given her a warning. She had to keep her head in the game. "Do you have tomorrow free so we can take those shoes to the kids in that village? If you do, I need to write up a flight plan so the major can sign off on it and then get it over to Ops, so I can be assigned a bird."

Surprised, Ethan considered her request. Sarah's eyes were clear, and he could see the feistiness was back in them. She didn't look any worse for wear after confronting the major. A slow smile tipped the corners of his mouth. "So, the major is punishing you for doing the right thing?"

"It's in his DNA," Sarah muttered defiantly. "Oh, and more good news. I called Bagram earlier and those two Marines survived. Both are being transferred to Landstuhl Medical Center in Germany shortly."

He couldn't help but grin. "That makes my day." And it did. Two families who were on tenterhooks, knowing their loved ones had been wounded, would now be informed they were not only going to live, but make recovery.

"Yeah, did mine, too." Sarah pushed her hair away from her cheek, holding his gaze. Just being around Ethan lifted her spirits. "So? I'm offering you me and my helo. Are you going to take advantage of it or not?"

Ethan grimaced. "I don't know. I'll have to talk to our chief. He runs the platoon and only he can give me orders to take a day off. I'll ask him a little later."

He pointed to the papers beneath his elbow. "Right now, I'm in the middle of planning an op for an upcoming mission and the chief's expecting it yesterday."

She raised one brow and nodded. "It's the same everywhere, isn't it?"

Ethan gave her a half smile. "Yeah, I guess it is." He looked at his Rolex. "How about I meet you at noon over at the chow hall? I should know what's up the master chief's sleeve by then and I can let you know his decision."

Ethan wanted any excuse to spend time with Sarah. Her eyes turned warm, her cheeks flushed and he sensed her happiness even though she wasn't smiling. Sarah was a complex person with a lot of depth and secrets.

Yesterday's talk had made him feel like a jerk. He hadn't wanted to see the tortured look on her face as she'd recounted her painful childhood. Somehow, Ethan wanted to make it up to her. And he sure as hell wasn't going to ask her any more personal questions for a while. She deserved happiness, not going into that vat of misery again. He could see her seriously thinking about his request.

Sarah slid off the stool, leaned down and retrieved her baseball cap. Straightening, she asked, "I'll see you then?" She put the cap on, drawing the bill down until it was almost level with her eyes. She felt a thrill move through her as she looked at Ethan.

"I'll see you out," Ethan said, gesturing toward the door. He was walking on air but keeping his game face on.

Sarah had already chosen the last table against the wall and gone through the chow line when she saw Ethan arrive. He spotted her immediately out of hundreds of people. Amazed, she nodded toward him, letting him know she saw him, too. Of all the black ops types presently in the chow hall, Ethan stood out. Sarah wasn't sure why. Maybe because he was so tall? His solid confidence? Or maybe the weapons he carried? He was the only man with a SOG SEAL knife in a sheath on his lower left calf and a drop holster on his right thigh with a SIG Sauer 9 mm pistol in it. That SIG was a calling card to everyone that he was a SEAL.

She enjoyed watching him. His movements were economical and fluid, his body honed into a male version of gracefulness.

As she sat there, her entire body began to come to life, as if hidden coals of feminine hunger were awakening, blazing brightly within her. Ethan's maleness, his rock-solid self-assurance, turned her on. It didn't hurt he was damn good-looking even though, like all black ops types, he wore a beard. They had to in order to blend in with the Muslim male population.

Ethan smiled at her as he took the bench so his back would be against the wall. That way, he could see the entrance and exit points in the building and observe what was going on. SEALs did not like to be caught off guard. "Sorry I'm late. Last-minute stuff I had to talk over with Master Chief Gil Hunter." He sat down. His tray was piled high with carbs and protein.

"No worries," Sarah assured him. "I have some bad news for you. My CO isn't going to let me land, stay behind and help off-load those shoes for your kids in that village. I can only drop you and the shoes off and then I have to leave. I can come back and pick you up when you make the call."

He saw she was bummed out. "You have a copilot, but it requires both of you in order to fly that bird."

"Don't go there. I want this to be an enjoyable lunch. Okay?"

His mouth twitched as he picked up a slice of bread and buttered it. "Fair enough. I have good news. The master chief is willing to give me the day off. He says it's a good nation-building exercise." He saw the dejection in her eyes. "You know, SEALs are famous for doing work-arounds? If we get stopped from doing something one way, we just figure out another way to accomplish it."

Sarah watched him dig into the chicken parmesan on his tray. Ethan had three chicken breasts piled high. Sarah knew the heat and long missions for any black ops men were brutal. They burned up thousands of calories in a day, she was once told by a Special Forces captain. "Okay," she offered, confused. "What does thinking outside the box have to do with me and my predicament?"

Grinning, Ethan said between bites, "I'll make a call to Captain Shaheen. Tell him the situation and suggest he call your major and ask for a free-floating pilot. His NGO owns two CH-47s. If he can get your major to let you fly one, then he shouldn't have a problem with it. That way—" his eyes gleamed "—you can fly in with us from Bravo to the village."

"I am CH-47 qualified," Sarah told him, excitement rising in her. Then she frowned. "But Captain Shaheen doesn't want that bird on the ground any longer than necessary, either."

"His wife, Emma, is the other pilot. She can drop you and me off at the village and fly in later and pick us up." Ethan liked the idea of having an entire day with Sarah. A slight glint flared in her eyes.

"If you can pull this off, Ethan, I'm good to go. I love kids. It would be nice to be among them." And it would. Sarah doted on children with good reason. She told herself she wanted to do this just for the children. And knew she was lying in part, because she also wanted to be around Ethan.

"I'll make it work," he gloated, meeting her tentative smile. He motioned to her tray. "Are you not hungry?"

Sarah picked up her fork, a feeling of tension washing through her. "A little." Ethan was easy to be around. He didn't threaten her. "It's your turn," she told him with a dark look.

"To do what?"

"To tell me about your childhood. It sounded wonderful from what little you shared with me yesterday."

"Yeah," he said, shrugging. "I was born in Anchorage, Alaska, where my dad, who was in the Navy, was stationed. After he retired, he bought a small ranch in Texas. My mother, Rose, is a grade school teacher. Me and my two brothers and sister were raised to work hard and play hard."

"It sounds idyllic," Sarah murmured. "At heart, you're a military brat?"

Ethan kept his emotions under tight wraps. It was disconcerting as hell because he could feel Sarah's genuine sincerity of wanting to know who he was. It excited him. It scared the hell out of him. "We were tumbleweeds for sure. I liked it. I have an insatiable curiosity about people and cultures. My sister, Julie, loved it, too. She's a linguist, fluent in four languages, and is a translator. My brothers, Mike and Dan, are in the military like me."

"You're lucky you have siblings," Sarah said, finishing her salad. Discovering she was hungry, which was unusual because combat usually dulled her desire to eat, she moved on to her bowl of beef stew.

"I think so." Ethan grinned. "We'd always had each other's back when one of us got in trouble. Looking back on those days, I'm sure my dad and mom knew, but they let it slide."

She studied him for a moment. "Is Julie in the military, too?"

"Just my brothers. Julie got her teaching certificate

and is following in Mom's shoes. She teaches French. Dan and Mike are in the Marine Corps."

"So you're the only SEAL in the family?"

Nodding, Ethan said, "I like the water."

"No water around here," Sarah pointed out drily. "You're a beached SEAL."

Ethan laughed heartily. He saw the effects of his laughter reflected in her expression. Did he see happiness lurking in those always shadowed, wary-looking eyes of her? It made him feel good. "I'm a landlubber for sure right now, but SEALs get trained in all aspects of black ops—sea, air and land."

"Do you like what you're doing?" she wondered.

"I'm passionate about it." Then Ethan became more somber and added, "Just like you're passionate as a medevac pilot about your mission to get to the wounded and give those guys a chance to live."

The words Ethan used made her think of the stanza of the poem. Studying him beneath her lashes, she saw the commitment in his darkened gray eyes. Sarah was discovering that when Ethan was passionate about something, his eyes took on more intensity. When he was happy, they lightened. It was a small discovery, but it infused her with happiness. As her gaze dropped to his mouth, her lower body ached. What would it be like to kiss Ethan? And if she did, Sarah knew her life would *never* be the same again. Fear of the unknown rose up in her.

Chapter 9

Sarah had set her alarm clock for 0500. Major Donaldson had happily given her permission to go as backup pilot on the NGO's CH-47 today. Somehow, Ethan had made it happen, and she woke up seriously looking forward to the day. The first place her gaze went was the front of her tent. And there, on the plywood floor, was another white envelope. Her heart picked up in beat as she sleepily pushed herself out of the cot and walked over and picked it up.

Her fingers trembled slightly as she opened it up. Anxiously, Sarah lifted the blue parchment, wanting to see the next stanza he had written.

Singing forever into spaces few could have imagined
Let alone foreseen. There are layers of mango
and gypsum

Marshmallow and honeysuckle, iridescent turquoise,
Fog and vapor, wisps and thunderclouds.

And it is given to us how foolish we were to ever
think
We had you pegged, as you unravel into affinity
and wonder,
Inhabiting rooms which here to now we barely
could have imagined.
(More as the busy poet has time)

Sarah felt Ethan had seen through her heavily guarded walls, that he saw the real person. He had even picked up the turquoise color of her eyes. His eloquence was driving her to confront him. She loved the words, and they meant so much to her.

Reluctantly, she set aside the poem and glanced at her watch. She was to meet Ethan at the chow hall in thirty minutes. The NGO helo would be coming in with Emma Trayhern-Shaheen at the controls. Excited about her day, looking forward to helping the destitute children, Sarah got dressed and ready.

Sarah sat with Ethan, watching him gulp down his meal as if he were starved. She forced herself to eat because she knew it was going to be a long day. When he finally slowed down, she narrowed her eyes and held his gaze.

"You've been writing those poems and putting them under my tent flap. Haven't you?" Her heart thudded because if she was wrong, she would feel foolish. Ethan stared at her as if stunned. And then a ruddy flush rose up his neck and swept across his face. For once, he was speechless.

"How did you know?"

"I was awake the first time you pulled the tent flap open to put the envelope inside it," she said, still tense, unsure of why he was writing such beautiful poetry to her.

"Oh…"

He looked so crestfallen. "What? You're a SEAL and you got caught in stealth mode?" A grin nudged at one corner of her mouth.

"I thought… I knew it was a risk. I was running late.… I had wanted to finish the poem and get the first stanza to you, but things went haywire at the HQ. I had to drop what I was doing and attend to other things. I didn't get back to it until after dawn." Ethan shook his head and gave her an apologetic look. "I meant it as a surprise. Something I hoped would make you happy after getting the crap beat out of you by that Army sergeant. I didn't want you to think all men were like that guy who attacked you."

Her heart warmed. This time, Sarah allowed it to fully embrace her. "Is that why you wrote me the poem?"

Ethan pushed his tray aside, then folded his hands, never more serious. "I've always been attracted to you, Sarah. I wanted to get to know you, but I didn't know how. I didn't want to hit on you like every other guy was doing. I knew you hated it, and I don't blame you. And just getting to hold you…carry you…to the E.R.,

I went crazy trying to figure out a nonthreatening way to reach you."

"Then why didn't you sign your name? It was a good thing I saw you, Ethan. I would have, for sure, thought it was the pilots in my squadron playing another dirty trick on me."

"I didn't think—"

"You didn't know what I've been up against in the squadron…the tricks…"

"I'm sorry, Sarah." Ethan searched her eyes. "Did… you like the poem so far? Or do you want me to stop sending them to you?"

Sarah had never seen a man be as vulnerable as Ethan was being with her right now. She knew he was unguarded, no game face, but authentic and honest. "I loved the poem, Ethan. I love receiving them. They're like new life being breathed into me when I read the lines." She quirked her mouth and looked away, a war raging inside her. "I so wanted to believe you. I knew you were writing about how you saw me. And—" she swallowed, her voice hoarse "—I loved how you saw me because that's not the way I see myself.…"

The children waited like wriggling, excited puppies as Ethan and Sarah carried the bulky cardboard boxes filled with shoes into the Afghan village. The sun was just edging the sharp peaks of the Hindu Kush mountains; slats of gold light shot across the green, narrow valley. The mothers of the children kept their charges away from the opened gate that led into the walled village of 150 Shinwari people.

The wife of the leader of the village had thoughtfully provided several large tables to place the boxes on, and, like a good leader, she asked mothers and excited children to line up. As soon as the boxes were on one table, Sarah sat down to begin to fit the shoes on the little girls' feet. Ethan sat at another table opposite her, ready to work with the boys. Muslim law didn't allow Sarah to work with boys. Ethan could never talk to or touch a Muslim woman or female child, either.

The coolness of the morning was delightful, and Sarah made sure her dark green scarf was over her head, honoring Muslim tradition. The village leader's wife smiled and provided tea. She had even given her a rare umbrella so that she could be shaded by the coming hundred-degree heat that would occur by noon. For that, Sarah was grateful.

She smiled over at Ethan, who was about ten feet away. He seemed ecstatic over being able to help the children. Her heart lurched in her breast because the heated look he gave her made her very aware that he wanted her. Swallowing hard, Sarah tucked the awareness away and focused on the little girls looking up at her, their eyes shining with excitement.

By early afternoon, in the heat of the day, Sarah had finished giving every little girl a new pair of shoes, and Ethan had done the same for the boys. She heard the CH-47 coming back to pick them up. Ethan had given the wife of the leader the cardboard boxes; they would use them as fuel for their cooking fires. Nothing was ever wasted in Afghanistan.

Ethan walked up to Sarah. He had never seen her

so relaxed, her blue eyes shining with such happiness. God, how he wanted to reach out, cup her flushed cheek and kiss her. She wore no makeup, but her natural beauty required nothing else. The green scarf had settled around the shoulders of her flight suit; her black hair was loose and free around her shoulders. He felt his heart pick up in beat as she looked up and smiled at him. A smile that told him she was honestly happy to be in his company.

"Hey," he said. "When Emma lands, we'll hustle on board and take off for Bagram."

"Bagram?" Sarah walked with him out the gate of the village, waving goodbye to the leader and his wife. "I thought Emma would take us back to Camp Bravo?"

Ethan responded with a feral smile.

"Okay, what's going on?"

Shrugging, Ethan grinned. "Hey, your major approved it. I sent him the flight info, that we'd be making an open-jaw stop. One at the village, one at Bagram and then flying back to Bravo."

Frowning as she walked at his side, Sarah said, "I didn't see the flight info."

Ethan took the flight report from one of his pockets and handed it to her. Was Sarah disappointed? She seemed worried as she took the orders and read them. "Are you upset about it?" he asked as they stood on an open field outside the village. He had plans, or so he thought, to be with her a little while away from the military world.

After reading the flight report, Sarah handed it back to him. "I'm in enough hot water with my CO. I just didn't want any more trouble." She looked up into his warm gray gaze, feeling herself go weak with longing. Ethan was tall; his shoulders were back with natural pride. The confidence around him was palpable. She'd struggled all her life with low self-esteem and was in awe of people like him who had that incredible self-assurance. It made her trust him a little more, when, ordinarily, she wouldn't have.

"I've got your back," Ethan assured her in a husky tone, giving her a concerned look. "If it's okay with you, Emma and Khalid are inviting us over to their villa for dinner tonight. I thought you might like to have some time off and just be with some of my good friends for a bit?" He peered into her widening eyes and saw them shimmer with sudden excitement. "I mean," he teased as the CH-47 was coming in for a landing, "you strike me as a woman of many facets and that you were up for a little adventure."

"I live for it," Sarah said. Again, the poem stanza gently rose before Sarah. The words… And they were about *her.* What would Ethan's mouth feel like beneath her lips? Taste like? She found her womb beginning to ache with need. The glint in his eyes sent flashes of heat through her. Ethan wanted to kiss her, too. Turning away, breaking the silent energy strung hotly between them, Sarah licked her lips, feeling scared and yet *wanting* him. She hated that tug-of-war feeling that always rose when she was with a man.

Emma flew them back to Bagram in the CH-47 helicopter. It was only a thirty-minute ride, and Sarah enjoyed the sun hanging low on the western horizon over the desert. Her heart, however, focused on Ethan, who rode in the back on one of the nylon seats. He wanted to kiss her. It was there, in his eyes. Just thinking about it made her heart beat faster, her body yearn for his touch. Sarah didn't know what to expect at Emma and Khalid's villa outside Kabul. Feeling excited, Sarah forced herself to stay alert. She knew the Taliban didn't care that this CH-47 was an NGO and not a military helo. They'd try and take it out of the air. NGOs were equally at risk in this country.

Ethan walked with Sarah in the fragrant garden of roses and jasmine after dinner at the Shaheen villa. Above them, the stars hung near and glimmered in the velvet black sky. He guided her to a stone bench along the tiled walkway. The villa was completely surrounded by a ten-foot rock wall with razor-sharp concertina wire strung across the top. Gurkha Indian security guards kept the villa safe from Taliban attacks. The fragrance of the jasmine wafted in the cool night air as they sat down.

"Did you enjoy dinner with Emma and Khalid?" he asked.

Sarah pushed her fingers through her hair. "I did. They're wonderful people. Very compassionate and caring." She felt his warmth and attention, but it didn't scare her as it might with other men. She studied Ethan's deeply shadowed face. The full moon rose in the east, its luminous light touching the garden here and there.

"So are you," Ethan said in a low voice, catching her glance. "Not everyone spends their free time or standby time finding the right size of shoes for a little pair of feet."

"I have a soft spot for children. It was fun today, Ethan. Thanks for inviting me along."

He smiled a little, holding her shadowed gaze. "I'll put you on my list of people who like giving back to others."

Swallowing hard, Sarah stared deeply into his gray eyes. She felt such strength and confidence around Ethan. Wanted it. Wanted him. "I'm in a quandary," she whispered. "About you."

"Me?"

"Yes." She sighed, frustrated. "You might as well know I'm gun-shy of men in general, but I think you already knew that." Frowning, Sarah stared down at her hands in her lap. "I've good reason not to trust them…."

Ethan heard the pain in her whispered words, saw it in her face. He sat for a moment, going over their previous conversations. "It has to do with Bill and Marge Caldwell?" he probed. Instantly, her lower lip trembled and she refused to meet his eyes. If Ethan hadn't seen her in action during the medevac rescue of those two wounded Marines, he would not have believed her shy response to his question. Sarah was bold and courageous as a pilot. Yet, here with him, a mere shadow of herself. As if… He dragged in a deep breath, hoping he was wrong about his sudden realization about her. His heart squeezed with pain, but it was for Sarah, not for himself. He felt as if someone had suddenly hit him in the chest. As he put all her conversations together, his stomach rolled with nausea. As a child, she'd been sexually abused by Bill Caldwell. He couldn't speak.

Moving her damp fingers, twisting them, Sarah finally said, "Yes." The word came out flat. Lifeless.

Ethan's chest tightened. He reached over, gently cupping her shoulders and turning her toward him. Sarah didn't stiffen. Didn't resist. For that, he was grateful as he tried to catch her lowered gaze. "Look at me," he rasped, lifting her chin with his finger. There was such anguish in her blue eyes. Indecision, an internal war, was going on inside her. Now Ethan thought he understood why. "You can trust me, Sarah. You're an incredible person, and I want to know you better."

Trust. Well, that was it, wasn't it? Trusting a man with herself? Not being hurt by them again? Her skin tingled where he'd lightly touched her chin, forcing her to meet his narrowed eyes. Her flesh warmed beneath his hand resting lightly on her shoulder. They were so close to one another. Sarah ached to kiss this man. Ethan had never done anything but protect her.

Her throat tightened as she lifted her hand and barely grazed Ethan's bearded cheek. His eyes grew more narrow as her fingertips lingered there for just a moment. She felt him tense. Her breath became shallower. She'd never craved intimacy with a man until now. And she sensed that he would be gentle with her. Pushing beyond her fear, Sarah leaned up, tilting her head and closing her eyes as her lips brushed his.

Heat exploded through Ethan as her full lips tentatively touched his mouth. Sarah was like a frightened animal, excruciatingly hesitant and unsure. His hands tightened around her shoulders, drawing her closer. He wanted to drag Sarah hard against him and kiss her senseless, but Ethan knew it would scare her off. His lower body hardened painfully and he wanted to groan, take her completely and fill her with himself. His heart beating hard in his chest screamed at him to do the opposite. Her mouth pressed softly against his, as if shyly asking him to participate, to return her risk of reaching out to trust him.

Sarah's fear melted away as Ethan curved his mouth over hers, taking her gently, moving slowly across her wet lips, savoring her. His mouth was tender, coaxing her to join in their celebration of one another. His calloused fingers traced the slope of her cheek, deepening their kiss. She felt flowing fire anchor deep into her womb as his lips took hers, his breath uneven against her cheek. Heart hammering, she slipped her hands over his shoulders. Instantly, she felt his muscles flex, tense, and she heard him groan. Wanting more, she strained against him, her breasts just meeting the wall of his powerful chest. Tiny flames licked through her, tightening her breasts, aching for his touch. Wetness collected between her thighs as his mouth rocked her lips open.

Her world anchored around Ethan as his roughened hand tipped her chin just slightly so he could get better access to her. She swam in the mounting fire of his mouth caressing hers, teasing her, asking her to participate and join the scorching heat growing rapidly between them. Sarah trembled violently as his tongue moved slowly across her lower lip and then invited her to respond. It was almost as if he were teaching her how a man could pleasure his woman. Her arms tightened around his shoulders, her breath becoming ragged. Ethan pulled her tightly to him; there was no space left between their straining bodies. Sarah arched fully against him, wanting more, much more. As his fingers trailed down her cheek, framing her face so that he could take her deeper, the last vestiges of fear dissolved.

Her breasts tightened almost painfully, her nipples aching, captured against his chest. As Ethan moved his tongue into her mouth, she felt a stab of heat that sliced swiftly through her, vivid flames erupting between her thighs, making her so damp and needy, she moaned. Sarah almost cried out when Ethan tore his mouth from hers. His eyes were dark obsidian as he pulled away just enough to meet her gaze. She could feel the thunderous beat of his heart against hers; his nostrils flared, as if taking in her womanly scent. The look in his eyes made her start coming apart in his arms.

"Sarah," Ethan rasped, framing her face with his hands. "I want to love you so damn badly I can't think straight. But this is your decision, not mine."

His words were guttural and heavy with desire. Sarah felt captured within the fire and need wrapping around them. She knew there were two suites in the villa. "But," she whispered unsteadily, "won't Emma and Khalid—"

"Sarah," he growled. "They know we're a couple. There is a suite available to us if we want it. Okay?" He held her startled gaze, which burned with need for him alone.

A couple? Sarah couldn't think, her mind tumbling

in tatters of fevered flames racing through her entire body from Ethan's one kiss. He'd triggered every possible button within her as a woman.

"Yes…okay…"

He gave her a very male smile. It was the look of a man wanting his woman. Was she his woman? Sarah didn't have the focus to feel her way through that life-changing question. All she knew was that she was trembling in Ethan's arms, and the twinge in her body was something she had no experience with. Gazing up into his hooded expression, his eyes gleaming with intensity, Sarah surrendered herself in every way to Ethan. He must have seen it because in one easy motion, he picked her up, then carried her around the tiled sidewalk to the rear of the villa where there was a door.

For the first time in her life, Sarah closed her eyes and trusted a man with her heart, her body. She leaned her head against Ethan's broad shoulder, a new sense of contentment flowing through her, her arms around his neck. She could feel Ethan breathing deeply, the span of his chest moving against her aching breasts.

As he opened the door and walked her down the dimly lit, carpeted hall, Sarah sank fully against him, no longer questioning Ethan or herself. Just once, Sarah wanted to know what it felt like to be truly loved by a man who wanted her for all the right reasons. She pressed a small kiss to his neck, inhaling his masculine scent, which only fed the ache, and her ugly past seemed to dissolve.

Tonight, Sarah was going to give herself to Ethan in every way that she knew how. Her heart told her that he would not only love her, but cherish her, as well. The sense of security around Ethan flowed through her, a sense of safety she'd never experienced before.

Chapter 10

Ethan laid Sarah gently on the large bed in the suite and sat down beside her, his hip resting against hers. The stained glass lamp on the antique dresser shed just enough light so he could read her shadowed expression. Her lips glistened. He wanted her so damn badly. Ethan reached out and brushed her lower lip with his thumb. "I want this to be good for you, Sarah," he told her. "And you need to know, you're in control here."

Her eyes widened slightly. He wasn't going to dredge up the past, or what he suspected had happened to her. He had to be careful since she might interpret any move as a threat. Never had he been more scared with a woman. Sarah was uncharted territory, and Ethan deferred to his heart and instincts to guide him.

When her pupils dilated as he whispered those words

about control being in her hands, he felt an immediate shift in her energy. Relief perhaps? More importantly, he saw it in her gaze.

Ethan slid his finger across Sarah's temple, moving strands of black hair away from her delicate ear. His heart lurched. Was it Sarah's blue eyes, that otherworldly color, that swiftly captured his heart? Or the sadness he'd seen in them the first time he'd met her? Ethan didn't know, but he wasn't going to stop his heart from guiding him where she was concerned.

Sarah deserved a good man in her life. And that is what gave Ethan the steel control over his own body. He didn't want her to associate him with men who had used her, either with her permission or not. Those men had selfishly taken her body, ignoring her heart and soul, not interested in giving back to Sarah or sharing anything with her. Ethan was damn well going to show her how a man could love his woman, make her his equal. And then they could soar together in one another's arms.

It was the tenderness banked in Ethan's gray eyes that convinced Sarah he meant what he said. No man had ever whispered those words to her. She felt suddenly vulnerable beneath his gaze, no longer defensive. He touched her heart. Ethan wanted to forge a trust with her she'd never experienced before, and it left her feeling inept. Just as she was going to say that, he leaned down. His mouth covered hers, sending fire scattering wildly throughout her body. She quivered while he threaded his fingers through her hair, the sensation bringing a moan of pleasure from deep within her.

In her fluctuating mind, Sarah felt a connection building. For whatever reason, as Ethan's mouth gentled hers, coaxing her lips open, the feelings of weakness and shame melted away. His fingers massaged her scalp, sifting her silky strands between them, wreaking new havoc on her unraveling senses. She felt incredibly loved by this man who was a warrior and someone she never believed could ever exist in her world. He was erasing her fears so that no barriers remained between them. Physical and sexual hunger increased as his calloused fingers followed the curve of her slender neck.

Ethan lifted his mouth a bare inch from her own, searching her drowsy eyes, his breathing irregular. "Sarah, are you protected?"

Barely able to speak, she whispered, "Yes, I'm on the pill."

"Tell me what you want, Sarah. What makes you feel good?" He saw arousal in her expression. Ethan could feel her quivering, her breath jagged, her eyes glazed with feeling her own body's need for him. He'd kissed her; that was all. Ethan was shaken at how sensitive Sarah was, to his mouth, his hands. He saw the yearning in her eyes for more of his touches, but he had to hear what she wanted.

Her voice came out wispy. "I like what you're doing…. I want you, Ethan. Please, don't stop…." Sarah swallowed, feeling her pulse leaping as he considered her words and his hands stilled on either side of her head.

"Sarah, I don't want to hurt you."

She smiled softly, lifting her hand, resting it against his cheek. "Ethan, you will never hurt me. I know that."

Her trembling voice tore through him. She'd given him her trust. "You can tell me stop at any time, Sarah, and I will. Just say the word."

She nodded and closed her eyes, dragging in a breath as she felt his fingers gently pulling open the top of her flight suit. "I trust you," she whispered. Trust. For whatever illogical reason, Sarah trusted Ethan with her soul. How to tell him that? She couldn't, too wrapped up in the ache and need of her body. Ethan continued to open the one-piece flight suit. Her flesh grew taut, igniting wherever his knuckles brushed against her sensitized skin. And when he slid his arm beneath her shoulders, drawing her upward into a sitting position to pull down her flight suit, he took her mouth.

Her skin leaped with pleasure as Ethan undressed her, his mouth wreaking new havoc against hers. Lust spiraled through her. Ethan eased her down on the bed and took off her flight boots. Sarah pushed the legs of the flight suit off with his help. He dropped it on the floor, leaned over and gently pulled off her socks. He laid them aside and slowly stretched to his full height, his eyes never leaving hers.

Sarah quivered with anticipation as his burning look drifted from her legs to her belly and up across her breasts and, finally, back to her eyes. Her body responded to his dark, hungry expression. He settled at her hip, watching her, absorbing her. Ethan slipped his arm beneath her back, lifting her against him as he fumbled for and found the hooks to release her bra. His fingers trembled. So did she as Ethan exposed her breasts. Sarah did not cringe from his gaze; the expression of wonder on his face touched her as nothing else ever had.

"You are incredibly beautiful," he whispered against her ear, lips touching her lobe, making her quiver. And then his mouth drifted to her cheek, then found her lips, curved against her, possessing her.

She felt her nipples grow hard. Needy. Her breath hitched, her heart crazily beating in her chest when his roughened hands moved with delicious slowness across her shoulders and then followed the curve around her breasts. His palms were calloused; her flesh was taut and growing hot beneath his exploration.

"Beautiful," he said again, the moisture of his breath flowing across her skin. She tensed, arching forward, straining upward to meet his mouth hovering over the tight peak of her nipple. He moved his hand beneath her hip, adjusting her toward him, giving him full measure of her breast, and he began to gently suckle her.

A cry, part surprise, part intense pleasure, tore out of Sarah's mouth. Her entire body spasmed beneath the electric shocks he'd created with his lips. Whimpering, her fingers sank deeply into his thick, tense shoulders. The sensations were so exquisite, so intense, she froze. He wreaked fire from her other nipple, his tongue rasping across it, making it tight and needy.

Her thighs became wet and her core tightened, wanting him. All of him. Sarah had never had love made so slowly, so deliciously, to her. Each of Ethan's grazing caresses was reverent, as if she were a beautiful goddess come to earth to make love with him. And Sarah felt exactly like that, starving, trembling with his continued ministrations, drawing her breath into his mouth and exchanging it with his. She felt a desire so deep, so undefined in her world, that all she could do was cry out his name.

His mouth left her breast, and Sarah slowly opened her eyes, disoriented, tangled in the webs of lust as Ethan left the bed and stood before her. Her chest rose and fell; her thighs anticipated his coming touch. She couldn't stand much more of this. He gave her a very male look as he shed his boots and pulled off his shirt, exposing the tan T-shirt and dog tags beneath it.

Sarah watched, mesmerized while he pulled off the T-shirt, exposing his darkly haired, powerfully sprung chest. She followed that line that moved across his slab-hard stomach and disappeared like a tease beneath the waistband of his trousers. She licked her lower lip, finding new pleasure in simply watching Ethan remove the clothes from his lean, athletic body.

As Ethan pushed the trousers downward, there was no mistaking how much he wanted her. Her heart quickened, her body erupting at the sight of his erection pressing against his boxer shorts. Her lashes lifted to his face, to his narrowed eyes that held her captive. She felt his hunger for her, but at the same time, she saw thoughtful regard deep in his gray eyes. It was tenderness. For her alone. The realization shook Sarah, opened her, increased her trust in Ethan.

Ethan removed his boxers and put them to the side. He could feel her eyes on him, feel her woman's fire igniting in the drowsy depths of those incredible blue eyes. He felt strong, his body in a painful knot of need. At the same time, Ethan had a primal need to protect Sarah. He placed his knee on the bed, the mattress dipping, and then he lay down beside her. He reached out, his hand curving over her hip, and slowly brought her fully against his body.

Her eyes flared with sensual realization as his erection pressed deeply into her belly. Ethan watched her carefully for fear, but all he saw was desire. Her lips parted, pleading silently for him to continue touching her. He wanted to whisper against Sarah's mouth that he was falling in love with her. Ethan kept quiet, didn't want to risk breaking the connection radiating between them.

He raised up on his elbow, leaned over and claimed Sarah's mouth as he brought her to rest on her back, his hand splaying out across her soft, rounded belly, claiming her. Sarah reminded him of the lush, large-breasted, ample-hipped women painted during the Renaissance era. That bulky flight uniform hid her curves, but God, she was a voluptuous Garden of Eden beneath his exploring hand. Sarah was even more exquisite than even he had dreamed, her flesh creamy white against his sunburned hands.

Ethan slid his fingers down beneath the elastic of her silky white panties and felt her shift. Tense. He went no farther, just allowing her time to get used to his moving teasingly beneath the waistband, feeling her relax, trusting him once more. His mouth went from her lips to capture one of her hardened nipples. Sarah's soft gasp, the arching of her back, told him she was in that pleasure zone once more. And it didn't take much for him to coax down that silky material across her hips and then push them off her lower legs. He sat up enough to pull them off and let them drop to the floor.

Ethan caught Sarah's dazed look as he ran his hand slowly up her long, shapely leg, feeling her muscles tense beneath the soft firmness of her flesh. He wanted her to get used to his hands, his calloused fingers that would only bring her pleasure. Skimming his hand around her thigh, he watched her eyes shutter closed, her breath hitching as his fingers slid closer to the juncture of her thighs. Sarah trembled, telling Ethan she'd enjoyed it.

A deep moan tore from Sarah's lips as she felt his large palm cover her mound that led to her core. His mouth captured one of her nipples, suckling her strongly. Sarah writhed in his arms, pressing herself wantonly against his hand. Her body burned white-hot, her womb contracting in spasms of need. As he moved his hand, his fingers curving around her thigh, he gently drew her open. And when his fingers met her wetness, she tipped her head back, crying out his name.

"Easy, angel," he whispered, his fingers melting into the silky heat at her entrance. Her face was flushed, her eyes tightly shut, her fingers digging frantically into his biceps. Sarah was ready for him, and that was all he wanted to know. Ethan moved between her creamy, taut thighs, stretching forward across her damp, restless body. He held himself in tight check as he framed her face with his hands. Her eyes were wild and unseeing, caught in the silken webs of lust. He kissed her slowly and then caressed her torso, across her hip, curving around her thigh, opening her a little more.

Their bodies were nearly fused and their hearts were pounding against one another. Ethan eased to her entrance and waited to see if she wanted more. Her eyes opened and clung to his gaze, her lips whispering his name, her hands sliding down his tense flanks, trying to pull him forward. It was so easy to feel her tight confines wrap around him, the heat of her sweet, scalding fluids making it effortless to flow into her.

A hoarse sound of pleasure tore out of Sarah as she felt him slide into her. Her body was so tight, and she could feel Ethan waiting, allowing her time to accommodate him. Her body stretched and burned, but the discomfort quickly dissolved into a cauldron of fire and pleasure. Wanting to be closer to Ethan, wanting him deeper, she flexed her hips upward, wrapping her strong legs around his. Sarah watched from beneath her half-closed eyes as his back arched and he clenched his teeth, a muscle leaping in his jaw. He was pulled into her feverish heat. He groaned, and the reverberations swept through her body. Ethan's response deluged her with her own power as a woman. For the first time, Sarah was in touch with her own feminine strength, and it sent a rainbow vibration of satisfaction and completeness soaring through her.

Little by little, Ethan moved more deeply within Sarah, feeling her body give and relax, the fluids surrounding him, driving him near the edge. He eased his fingers through her black hair, cupped her cheek in his palm. Her breathing was uneven, her lips pouty from his kisses. Flexing his hips, Ethan began to move just enough to engage Sarah. A sweet sound caught in her throat, and he smiled, asking her to meet and match his rhythm. Her fingers sank into his shoulders, and he could tell she was lost in the haze and heat of their melting into one another.

Ethan slid his hand beneath her hips, and Sarah sank into his large, rough hand, surrendering herself to him. He angled her hip, finding that sweet spot within her that sent an avalanche of inner sensations vibrating intensely throughout her. She strained against him, wanting to disappear into his hard, driving, sweaty body. The explosiveness, the tension in her womb built until she felt as if she would burst from the inside out as he drove her straight toward that cliff. Sarah sobbed out in desperation; his deep, quick thrusts led her so close to the edge of oblivion. Suddenly, an imploding fire erupted throughout her lower body, tightening around him, feeling her scorching fluids race outward like an unleashed tidal wave. A scream tore from Sarah's lips as she found herself captive to her willful body, to Ethan's undulating thrusts. His hand held her hips tight against him, milking every bit of pleasure he could from her body. Her head sank deeply into the mattress, her entire body bowing upward in spasm, pressed against him, caught within the cauldron of one orgasm after another that shook her to her soul.

Ethan felt Sarah begin to go limp and watched with satisfaction as her skin flushed from the last orgasm. She was so incredibly beautiful, so mind-blowingly responsive to every touch and twist of his body as he remained within her. Finally, he felt his control dissolving beneath her body's honeyed demands. Gritting his teeth, he thrust as deep as he could go and felt his world shatter, spinning out of control, trapped by her strength and heat. Ethan was hurled into the explosive lights he saw behind his tightly shut eyes. Burning heat tunneled down his spine, slamming through him, spilling hotly into her. A growl of utter relief and satisfaction ripped out of him as he finally sank against her warm, soft body, tasting the dampness of her cheek, finding her mouth, plunging his tongue deep into her. A guttural sound of animal satisfaction rippled through his chest.

Sarah floated. Ethan was a warm, heavy blanket across her. Their hearts pounded as one; his arms were around her, holding her tightly. Sometime later, Ethan eased his weight off her, removing himself from her, then drawing her back into the circle of his arms. So weak she couldn't speak, Sarah was surrounded by his hard, protective male body. She rested her cheek against his chest. His long leg crossed over hers, keeping her possessively against him in every way possible.

Is this what love felt like? The question was like magical fog moving slowly through her mind.

All Sarah wanted to do was inhale Ethan's scent, drag it deep into her body like the rarest of perfumes, feel the dampness of his hard flesh against her cheek, his beard rasping against her cheek, his fingers trailing lightly across her shoulder and tracing fire down her arm where it curved across his abs.

Sarah felt cherished. She'd never felt like this before. How could a man be so powerful and yet so gentle with her? And every particle of her being opened up to Ethan, like a flower finally blooming in the sunlight of his hands, his body and that heated smile of his. He had brought her such exquisite pleasure.

She sighed, utterly spent, utterly satisfied, her body continuing to ripple and glow. She luxuriated against Ethan, feeling his erection pressing against her belly once more. How could this not be love? Every other sexual experience she'd had paled in comparison. Not that she'd had that many relationships. But Ethan... Sarah quivered like a cat still purring after being so lovingly stroked and fulfilled.

Finally, their collective breathing returned to normal. She nuzzled against Ethan's chest, the hair tickling her nose and cheek. His long fingers ran slowly through the strands of her hair as he continued to hold her gently against him. Sarah closed her eyes, the feeling of safety and protection within his arms overwhelming her. She'd never felt safe with a man before this. Ethan had given to her, not taken from her. Ethan had known. Somehow, he'd known how hurt she had been by a man at such an early age. And he had given her the gift of himself.

He had educated her about her own body, the beautiful, remarkable gifts she held within herself.

Sarah leaned over just enough to press a kiss to his chest. She could hear the strong beat of Ethan's heart beneath her ear. She tasted the salt of his flesh, the dampness created by their lovemaking, and it made her again sense the power of her femininity. She'd shaken his foundation just as he had dismantled hers. Streaks of heat, light and pleasure flowed through her as she felt Ethan adjust enough so that he could look down into her eyes. Sarah melted beneath his male smile and saw the satiation in his clear gray eyes that burned with tenderness for her alone.

This is what it felt like to be worshipped, Sarah thought, still caught in the arms of the lust that had exploded between them.

"I knew from the moment I saw you," Ethan rasped, his fingers moving the silky strands away from Sarah's half-closed eyes, "that you were an extraordinary woman." He melted beneath the coals of arousal banked in her soft- ened blue eyes. Ethan felt himself responding, wanting to fill her once more, the pleasure thrumming through him. "Sarah, you are an incredible woman. You're beautiful inside and out, angel. And you have no idea how you can make a man want to cry just to be near you…."

His words were like tender strokes across her wounded womanhood. Ethan was so sincere, so heart- breakingly honest that it tore the last vestiges away from her tightly guarded heart for this exquisite mo- ment. All Sarah could do was be held captive by sweet- ness. She felt a new, powerful heart-centered sensation tunnel through her. She saw it reflected in Ethan's eyes, too.

How could what they had, whatever it was, stand a chance in combat? They led lives where they were al- ways in harm's way. Throat tightening, Sarah wanted so badly to tell him, but a new, unsettling fear reached out to imprison her. She'd already seen Ethan in a fire- fight. He ran toward trouble, not away from it. SEALs lived to fight. He fiercely protected those who couldn't protect themselves. Just as he had protected her as he loved her. And now that sense of protection was even more intense surrounding her. She felt branded by his essence as a male, felt his stamp on every trembling, satiated cell of her being.

Swallowing, Sarah whispered brokenly, "You touched my soul, Ethan."

Closing his eyes, Ethan rested his jaw against her brow, an emotion filling him, surrounding his heart, deluging his soul with equal relief and gratefulness. "Angel, we're good together. There's no denying that." He smiled a little, comforted that he'd been able to maneuver through that minefield of her past. Ethan felt lucky. There was so much that could have gone wrong.

"Good?" Sarah stirred, smiling. Their bodies were still damp against one another, simmering, waiting. "I've never been loved so thoroughly, Ethan. I never knew it could be like this...."

Her halting, husky words tore at his heart. It confirmed what he already knew without her saying anything else. No wonder Sarah held sadness in her blue eyes. Caldwell had fractured her soul, ripped her spirit apart as a child. He stilled the rage building in him over the injustice done to Sarah. Ethan knew he could not repair her past. But if she would let him, he could help her build a healthy, solid, happy foundation for the future. With him. But he wasn't sure she trusted him enough to go the distance.

Kissing her brow, Ethan whispered, "What we have is special, Sarah. It doesn't happen often." Only when two people love one another did it get this good. But he couldn't say that to her yet. And God knew Ethan wanted to. He was drowning in her turquoise eyes, which shimmered with unspoken joy. Sarah made him feel so damn strong and good about being a man. There were no games or manipulation with her. She simply was her natural self without the walls she'd hidden behind all her life. And he was privileged—blessed, really— to see her in all her beauty. She made his heart dream with possibility.

"Mmm," Sarah whispered, content to be held. It felt so good to find an embrace that made her feel safe. That made her feel good about herself. "You're pretty amazing, Ethan."

He chuckled, smiling against her hair. "Just remember that if I ever make you mad." He felt and heard her laugh. God, Sarah had such a sensual, smoky laugh. Absorbing the sound of her against his chest, Ethan just kept smiling because he felt like the luckiest man on the planet.

Sarah slowly slid her fingers through the damp, tangled hair across his chest. "Ethan...what are we going to do?"

He understood the brevity of her question. Her hand stilled against his chest, as if waiting. Not wanting to hear reality. And in a war zone, the only way to survive was to remain realistic. Ethan shifted away from her, still cradling Sarah within his embrace, holding her concerned gaze. "I want a serious relationship with you, Sarah. Our jobs are going to tear us apart more than give us time together." He saw her lips part, that pouty lower lip calling him once more. Sarah hadn't done it on purpose to tease him, he realized. Her eyes looked worried as she held his somber gaze. Ethan prayed she felt the same as he did. "We'll find the time. Just like today. We took advantage of it."

"Reality's a bitch," Sarah finally muttered. She closed her eyes for a moment because what they'd just shared was so wonderful, a gem in the desert of her life. "I'm still afraid, Ethan. Ever since you saved me from that guy…" The words jammed up in her throat. She felt tears burn her eyes. Forcing herself past all of that, Sarah whispered unsteadily, "There's something about you…. You're different. A part of me wants to know you. All of you. Whenever we can get some time off together. The other part of me—" she lowered her gaze as shame flowed through her "—is so scared."

Ethan's heart twisted in his chest at the tears glimmering in her blue eyes. From his vantage point, she was an emotional minefield, with so many scars and bad memories. "It's all right," he managed. "We'll make it work. We'll figure something out. I don't want to lose what we have, Sarah." And then Ethan leaned closer. He wanted to say so much more but he saw the fear in her expression. One step at a time….

Chapter 11

Sarah didn't want the night to end. Ethan must have seen the disappointment in her eyes.

"Why so sad?" he whispered, nuzzling her hair, inhaling her scent.

"Time," Sarah uttered, feeling his lips caress her hair. The luxury of being so incredibly cherished was new and beautiful to her. "We have to get back to Bravo, and I don't want to move. I wish…" Sarah sighed, feeling Ethan draw her closer to him, his hard, warm flesh strong and steady against her softer curves that gave way against him.

"That we had more time together," he breathed, finishing the sentence for her. Ethan tucked her head beneath his chin, wanting her to fully feel his protection. "We don't have to be back to Bravo until 0800." He raised his head, reading the digital clock opposite the bed, high on the dresser. "It's 0100. We have seven hours."

Stirring, Sarah admitted, "I feel like I've just been given a gift of you." She smiled softly, eyes closed as she slid her hand across his chest. His muscles flexed, responding beneath his skin to her fingertips.

"You're the treasure," he growled, kissing Sarah's parted lips gently. "I'm the luckiest one right now." He felt her full lips draw into a smile beneath his. "And you're such a fierce warrior," he added, meaning it.

Rousing herself, Sarah tipped her head back on his broad shoulder. "No more than you, Ethan. Remember? I saw you in action, too."

"Mutual admiration society, then," he murmured, sliding his mouth across her lips, feeling her respond. How could Sarah be this sensitive and still do the job she did? They were like separate puzzle pieces within her: the woman warrior and the lush lover who came apart in his arms. "How did you get so fierce?" he wondered against her cheek, the velvet warmth against his mouth.

"I don't know," she admitted, her voice sounding far-off. Sarah simply absorbed Ethan, his holding her, never wanting the night to end. "Maybe…maybe because of my past." And then she gave a short, bitter laugh. "When you get left in a Dumpster after being born and then found by two winos searching for some food… Maybe that beginning branded me. I feel a baby picks up on everything, whether they are loved, hated, stalked."

"You," he whispered, his voice filled with emotion, "had a rough start in life, Sarah. But when you felt thrown away, you were really the gem hidden within that trash. I can't imagine how you felt when you were told that. I can't…" God help him, his sense of protection became even more intense within him. Ethan felt driven to somehow heal her, to allow Sarah to see who she was today, help her discover the inner beauty of her soul whether it was fractured or not.

"All my life," Sarah said against his chest, "I wanted to prove I was worth keeping, Ethan. Maybe that's where my drive to show everyone I'm worth having around originated."

Her words tore Ethan apart. Shutting his eyes tightly, he struggled to get his own emotions under control. Sarah didn't need his pity. What she needed was something very different. "Listen," he told her, his voice dark and impassioned. "You just saved two Marines from dying out there the other day. I saw it. I saw *you*. Nothing rattled you as the bullets were flying, Sarah. You were like a rock, holding that helo steady, holding the tenuous threads of your medics running to help us get those Marines on board. You are so damned powerful in a crisis—it just blew my mind. You didn't care what was being thrown your way. It was your quiet, steadfast courage that made it all work and have a happy ending." He moved his hand down her long spine, feeling her strength beneath his fingers. "You are incredible in my eyes, my heart…." And Sarah was.

Ethan's vibrating words filled her heart, touched her soul that was so hungry. "All I felt at the time I was sitting in that right seat was a very different emotion, Ethan. I was damned if those Marines weren't going to be protected, to be given every chance to live." Her eyes flashed with anger, and she felt it deep in her body, in her passionate soul. It was that pit bull power that had always been with her since she could remember. It had gotten her through every hell she'd been forced to experience in her life. It had gotten her to tonight, into Ethan's caring arms, being given access to his incredible heart.

"That's because no one protected you as a little girl," Ethan told her huskily, sliding his hand against her hair, holding her a little more surely against his body. "Because you never received the protection you deserved, Sarah, there was something good and clean in your soul that recognized you could turn around and become someone else's protector." He wanted to cry for Sarah but simply squeezed her to let her know she had his protection. And SEALs damn well knew how to protect their loved ones.

They lay in one another's arms for a long time, and Sarah absorbed every cherishing movement of his hands whispering across her body. How was it possible to have met Ethan? She could literally feel him giving to her, and it brought tears beneath her closed eyes. "How do you exist?" she whispered unsteadily against his chest, his slow heartbeat soothing her.

Ethan laughed softly. "What do you mean?" He could feel her thinking, not by mental telepathy, but something else, a vibrant connection between their souls.

She frowned. "How did you get to be the way you are?"

Ethan's mouth quirked. "I don't know, Sarah. I'm just me."

"But you *see* me."

He sighed. "My heart saw you first."

"Your heart has eyes then," she said, absorbing his embrace. Sarah had never felt so profoundly safe in her life. It was him. Ethan. Who he was.

"I believe the heart should always lead us, be our eyes in our life," he murmured. Ethan watched the strands of her hair fall like gleaming black ribbons against the others. "I guess my parents taught me that. Especially my mother." His voice grew amused. "I can remember her always telling us kids that our heart was our compass. Our head was secondary, but to always listen to our feelings, our instincts. She was a mother bear about that." He chuckled quietly. Their time with one another was never going to be guaranteed. Right now, Ethan was like a greedy beggar, absorbing every precious second with Sarah. He would not know when they'd ever have this kind of time again. Ethan felt as if he were in some radiant dream, transported to another realm with her.

"You are different," Sarah said in a hushed tone. "When you came into that canteen, I felt you before I saw you. I looked up, and there you were. For the first time in my life, Ethan, I didn't feel so threatened by a man. I felt you look at me, but I can't explain it." Sarah moistened her lips, searching to articulate her feelings. "You sat down opposite of me. You never looked at me directly. But I felt you watching me, and I didn't feel as defensive about it, as if you weren't stripping me with your eyes, wanting to take something from me that wasn't yours to take."

Ethan struggled to contain the pain he felt for her. "I wanted you, Sarah. Every man in that canteen wanted you." He caressed her shoulder. "Maybe the difference was I was attracted to you for a lot of reasons, not just the physical." Ethan's voice became derisive. "I'd be a liar if I told you I didn't want you, too, Sarah. I did, but what threw me was that I saw the sadness in your eyes, felt it go right through me like someone had shot an arrow straight into my heart. The sadness I felt in you was soul-deep, nothing light, nothing unimportant."

Ethan eased her away from him to drown in Sarah's moist blue eyes. "Maybe I was feeling your beginnings in your life? Being thrown away, thinking you weren't good enough to be loved or not be taken care of? I don't know—I honestly can't give it words." And then his mouth drew into a wry smile. "And I'm pretty good with words. Or I like to think I am." Ethan gave her a sheepish look. He knew she loved the words in the poems he gave her.

Sarah stared up at him. His expression glinted with an intelligence she'd never found in another man. His mouth was so strong, one corner pulled inward, as if he was experiencing her pain, perhaps. "Your words always lift me, Ethan."

His cheeks glowed a dull red even in the shadowy light of the room, and a sudden shyness fleeted across his gaze. It was his mouth, however, that touched her.

His lips twisted into a wry position, as if he was unsure in that moment. *Of what?* For a split second, the confident man wasn't there. She saw a shy young boy, his heart on his sleeve.

"From the first day when I saw you at the canteen, Sarah, I thought of you as an angel with wings. Only your wings were the blades on your helicopter. I wanted my poem—how I saw you—to make you feel good about yourself," Ethan admitted, seeing the realization make her eyes shimmer with an incredible rainbow of emotions.

Sarah lifted her hand, sliding it against his clean jaw. "I love them. You can't know how your words touched me…." She held his gaze, seeing hope flare. "You can't know how, after a while, I didn't believe they were a trick, but coming from someone who really saw me. Not my body. But me. And every day, your words just melted into my heart a little more, and for the first time in a long time, I felt hope. I felt—" Sarah's voice broke "—I felt you saw something in me that was so beautiful. And I wanted to believe in what you saw." Tears ran down her face.

Drawing in an uneven breath, Ethan lifted his hand and, with his thumb, removed the warm tears from her flushed cheeks. "Sarah, I wanted to touch your heart and your beautiful soul. To share with you what I saw within you. I lived in hell wondering if you didn't understand my words. I was afraid you'd think I was like every other poor bastard at that camp, wanting you and tricking you into being trapped in my snare I'd laid out for you."

His touch was so incredibly light against her cheek. Sarah sensed he fought his own emotions. "Your words were so insightful, and somehow I knew you were sincere. I—I just haven't ever met anyone like you, Ethan." And it scared her even now because she was on new ground and had no experience. Sarah didn't ever consider herself beautiful. She'd always felt ugly.

"Words are powerful," Ethan agreed, leaning down, barely brushing his mouth against hers. He felt Sarah tremble, felt her body awakening once more beneath his hands. The soft lushness of her lips glided against his own, enjoying him in so many ways. Her courage to open up to him, to trust him, was a special gift that he always wanted to cherish and build on with her.

"Your words are healing to me, Ethan," Sarah whispered unsteadily, feeling his mouth becoming more possessive, reigniting her body, making her womb ache with renewed hunger, wanting to love him once again.

As he eased Sarah down upon the bed, her hips flexed against his and her eyes changed to undisguised raw hunger for him. He gave her an intense look; his erection was trapped against her soft belly. She lay beneath him, her blue eyes glistening with some unnamed emotion. Helpless to fight the possibility of love, Ethan allowed his heart to interpret her expression, her soft, parted lips, her hands calling him to him, wanting him to take her once more.

As he leaned over, whispering his breath across her taut breasts, watching the peaks harden beneath the rasping of his beard, his heart burst open with such an avalanche of possessiveness toward Sarah. The power-

ful sense of wanting to claim her as his woman, wanting
to always protect her, overwhelmed Ethan. Sarah had
given him her heart and soul tonight. But Ethan also
recognized, just as starkly, how the specter of Sarah's
past ran her life to this day. Could he compete with that?
Could he win her trust? Everything was so tentative.
So damn fragile between them.

Chapter 12

Sarah arrived back at her tent after flying all day. To her delight, she found Ethan's white envelope on the floor of her tent waiting for her. A soft smile came to her mouth as she scooped it up and went inside the hot, stuffy interior. It was 1800, and she was starving. Sarah had been flying medevac missions from 0900 onward. Her hand shook slightly as she sat down on her cot after placing her helmet bag on the floor. Last night had changed her life.

Her body still glowed from Ethan's lovemaking. She had hated saying goodbye at Ops at 0700. Wanting to kiss him but unable to; she was back in the military harness with too many eyes watching them.

She opened the blue parchment, hungrily reading his beautiful words.

These are the shining mansions and palaces
Dwelling within the house of your consciousness,
Where colors run riot, and the rigidity of rules
And restrictions have no sway. I am forever
touched by gladness
That you allowed my antenna to slip in for a short
stay
To this hidden oasis, this rainbow retreat
Where jewels of yourself are unrestrained
And your spirit engages in endless delight and
play,

Say what you will that you are an ordinary person:
We will tell none of your poker face desire
To blend into normalcy and proper station

Say what you will
Yet we hear the whisper of enchanted blustery
breezes
To careen and dance between your atoms' space
And for the blazing, coursing tides of ardent
expression
To kiss as dew into your untrodden, spiraling
paths and passageways
Hidden beneath the winking sphinx of your
countenance...

(Ethan)

Closing her eyes, Sarah pressed the paper to her
heart, feeling Ethan's invisible arms around her, hear-

ing his low voice whispering those words in her ear and heart. She took a deep breath, opened her eyes and carefully slipped the poem back into the envelope. She stood and placed the letter with the others in a small bundle that she'd wrapped in some twine to keep them together. Her heart ached for Ethan's nearness. He fed her on so many levels, so unlike other men. Perhaps it had been his mother who had made her boys sensitized toward women, taught them to treat them as equals.

She put all her gear on the cot and pulled on her dark green baseball cap. Settling the cap on her head, she decided food first.

Would Ethan be there? He had given her the number to call him over at SEAL HQ if she needed anything. Sarah had decided not to call him. On something important, definitely. A huge part of her wanted to keep what they had secret. Sacred.

A new vulnerability opened deep within her and Sarah wanted to protect it, give it a chance to take root. To flourish for the first time in her life. And just when she would experience that high, heady feeling, her past would crash into her, destroying all those fragile, new feelings.

Sarah awoke the next morning. Automatically, her gaze went to the tent floor. Her heart bounded. There was another envelope from Ethan. She felt an incredible wave of desire. How she wished he could steal silently into her tent, but someone would see him. And then gossip would start. It wasn't something Sarah wanted. Not here. Not with the other medevac pilots who just waited for an opportunity to mercilessly tease her. If they ever got wind that Ethan was the man in her life, hell would rain down on her. Better that he stole like a silent shadow in the night, long after everyone slept, to deliver his beautiful poetry to her. It was enough.

Sarah sat up, rubbing her eyes and walking to the door to retrieve it.

I might seek to tell others

About the lush vibrant peaks of your blossoming soul
But until they see your gardens,
They are likely to take you at face value

That you are ordinary...

Do not believe it.
You are extraordinary
You are a testament and reminder
that in the seed of all of us

Are the blooms to come
Reaching as effortlessly as sunflowers for the sun

And here on out you need not ask me
If I can come out and play. The Answer is YES.
And it has always been YES—You are luminous.

(to be continued by the poet who is currently on Rollerblades...)

Sarah's heart burst with such raw emotion for Ethan that she felt breathless for a moment. She closed her eyes, fingers against the envelope and paper, her heart wide open to him. To all possibilities.

Ten days later Ethan scowled as he was handed a summons for a court-martial. He was ordered to Bagram for an interview. He saw it involved the man who had assaulted Sarah. His mouth automatically tightened. He wondered if she'd just been given the summons because Tolleson and about thirty other individuals were named. Probably the whole damned canteen of men on that day had been given this summons. The Army sergeant who had assaulted her had been in the canteen prior to her leaving it.

It was near noon, and he missed Sarah acutely. After spending the night with her in his arms nearly two weeks ago, Ethan could barely think about anything else. Luckily, the platoon had just come into a rest cycle and he could clean his equipment, replace items in his ruck to prepare for the next mission coming up shortly. And finally get a chance to meet Sarah at the chow hall.

His mind always lingered on her. He worried about her flying, even though he knew her bravery was unmatched. She would rush into situations other medevac pilots might deem too hot and dangerous. Ethan scowled, beginning to realize a romance in war had its highs, but the lows sure as hell sucked. Big-time. It gave him satisfaction to write the poem stanzas and then move like a shadow to her tent in the early morning hours. Now he knew his words touched her heart, and that made him feel good in so many ways.

Looking at the summons again, Ethan realized all of them had to be in Bagram on the same date. He wondered how all the witnesses were going to testify in one day. It was just too many people to interview at one time.

Someone approached and turned. It was Tolleson, scowling as he read his summons.

"Damn, this is going to screw our patrol that's scheduled on that day," he muttered. "There's no way all these witnesses are going to give their testimony in one day."

"We might be there two days," Ethan agreed.

Snorting, Tolleson growled, "Three or four friggin' days. I know how these little investigations work. They'll only have three investigators and your name will be called and you'll be led to a little room to be interviewed. It's such a waste of our valuable time."

"That Army sergeant has whatever they hand out to him coming," Ethan said. "I know we have a mission coming up, but I think we owe Chief Benson our testimony. Don't you?"

Tolleson grimaced. As LPO, his duty was to get the shooters prepared and ready to go. He didn't like to be blindsided. And Tolleson had no idea Ethan and Sarah had a relationship. Ethan was remaining mute on that one. He had Sarah's back.

"Yeah, she's the victim in this," Tolleson finally muttered apologetically, scratching his head. "It's just coming at a friggin' bad time is all."

* * *

Sarah awoke early. She'd slept restlessly because she'd received the summons to go to Bagram and testify against the man who had assaulted her. She wished Ethan were around. Being in the limelight scared the hell out of her, even if she was within her legal rights. As a child, if Sarah drew attention to herself, Bill noticed her. And when he noticed her... She whispered a curse and stood up. She saw Ethan's white envelope on the deck. A rush of emotions, all good, pushed her ugly memories aside.

Her heart pounded briefly as she unfolded the creamy parchment.

As you gain momentum for your magnified daring
I encourage you to invite others to your hidden
gardens
To receive a taste of the leafy wonders unraveling
there

You need no longer hide your head
Under sheets of practicality—
It is a given for you to dazzle
And expand beyond all that you had once dared
To have seen. Infinity is yours for the asking.

Just as you cannot help but grow
Into the break dance of light as it embraces day,
Shining into infinite prisms of magic and of light.

*And to answer your question, there is no end to
growth
As your petals continue to open and magnify
Beyond everything you have ever seen, or hope
to be
To encompass and caress.
As long as I breathe, I will seek the diamond of
your heart.*

*Chow hall 1900 tonight?
(Ethan)*

Sarah tried to keep her game face on as she searched
the busy chow hall, which contained at least two hundred people at dinnertime.

Where was Ethan? She felt dread and didn't know
why. They hadn't seen each other in over two weeks.
Sarah felt that ugliness creeping back into her emotions
and mind. She'd always felt dirty and discarded. Ethan
had made her feel clean and beautiful. Now their relationship seemed as if it had been a dream, now shattered by reality as she came back down to earth. She
had come home to Bravo and that toxic, hungry animal that lived within her was awakening again. Ethan's
love had tamed it. And that pain-filled animal within
her always reminded her she was ugly. Sarah couldn't
put into words the feelings that came with it. That dark,
flowing river of emotions experienced as a child was
always there.

Would Ethan one day see her ugliness? Sarah lived
in dread of that. Her desire to see him turned into anxi-

ety. She didn't want to look obvious as she went through the line with her tray. Too many men stared at her. And now their stares had the same power over her as they had before.

As Sarah left the line, she still hadn't spotted Ethan. He may have gotten orders for a QRF. She tried to find a quiet, safe place away from all the men.

"Sarah?"

Ethan's low voice was close, and she turned, surprised. He was standing nearby, his expression solemn, his gaze trained on her. His look moved down through her like a bolt of lightning. He was in his SEAL cammies, the SIG pistol riding low on his right thigh, a small knife in a sheath strapped to his lower left leg. Everything about him shouted danger. But he wasn't dangerous to her.

He had been her tender, sensitive lover. He knew how to please her, release her from her dark past and give her hope. Sarah's smile was halfhearted as she looked up at him.

"This way," Ethan urged, turning and leading her out of the main room.

There were several smaller rooms out of view of the patrons in the chow hall. To her relief, he led her down a brightly polished hall and into a room on the right. Inside, Sarah saw one table and his tray on it.

"Is this called a SEAL ambush?" she asked, walking over and sitting down opposite him.

Ethan closed the door. There was a window in it and no way to stop people from looking in on them.

He wanted to kiss Sarah. "You could say that," he murmured, giving her a warm look of hello. His body burned and ached. God, he wanted her right here, right now. Ethan had to erase the visualization of Sarah naked, lying on top of the table. He took a deep breath, willing his control back into place. It didn't matter what she wore, he knew the voluptuous, soft, velvet body hidden beneath that green flight uniform. A wariness returned to Sarah's eyes. His gut knotted. What had happened? She didn't look happy to see him. Almost… shy in his presence once again. Something was wrong.

Ethan sat and gazed at her. "You look incredibly beautiful. I've missed you."

Sarah felt heat move into her cheeks, meeting his narrowing gray eyes. "Your poem—it was wonderful. I sat there this morning and cried because it was so un-believably sincere. I knew it was your heart speaking to me." She forced herself to pick up her utensils and eat. Just looking at that well-shaped mouth of his, sent her body on alert. Remembering.

"I don't have any more written," Ethan apologized, cutting the roast on his tray. "What did you get out of the poem?" He held her moist gaze. Sarah, he was dis-covering, was easily touched. But a woman's heart and soul were wired differently than a man's, and it was something he had always appreciated.

"It's as if you took one look at me and knew I was trying to hide. Trying to not be noticed. That you felt I should come out of that hiding and bloom, be myself no matter what anyone else thought."

Ethan shook his head. "Damn, you're good," he praised. "Bingo. I wrote the poem after that first day I saw you in the canteen. I could feel you hiding." And then his voice softened. "But now I know why." She still was to a degree.

"It's in the past." She shrugged.

Ethan said nothing, knowing Sarah's past still haunted her. He marveled at how fearless she was as a pilot.

Unstoppable. To look at her classic face, to fall into the depths of her blue eyes—she moved every particle in his hard, aching body to vibrant, throbbing life. "There are so many sides to you," he said, taking a drink of his water. "I find myself lying awake at night on my cot wondering what you did as a child that made you laugh. What fascinated you? What got your attention?"

She smiled a little, carried on the caress of his low voice. Sarah recognized the smoky-gray color of his eyes and knew what it meant. Ethan wanted to love her. And how her body was blazingly pleading with him to do just that. "I love butterflies," she admitted softly, picking at her salad with her fork. "And rainbows…. I like to go for a walk in a soft rain and feel the drops on my face. I feel like the sky is washing anything dirty or sad around me away."

When she looked up, Sarah saw the serious expression on Ethan's face, as if he were memorizing her words and placing them in his heart. "What about you?"

Ethan raised his brows. "Riding a horse at full gallop

over the hills, the wind cutting against my face, feeling the horse flying under me." He dabbled with his corn, staring down at it, feeling her warmth and attention. Those beautiful blue eyes, so filled with awe. And there was undeniable life in their depths now. He understood loving Sarah had, in some small way, released her from the dark chain from the past that had held her prisoner for God knew how long. But it also raised the whole issue. Understanding he could continue to love her, open Sarah up to the wonders of a man fully loving his woman as equal and partner, would allow her to come from beneath the shadows she'd hidden beneath all her life. And Ethan wanted to be the man to trigger those changes in her, to give her the freedom that she so richly deserved. But would she let him?

"That sounds wonderful…the freedom," Sarah admitted, carried away by his words and descriptions. "Tell me more. What else makes you happy, Ethan?"

Just the way his name rolled off her lips sent an incredible fire from his heart straight down to his tightening body. Damn good thing he had on bulky cammies. Looking up at Sarah, he realized she didn't understand her impact on him.

"I like walking out in the middle of a hellacious thunderstorm," Ethan admitted. "It would drive my parents crazy because they'd always think I'd get struck by lightning, but I never did. I just reveled in the awesome, natural power of the clouds, wind and rain swirling around me. I could feel the wind gut punch me, the rain tear through my hair as I ran, the sweet smell of dried earth being drenched with life-giving water."

"You like chaos."

Ethan chuckled a little. "I suppose I do." And then he grinned. "SEALs own chaos. SEALs are chaos in action. It's what we're trained for—the unexpected and dealing with it."

Sarah finished off her main course and moved to her buttered peas and small, dainty onions. "I'm chaos, too." A dark, ugly storm that lived within her. It scared her that someday Ethan would see that part of her. And he would walk away.

"You are," Ethan agreed, his voice turning low with feeling. "You're an amazing thunderstorm in your own right, with incredible downdrafts of pleasure and then violent updrafts of flying loose and free. The sky isn't even your limit."

Her heart wobbled with fear, saturated with emotions she'd never experienced before. Sarah set her flatware down, feeling tears leak out of her eyes. "You even speak in poetry, Ethan. My God. I can't hardly stand it because your words, the pictures you see in me…"

It took every bit of his control not to reach over and touch Sarah's flushed cheek at that moment. Her lower lip quivered, and Ethan saw his words touch her as surely as he'd drawn her in his arms and kissed her. "I want you to know just how incredible you are as a woman." His eyes became hooded as he held her gaze. "Every second I can find in my day is devoted to you, discovering who you really are. I see you. But you don't see yourself." His voice dropped to an intimate growl. "I'm going to watch you open up, grow, gain confidence in yourself as a woman. It's a tough task," he teased her gently. "And I want to do it." *Because I'm falling in love with you.* Ethan ached to whisper those words to Sarah, but it was far too soon. He felt an urgency to tell her because he knew a SEAL's last breath could be one bullet away. One RPG away. One helicopter crash away. They were not afforded the luxury of time, but his intuition told him to wait and continue to be patient.

Sarah sat there, wrapped in his warmth. She saw it in the tender expression of his face, felt it in the huskiness of his voice. She shook her head. "You're a dream, Ethan. I swear, you're a dream I've concocted because I couldn't stand the pressure of being looked at by hundreds of men every day."

"I'm real, and you know it." Ethan gave her a heated look. "We're good for each other. And I'm no mirage. It doesn't get any more real than the night we spent at the villa, does it?"

Straightening, Sarah whispered, "That was the most wonderful real I've ever experienced, Ethan. You know that."

"Then hold that night close to your heart, Sarah." Ethan grimaced and looked around the small, quiet room. "I find myself wishing we'd met so many other places or at another time." He shared a frustrated look with her. "Why now? Worst place on earth to try and start a relationship. Don't you think?"

"We live in chaos, Ethan. That's what we've chosen for our careers. I worry about that."

"You have to have faith."

"I had to have that," Sarah answered, her voice turning bitter. The memories started to return and she pushed them away, focused on the present. Focus on Ethan, who was a ruggedly handsome warrior. And he liked her.

Did he feel what she felt? Sarah wanted to share her feelings with him, but she hesitated. What they'd found in one another was life giving. But fate could cruelly take it away from them in a heartbeat, too. Sarah pressed her lips together to hold the secret in her heart.

"You got the investigation summons?" Ethan asked her. Sarah's eyes went dark.

"Yes. You, too?"

"Yes." He saw fear in her eyes and knew she was thinking about what might have happened to her. "How can I support you?"

The question startled her. No one had ever asked her something like that. But the seriousness in Ethan's eyes, the set of his mouth, told Sarah he had her back.

"You've done so much already," she said, finishing her food and setting the tray aside. "I need to go, Ethan. This was a nice place to meet. Thank you."

She felt such a rush of anxiety, it made her stomach feel icy. It became apparent that the more she remained with Ethan, the more she knew she had to break it off. This was all just too much.

"The galley chief owed me a favor. Can't do it often,

but tonight…" Ethan ached to kiss Sarah's soft mouth, to feel her lush body against his.

Glancing at her watch, she said apologetically, "I really have to go."

Ethan stood. "Just leave the trays. The guys will come by and pick them up. Follow me?"

Sarah gave him a quizzical look. "Are we going out front?" Out to all those male eyes following her.

"No, we're going into SEAL stealth mode." Ethan grinned. "Trust me."

"With my life."

Ethan opened the door and stepped out, looking up and down the empty hall. He caught Sarah's small hand for just a moment and said, "This way."

Her heart beat a little harder in her breast as he moved quickly and silently, like the shadow he was, down the empty hall. Abruptly, he turned right. He opened a door and slipped through it. He turned, holding out his hand to her. She took it, feeling his strong fingers wrap around hers, sending electric tingles up her hand and arm.

As Ethan drew her into the room, Sarah noticed they were in the maintenance room, where all the machinery, the air-conditioning, plumbing and pipes were located. A hungry look filled Ethan's eyes as he turned and locked the door behind them. They were alone. She met his burning look. Though she wanted to run, she was anchored. Ethan was going to kiss her. How badly she wanted it. One last kiss. A goodbye kiss. Without a word, Sarah walked into his opening arms and felt his mouth press hotly against hers.

She relaxed in Ethan's arms, surrendering to him. Sliding her hands up across his broad shoulders, Sarah strained, wanting to be closer, wanting him inside her. Wanting the pleasure he had given her before. Ethan's breath was uneven as he opened her mouth, moving his tongue against hers, teasing her, asking her to dance with him. His hand ranged down across her back, coming to rest on her hip, hauling her tightly against him.

She moaned, feeling how hard he was, pressing into her belly, her womb tightening with an ache that dived down between her thighs and made her go weak with need.

Sarah couldn't get enough of his mouth, how he possessed her, rocked her lips open, tasted her, shared his breath with her. Ethan was making her ache so much she wanted to cry for relief. As he cupped her face, drinking of her mouth, giving everything he had to her, Sarah quivered in the face of his incredible energy, his protection, flowing through her.

Finally, as Ethan eased from her mouth, giving her lower lip soft nips and then moving his tongue across it, Sarah opened her eyes to stare into his narrowed, stormy gray ones that held her a willing captive. She inhaled his male scent, the sunlight on his flesh, the heat of his skin. She never wanted this moment to end.

Sliding his fingers through her loose, dark hair, Ethan shook his head. "You make me burn. I want you so damned badly I can't think, Sarah." He brushed his mouth against her cheek, feeling the soft velvet of her skin, inhaling her scent. Sarah was so damned exotic. Those blue eyes of hers would melt a glacier in ten seconds flat, no problem. He bussed her cheek, nuzzled into her temple, her hair tickling his face.

The unexpected kiss only tormented Sarah more. Ethan was like sunlight to her dark world. He shed light into her, filling her with radiance, with hope. Her throat constricted, her voice coming out strained. "We need to talk—"

"Listen," Ethan rasped, his hands sliding around her waist, pinning her lower body hotly against his own. "We've got a long-range patrol, several of them, coming up in a week. I'll be gone. I don't know how long, Sarah, but just hold good thoughts for me. I won't be able to contact you." He flexed his mouth. "Not as much as I want to, but where we're going, comms is going to be sporadic at best."

The hair on the back of her neck rose. Sarah frowned, sensing this mission was dangerous. But which one wasn't? "Will your patrol take precedence over this summons?"

"I don't know yet. My LPO is trying to find out. This particular mission is based upon perishable intelligence. It won't wait. I think he's trying to get the court-martial board to give us a waiver. When the mission's complete, I can fly into Bagram and be interviewed." Ethan gave her a sad look. "So, maybe that villa will have to wait."

Sarah was even more confused. Ethan was going into danger. She cared so damn much for him, but at the same time, she felt pulled between that and her own terror over their budding relationship. "We have to talk," she said more firmly, pulling out of his arms. Wincing when she saw the sudden puzzlement come to his gray eyes, Sarah had to step back, against the wall. "I—I can't do this, Ethan."

"What are you talking about?" Panic began to eat through him as he saw the old wariness and distrust in Sarah's eyes. "What's wrong?" He forced himself not to move toward her to try and embrace her. She stood tense, shoulders up, as if expecting to get hit. He'd *never* hit a woman in his life.

"I'm afraid, Ethan," Sarah whispered brokenly, forcing the tears back. "I've never met someone like you before. I feel...out of water.... I'm afraid...." She curled her hands into fists for a moment at her sides. She saw shock and then hurt in his expression. "It's not you," Sarah rushed on in apology. "It's *me*. It's me, Ethan. You really don't know me. I feel so ugly inside. I—I have so many issues that are still stalking me. I don't want to hurt you!" she choked out, pressing her hand against her mouth, trying not to sob as she stared up into his anguished face.

"No," he rasped, his voice breaking. "Sarah...no... Just hear me out? Please?" he pleaded with her. The tears glittered in her eyes. Ethan suddenly got it. Sarah was caught in the past. She was trying to break free of it, but she wasn't there. Not yet. "We can slow down—"

"No," she cried out. "No! I'm not beautiful like you think, Ethan."

He blinked, as if physically slapped in the face. "What?" And then he drew in a deep breath, willing his emotions aside because all it would do was escalate the terror he saw in her eyes. "You are beautiful to *me,* Sarah. I see your beauty. I saw it with those little girls you put the shoes on. I saw your beauty with the women of that Afghan village." He halted, his mind spinning with what to say next. And not chase her off.

"I'm not good for you!" she cried out. "Don't you see that?"

Ethan winced at her cry. It tore through him, shredded his pounding heart and ripped into his soul. "Sarah—"

She closed her eyes and shook her head. "It's over, Ethan. I can't move forward with you. I want to, but I can't. All I'll bring you is unhappiness." She touched his face, tears streaming down her pale cheeks. "All you see is this. Beauty is skin-deep. I'm not beautiful inside, Ethan. I'm not. And I think too much of you to hurt you. And I know I will." She angrily wiped the tears off her cheeks. "This is over. I need it to be over. Don't send me any more poems. Don't try to sit with me at dinner. I—I need space. Time to think. So much has happened so fast."

Ethan watched her turn and swiftly walk to the door, jerk it open and disappear down the hall. *Oh, God.* He slumped against the wall, hand pressed to his face. He'd pushed Sarah too fast. Asked too much of her too soon. Ethan felt tears burning in the backs of his eyes as he tried to forget the night of the most incredible love he'd ever shared with a woman. But Sarah… Why did he push her so fast?

He'd taken advantage of her because she was starting to trust him. He cursed softly as grief rippled through him, stunning him, making him feel as if he were being skinned alive, so vulnerable, so damned open to Sarah.

Ethan got ahold of himself. He swallowed his tears. He forced himself into that box of no emotions to look dispassionately at what had happened. Worst of all, he loved Sarah. Loved her. And she wouldn't want to hear that. Ever.

Chapter 13

The next morning when Sarah woke up, there was an envelope at her door. Her heart sank yet also swelled with joy. Miserable, she rolled out of the cot. She knew Ethan had no other poems to share with her. So what was this? Sitting back on the cot, Sarah opened it up.

Sarah,
Am on a long-range patrol into a hot area. Don't
know how long I'll be gone. My testimony was
granted a stay and I'll give it when we get off this
direct action mission. Stay safe out there?
Ethan

Sarah drew in a shaky breath, a bad feeling moving through her. She had told him she didn't want any more of his poems. Her heart broke over what she'd done. She'd never met a man nicer than Ethan. Never been loved like he had loved her. He'd cherished her. Worshipped her heart, body and soul. Why the hell was she letting this old fear run her life? Tears jammed into her eyes. She had hurt Ethan. She'd seen it in his eyes. Heard it in his voice. Felt the desperation to keep her, not let her run. In the end, he'd stepped aside and re-spected her request. Sarah almost wished he'd fought to keep her. But if Ethan had done that, then she knew that whatever little trust that had grown between them would have snapped and broken forever.

"God," Sarah muttered, slowly rubbing her face. Her eyes were puffy from crying so much last night. Slowly lifting her head, Sarah felt so alone. So abandoned. But this time, she'd done it to herself. Ethan had wanted to stay at her side. He was a fighter. He didn't give up. She knew that about SEALs. You had to kill them to stop them from coming at you if you were the enemy. Sarah had seen that determination in his eyes, but he'd released her.

She missed him so much already. She wanted to find him. Apologize. It was her fault. He didn't under-stand about the ugliness inside her. How it made her feel. And Sarah didn't want Ethan ever to feel how she felt. It was bad enough she did. He was too fine a man to take down like that.

Her other two lovers had accused her of never being good enough. She couldn't please them. They never knew what she'd told Ethan, but both had accused her of being damaged goods. Not worth sticking around. All she was good for was sex.

Her focus shifted back to Ethan. He had told her about DAs, or direct action missions. It meant they were going to take the fight to the Taliban. There would be skirmishes, firefights and deaths. Her eyes grew cloudy with fear for him. Sitting there, Sarah understood now how a SEAL's loved one felt. Or indeed, the spouse or family of any service member who went into harm's way. They knew even less than she did, but the fear of losing Ethan was just as heart-wrenching.

They were still short two pilots at her squadron. As a result, the major was determining which missions to fly. She wondered just how far Ethan and his team were from Camp Bravo. More than likely they were heading to the border to stop the influx of Taliban and al Qaeda from flowing into Afghanistan. Mustafa Khogani and other leaders were always willing to take on any American group, whether Army, Marine or black ops. Their fierce, fanatical bloodlust left her stomach in knots. Mustafa was a cousin to Sangar Khogani, who had been killed earlier by another SEAL sniper team. He had replaced him and was even worse, from what she understood from Ethan.

Sarah decided to try and find out more. She didn't know if the SEALs were aware of her relationship with Ethan. It made her fearful, but her worry for his safety pushed her forward.

Master Chief Gil Hunter got called out of his office by one of his SEAL shooters. Standing at the front desk of their HQ was a woman pilot. His gaze quickly absorbed what he needed to know. She was an Army medevac pilot, a warrant officer. And then, as his gaze swept upward, he met her turquoise blue eyes. Smiling inwardly, Hunter realized this was the infamous Blue Eyes his men were always talking about.

"Chief Benson?" he said, halting in front of her.

"Yes, I am. Master Chief, I'm sorry to take up your valuable time, but I was wondering if you could tell me anything of where Petty Officer First Class Ethan Quinn is headed?"

He put his hands on the desk, considering her request. She stood tense, and he felt her worry. SEALs had this finely honed sense and could pick up on anyone in a hurry. "And Quinn is what to you, Chief Benson?" Hunter wondered if the impossible had happened and it had completely escaped his scalpel-sharp radar. Had Quinn captured Blue Eyes's attention? Judging from her reaction, the lowering of her lashes, the blush sweeping into her cheeks, he got it. What a lucky bastard Quinn was. But yesterday Quinn had acted differently. He'd been glum. Upset and trying to hide it. Did they have a fight?

"Look," Hunter said, lowering his voice, trying not to sound as gruff as before. "I can't give you any info, Chief Benson. We work in top secret black ops. I think you know that." He tipped his head, catching her incredible blue gaze.

"I do, Master Chief." Sarah took a risk and whispered, "I'm flying the border area for the next seven days. Could you at least tell me if he and his team are in that area?"

He smiled a little. "I can tell you, generally speaking, that Hawk is in that region. Yes."

Sarah nodded, compressing her lips. "Okay, Master Chief, that's good enough. Thank you for allowing me to speak to you."

"Wait," Hunter called as she turned to leave.

Sarah slowly turned, looking into the man's bearded face. Hunter was about forty-five years old, deeply tanned, his face a living testament to being a SEAL. "Yes, sir?"

He reached into the pocket of his cammies and produced a business-size envelope. Handing it to her, he said, "Ethan, who is called Hawk by all of us, asked me to give this to you, should you show up here." He held her startled expression. "He asked me to tell you to carry this with you when you flew." His voice lowered. "And he asked that you *not* read it."

Shaken, Sarah took it. A chill ran through her. "Master Chief, is this a death letter?" She barely got the words out; her voice sounded strained even to her. Every SEAL was required to write a death letter to his loved ones in case he was killed in action. That death letter would then be presented to the surviving family, a comfort to have a last letter from their SEAL warrior who they loved.

He scowled. "I don't know, Chief Benson. Hawk has a tendency to journal a lot." He tried to give her a reassuring smile as her face went pale, staring at the letter in her hand as if it were going to bite her. "He's our journalist here in the team. I asked him one time what he was writing about. He told me he wanted a daily log of his being a SEAL so that when he had a family someday, they could read his journal and understand what he had done. Kind of like a forward-future kind of thing his children would someday have. A treasure from their father, I suppose."

"I—I didn't know," Sarah said, feeling a pang of anguish move through her heart.

Hunter nodded. "Look, he's a solid SEAL. He's been around the block a couple of times when it comes to taking down bad guys. I wouldn't worry too much about him. Okay?"

"I know how good he is, Master Chief." Her voice grew stronger as she stared at him. "I was the medevac pilot that flew into that hill where the Marines were almost overrun. Ethan was the comms guiding me in to pick them up."

Hunter's brows rose. "So, it was you?"

Sarah couldn't quite translate his husky statement. But she saw something less harsh in the SEAL's eyes. A realization, maybe. His hard mouth softened just a bit. There was a change in his demeanor toward her, and she didn't understand why.

"I was on the radio that day," Hunter told her. "I heard it all go down. I'd heard a woman's voice, but I didn't know it was you." He gave her a look of pride. "I think Hawk deserves you, Chief Benson."

Just the way he said it, Sarah knew the master chief understood that there was a relationship between her and Ethan. He must have seen her terror over him realizing their personal connection. He didn't know they'd broken up. That she had gotten scared and run.

"SEALs take care of their own, Chief Benson. If I'd have known that, I would have been a little less growly with you." He smiled. "Your secret is safe among us. It will go nowhere, okay?"

Relief and guilt surged through Sarah. "I'd appreciate it, Master Chief. Thank you." Because she'd had enough hazing and grief.

"Look," Hunter said, pointing at the letter. "When Hawk brought this to me last night with his instructions, I knew something was up between the two of you. He didn't say anything, but as a master chief of this SEAL platoon, not much gets past me." His green eyes gleamed with amusement. "I don't think that is a death letter, if you want my gut check. Okay?"

Relief plunged through Sarah as she stared down at it, her fingers damp. "That's good to know, Master Chief. I appreciate your insights." And she did.

"Maybe," Hunter murmured, his grin widening a little, "it was Hawk's way of keeping you close to him. Or maybe he's wanting to be close to you when you fly. You aren't exactly a conservative medevac pilot from what I hear."

Sarah managed a lame smile. "No, Master Chief, I'm not. I'll never be. If men or women are wounded, I'm flying through a lead curtain if I have to and getting them the medical help they deserve."

Hunter grinned. "I think Hawk and you make a good team." And then his smile disappeared. "Leave me your tent number and a phone number where I can touch base with you at your squadron if I need to."

Sarah's heart shrank in fear. He wanted that information in case Ethan was wounded or, worse, killed. She saw it in his eyes, which betrayed no emotion. "Yes, of course...."

Five days later into their patrol Ethan lay prone just below a ridgeline with his team. Tolleson was at his elbow, looking through his Night Force scope on his M4 rifle. It was 0100, and they were watching a group of fifty Taliban carrying huge sacks over their shoulders. Interspersed between them were donkeys carrying such heavy loads they swayed and staggered beneath the weight. To the rear were ten double-humped camels carrying similar loads.

"Fertilizer," Tolleson growled softly.

"Gotta get that stuff to their bomb makers over here," Ethan agreed tightly. Behind him were six other SEAL shooters, waiting, crouched and silent. They had gotten perishable intel that the Hill tribe leader by the name of Mustafa Khogani was going to bring a resupply of fertilizer to make bombs in Afghanistan. Word was it would happen tonight under the blackness of the new moon. The asset had been right.

"What do you want to do?" Ethan asked. He was their communications specialist and he knew he'd probably be calling in the B-52s with JDAMs, laser-guided bombs, to blow this group to hell.

"Let me call HQ," Tolleson said in a low tone, setting his rifle aside.

Ethan listened to the LPO discussing options with Master Chief Hunter and the OIC of their platoon, Franco. The plan would then be called into Bagram Air Base near Kabul, where the SEAL HQ would look at it, analyze it and either give a go or no go on their attack. Ethan sat back, feeling the near-freezing wind cutting across the rocky ridge. He had on his NVGs, night vision goggles, like everyone else. The Taliban were on another mountain, a mile separating them from one another. This was a new line that had just been created, and they were on it with the biggest load of fertilizer supplies he'd ever seen.

He listened with one ear as Tolleson spoke quietly into the mic to the master chief. Ethan heard all the back-and-forth about a plan to take out the Taliban.

The hair stood up on his neck. Ethan twisted around, looking beyond the SEAL shooters waiting patiently fifty feet down from where they were laying on their bellies. *What the hell?* What was he sensing? Whatever it was, it was dangerous. Mouth compressed, Ethan tried to see anything moving down farther on the rocky slope. Only tough, small bushes lived on this cold, windswept ridge. He saw nothing.

To his left was a wadi that was a hundred feet from where they were. Damn, they needed a drone up in the night sky. They had thermal imaging ability and could spot hidden Taliban anywhere, even in a brush-choked ravine.

His mind automatically swung to Sarah. His heart contracted with pain so deep that he rubbed the center of his chest. Sarah had run. He'd pushed her too fast.

Why the hell did he do that? He loved her. Ethan wasn't going to lie to himself anymore. He loved the woman. And he was damned if he was going to let her run away from him. Somehow—and he didn't know how—he was going to walk back into her life.

His poems had gotten her to trust him. It had been a slow, easy introduction, and Ethan would bet his words had built a connection between them. If he just hadn't gotten in such a damned hurry. He hissed a curse beneath his breath, angry with himself.

"Hawk, call in the BUFFs," Tolleson ordered.

He turned, scowling. "Hey, keep an eye on that wadi while I do the calling? I got a bad feeling about it."

Tolleson grunted and slowly slid back off the ridge and then sat up. "Got it," he growled.

Ethan turned, pulling out a special radio from his H-gear that would put him in touch with the B-52s loitering on a racetrack, an oval flight circle, that they flew at thirty thousand feet above them. It would be up to Ethan to provide the laser light, a thin red beam from his rifle, on the target so that the JDAMs could lock onto it once they were dropped out of the belly of the bomber. And then those five-hundred-pounders would accurately drop exactly where they needed.

Just as he made the call to the lead bomber pilot, shots rang out behind him. A bullet snapped by his head. *Damn!* Ethan heard Tolleson snarl quiet orders, and the SEALs flowed out silently into a diamond formation. He was exposed. Taliban bullets were originating from that wadi, directed at them.

Ethan found a few boulders, four feet high, and

crawled behind them for protection, continuing his call. Now it would be up to him to provide the laser light to guide in the bombs even if they were under attack. More firing began. *Sonofabitch!* Somehow, the Taliban had found them! How? His mind leaped to the fact that someone *knew* they'd be here. Had the asset they trusted told the Taliban? Was it a friggin' setup to take out part of a SEAL platoon? Anger rolled through Ethan, but he kept his mind on the job of directing the B-52s to the target.

Just as Ethan flattened out against the hard biting rocks beneath his lower body, he heard the bottle rocket sound and knew an RPG was being fired at them. He released his M4, pressed his hands against his ears and opened his mouth. The air pressure from any explosion could liquefy and destroy a man's lungs if it wasn't equalized with outside air. By opening his mouth, he was equalizing inner and outer pressure, avoiding ruptured lungs and potentially being killed through suffocation as the RPG landed.

There was a powerful explosion; the entire night erupted into orange-and-yellow fire. Dirt, rock and brush blew into the night, raining down heavily around him. Cursing, Ethan jerked his M4 with the scope and turned on the laser. The thin green beam shot across the valley between them and he settled his eye against the scope, getting a range. Quickly, he gave the bomber navigation officer the numbers. They'd be dialed in on the JDAMs. His laser light would have to remain steady and on the target.

Ethan couldn't move and couldn't stop what he was

doing or the JDAMs would fly all over the place, maybe not hitting the target. Maybe hitting them instead. His heart pumped hard in his chest, the adrenaline pouring through him like a drug, giving him clarity and the ability to hold his focus.

The battle behind him was picking up in intensity. He heard yells and screams of Taliban in the wadi as the SEALs poured concentrated lead into the area. He wanted to hurry, to call in Apaches…anything to get them relief from this unknown force. But Ethan couldn't do anything at the moment except work the radio with the bombers and hold the laser steady on the caravan across the valley. He felt helpless, knowing they needed support. Now.

Sarah was sleeping in the ready room at the medevac squadron when the alarm buzzer went off. Instantly, she jerked upright, knowing she and her medical crew had been alerted to fly an emergency night mission. Her copilot and crew would get their gear and run for the Black Hawk. As air commander of the flight, she had the duty to get the intel on the mission.

She glanced at her watch as she swiftly jerked on her flight boots, shrugged into her survival vest and grabbed the .45 pistol, jamming it into the shoulder holster. She picked her helmet bag and kneeboard up in one hand. It was 0130. Her mind flew to Ethan. Her gut told her it was him and his team.

After hauling her go-bag—a ruck that was filled with water, food, first aid supplies and six magazines of bullets for her pistol—Sarah raced out the door and ran down the hall toward the flight desk. She saw Major Donaldson was the flight commander for tonight. He was scowling.

"Benson, mount up," he told her. "This is a nine-liner mission." He handed her the GPS coordinates. "There's a SEAL team pinned down just below a ridge near the Afghan–Pak border. They're in the process of setting up to blow a fifty-man caravan a mile on the other side of a valley with laser-guided JDAMs. There's an unknown-size force of Taliban about a hundred feet from where the SEALs are dug in on a hill. They've got two men down. One critical." His eyes narrowed. "You got this mission."

Her heart hammered, sending fear arcing through her. "Yes, sir," she murmured, grabbing the paper. She made sure the target information was there, call signs, radio frequencies and status of the two patients. The good news was the weather was clear. That was a piece of good luck. "No Apache escort?" she demanded of the major. Usually, on a firefight, the Apache came in first to make the difference, make it safer for the un-armed Black Hawk to land and pick up the wounded.

"None available. You're on your own. Your crew is already out there on the tarmac waiting for you," Donaldson said. "Tait is your copilot. It's his first night mission."

"Got it," Sarah said, turning and sprinting down the hall. She turned left and pushed open the door that led to the tarmac. The Black Hawk was already spooling up the engines, the blades turning faster and faster. She was relieved to see Pascal was her medic, and he held out his hand to help her up into the bird.

Sarah was all business. The crew chief slid the door shut. She squeezed into the right seat. Pascal handed her the helmet from her bag. Pulling it on, she quickly plugged into the ICS system and strapped it on. Tait's hands were flying across the instrument panel as well as tweaking the overhead fuel throttles. He'd linked her to the SEAL radio operator on the ridge.

Her heart stumbled. She heard Ethan's low, strained voice, calling for medevac over the radio. *Oh, God...*

"Take us up," she told Tait in a low, firm voice. "Pascal? You and the crew chief set back there?"

"Yes, ma'am. Door shut and locked. We're strapped into our jump seats. We're good to go."

Sarah pulled her NVGs down across her eyes, and flicked them on; the world became a grainy green in the blackness of the night. "Tait, I'm putting in the heading on the computer," she told him, punching in the latitude and longitude of some unnamed ridge in the Hindu Kush mountains, where Ethan and his men were fighting for their lives. The computer would then give her the waypoints, invisible positions that would be route markers to get her to the hill in the shortest amount of time.

"Yes, ma'am," Tait murmured, his Louisiana Cajun voice a combination of fear and adrenaline.

Sarah's job was to ensure everything in the cabin of the shaking, shuddering Black Hawk was ready to receive wounded. She worked with Pascal, who knew the drill. The aircrew chief, Potter, verified two litters were attached to the wall and ready to receive the wounded. Her mind revolved around Tait's being scared. Her crew chief would handle any emergency in the rear, behind their seats. Pascal was the best in any medical emergency.

She had a green copilot up front with her on his first night flight. It wasn't a good formula to have under the circumstances. Night flying was the most dangerous of all because the NVGs did not give the pilots depth of perception. All a pilot saw was a flat, two-dimensional surface, when in reality, it could be anything but that. Sarah wasn't going to let Tait do the actual landing. There was no way. *Not tonight.*

Ethan was out there. Was he wounded? His voice had sounded harsh. It took everything Sarah had to push her own personal feelings out of the way. Why had she run away from him?

After receiving permission from the tower, the Black Hawk lifted off; gravity pushed them down into their seats. She'd let Tait fly them in. No harm in that, but Sarah still watched the instrument panel, the FLIR, which was infrared radar that showed elevation of the mountains, and she constantly checked their altitude.

Many young pilots unused to night flight could lose the horizon, lose their sense of up and down. It was called spatial disorientation. And when that happened, and it would sooner or later to a new pilot, they had to trust the horizon indicator in the helo to stop them from crashing. She switched radio frequency to TOC, Tactical Operations Center, at Bagram Air Base. They would be their clearance and where they'd get their final orders.

She switched another channel, connecting with the SEAL team. "Gator Actual, this is Falcon Actual. Over." Her heart pounded, waiting for Ethan to reply. When he did, she heard screams, yells and bullets being fired in the background.

"Falcon Actual, this is Gator Actual. Over."

Ethan sounded so damned unruffled. As if he were talking to her over a meal at the chow hall. SEALs had nerves of steel. Closing her eyes for a moment, Sarah heard a massive explosion. Her ears rang from it. An RPG had exploded nearby, and she waited seconds for the booming sound to dissolve. "Gator Actual, we're on our way to your position." She read him off the co-ordinates, making sure they were the same as what Donaldson had handed her earlier.

"Roger that, Falcon Actual. GPS position is accurate."

"Our ETA is thirty-one minutes. Over."

"Roger."

She heard the calmness of Ethan's voice, but the strain was there. Sarah could feel his worry, his attention elsewhere. "Gator Actual, give me a tally of wounded? Over."

"Two down, one critical. Head wound. Thigh wound, no broken femur. Over."

Her heart tore over that information. "Roger, Gator Actual. This is a casevac. Will radio Bagram hospital with details. Over." Sarah wanted to say so much more. So much. God, if she could only apologize for being so afraid of a relationship with him. Mouth tightening, perspiration popping out on her upper lip, Sarah knew all their transmissions were monitored by all parties back at Camp Bravo as well as SEAL HQ at Bagram Air Base. She could say nothing. "Gator Actual, will apprise you five minutes out from your position. I'll need landing GPS coordinates from you. Over."

"Roger that. It will be ready for you. Gator Actual out."

She wondered if that would be the last time she heard Ethan's voice. Terror gripped her heart, but Sarah automatically watched the instruments. She gave a swift glance at Tait, who seemed all right now. He knew how to fly this bird. She glanced over her shoulder. Pascal was sitting at the rear of the cabin in one of the jump seats, his hands draped over his drawn-up knees. He'd heard the transmission and already had supplies laid out nearby for both types of wounds on the individual litters. Sarah was proud of her crew. She trusted Pascal. Often, on firefights, the two medics who normally flew in would reduce to one. The helicopter could only carry so much weight, and Donaldson had made the decision tonight to carry one medic. That way, if other SEALs became wounded, they could be brought on board and safely carried out. Weight was always a contentious beast in a Black Hawk. Sarah was glad Donaldson had made the decision he did.

She switched to SEAL HQ at Camp Bravo and heard Master Chief Hunter's calm voice speaking to Ethan, giving him intel. In the background, Sarah listened to the escalating firefight. The patrol was pinned down by a large, unknown-size force. The CIA was trying to get a drone into place over the ridge to give them thermal imaging capability of just how many Taliban were hiding in that wadi. Frustration moved through her.

They were twenty minutes into the flight and Sarah could now see the area ahead of them. The FLIR display on their computer screen showed the mountains and valleys in front of them. These were high-altitude, rocky, miserable areas to land on, and Sarah knew it.

Ethan's voice came over her headset. "Falcon Actual, this is Gator Actual. Over."

"Falcon Actual. Over."

"Be apprised there will be JDAMs falling in two minutes." He gave her the GPS coordinates. "Fly clear of that area. Over."

"Roger, Gator Actual. Received the info and will redirect our flight." Sarah turned and told Tait to bank right, away from that mountain ten miles away from them. She'd seen JDAMs light up the night and take out the whole top of a mountain before. The concussion waves of the bombs exploding would ripple through the air like invisible fists. If their helo was too close, it would cause hellacious turbulence, throwing crewmen around in the back and causing major and sometimes dangerous havoc. She quickly reset the GPS to create different waypoints that would still get them to that ridge, just a different flight route.

"I'll take over," she told Tait. "I have the controls. Potter, Pascal, strap in."

"Strapped in, Chief," Pascal confirmed.

"You have the controls," Tait said, releasing them to her.

"I have the controls." After wrapping her Nomex gloves around the cyclic and collective, boots on the rudders, Sarah felt better. She knew her bird as intimately as she knew her own body. Although she flew with instruments, there was another invisible connection she had to her Black Hawk and that was the seat-of-the-pants one. Sarah could feel the shuddering vibration running through her bird; she sensed its stability, the strains on the two engines, the sound and pitch of the blades above them. She melded, metal to human, with the helicopter. Now, they were one. Now she would feel subtle changes, shifts, stresses and anything else that would impinge on her bird. It was years of experience, intuition, that would keep them alive as they flew toward hell.

Tait gasped. "Man, look at *that!*" He pointed out the Plexiglas.

Sarah refused to look. The JDAMs had hit their target. Her hands grew firmer around the controls; her booted feet monitored the rudders. "Don't watch," she snapped at Tait. "It will destroy your night vision!"

"Damn," Tait rasped, amazement in his voice. "What a helluva show!" He turned away and followed her order.

Sarah knew what it looked like. There would be massive yellow, orange and red roiling, fiery clouds bursting out into the night sky. It would resemble a nuclear bomb, lurid red, dirty orange and yellow colors and fire churning upward into the blackness.

"Make sure your harnesses are tight," she warned her crew over the inter-cabin frequency again. Sarah knew what was coming. And so did Pascal and Potter. Tait didn't.

Tait quickly tightened down his harness, pushing his NVGs up because watching the string of blasts had destroyed his night vision. It would take precious minutes for his eyes to readjust.

Sarah felt the concussion wave of the JDAMs' energy stalking them. In seconds, the first one struck the Black Hawk. One moment they were flying level. The next, an invisible fist lifted the bird nearly five hundred feet straight up. Sarah wrestled with the controls. She heard Tait gasp and curse. The first wave rolled past them, and she got her bird straightened out once more, flying level and straight.

"Holy hell," Tait gasped. "What was that?"

Sarah grinned a little. "Blast concussion waves. They travel faster than the speed of sound. And they tend to suck you *back* toward them." Sarah knew he'd never experienced them before. "There's more coming. Hang on…."

The Black Hawk shuddered violently as two more concussion waves struck them in a row. The helicopter's engines changed, strained, and the bird got thrown sideways, sliding through the air on its starboard side. Tait was on the engine throttles, monitoring and changing them as demanded. Instantly, Sarah corrected with hard left rudder, jamming her boot down on it, swiftly making corrections with the cyclic and collective between her gloved hands. This was where physical strength counted. If she couldn't stop the helicopter from wanting to roll, which would put them into an out-of-control situation, it was brute strength that would help right the bird. Gasping, Sarah tightened her grip, her arm muscles tensing. Her boot held down that left rudder to stop the skid, and her hands finessed the bird such that it would respond to her efforts.

"Damn!" Tait yelled, gripping the fuel throttles.

"Relax," Sarah said. She hauled the Black Hawk around, feeling it respond. In such a flight situation, rough, quick jerks and pulls on the flight controls would send them into an even worse crisis. Knowing it had to be subtle, minute movements to not yank the helicopter around, Sarah felt the helo responding, righting itself. She heard less strain on the floundering engines. The blades were working hard, sucking air beneath them in order to rebalance. Some of her tension bled off, easing as the Black Hawk finally smoothed out to stable flight once more.

Tait was breathing hard, his eyes huge as he stared over at her. "Jesus, that was close!"

Sarah's mouth quirked. Tait was getting a hell of a lesson tonight, something every medevac pilot would potentially encounter sooner or later. "Get your goggles down, Tait. I'm going to need your eyes on the landing zone in a minute." Sarah's heart began a long, slow thud in her chest. She told Tait to switch channels so she could talk to Ethan. He was going to have to bring her in, guide her into the blackness of the night into somewhere on that rocky ridge to save SEAL lives. The FLIR would help her once he chose the spot.

Sarah's gaze moved to the digital clock on the instrument panel. "Gator Actual, this is Falcon Actual. Over." She would use the clock's seconds as a countdown to landing.

She waited. Nothing. *Damn.* Sarah called again, her heart rate amping up with fear. Was Ethan down? Wounded? *Oh, no...please don't let that be.*

"Falcon Actual, this is Gator Actual. Over."

Sarah heard the rasp in Ethan's voice, and the gunfire was loud and clear. What was happening? He sounded out of breath. "Gator Actual, I'm four minutes and thirty seconds out from your position. Give me GPS landing instructions. Over."

Tait wrote down the information, then quickly punched in the position into their computer on board the helo. He then called Bagram and received authorization to go in. Sarah's gaze whipped to the display showing the nine-thousand-foot mountain they were approaching. There was a crest-like ridge, and she memorized the land just below. There was nothing but rocks and very little soil and only some struggling brush trying to survive at that harsh altitude. Her worry focused in on the landing site. She saw the wadi two hundred feet away, to the north of the LZ. There was a slight knoll, about twenty feet high, just enough to set the two front wheels of her bird down on, but that was all. She'd have to keep the tail up in the air. Tait was running up the fuel throttles, giving the bird takeoff power to hang there and yet keep the front wheels on the earth so the men could be loaded on board. This was going to be dicey.

The surrounding area had fallen away, giving the blades of the helo enough room so that they would not accidentally strike any of the land formations, shattering the rocky outcrop and sending her and her crew into a crash. Judging from all the surrounding terrain, Ethan had chosen the best landing spot out of a bad situation. Sarah noted a hump of land to the north of her landing spot. She quickly estimated there was less than ten feet between that rocky cliff that jutted outward and the length of her bird's rotor blade tip. If she didn't set the helo down very carefully, her blade could strike that massive rock. And then they'd all be lost.

Sweat began to trickle down inside her uniform as she melded herself completely with her Black Hawk once more.

"We're committed," she told her crew, her voice tight. Somewhere down below, Ethan had the wounded SEALs waiting to be brought on board once she got the bird on the ground.

As she swung the Black Hawk around, banking in, Sarah knew they'd take on enemy fire. Praying that the Taliban would not shoot and destroy the Jesus nut on the rotor assembly, thereby causing them to crash, her mouth thinned into a single line, her eyes narrowed. They were going in....

Chapter 14

Ethan's heart wrenched as he followed the progress of the Black Hawk being flown in by Sarah. He crouched behind rocks; the two wounded SEALs were nearby. The firefight behind him was furious and escalating—the Taliban threw everything they had at them. Breathing slowly, the adrenaline giving him that cold, unemotional focus needed in battle, he heard the *whapping* of the blades puncturing the skin of the night. He worried about RPGs being fired at her helicopter from over the hill.

Tolleson was going to order the team into fire suppression mode, sending a wall of bullets into the wadi, hoping to stop that from happening. The LPO gave the order quietly over his mic to the SEALs. A roar of concentrated gunfire into the wadi began, booming thunder, lacerating the night.

Ethan knelt, waiting, rifle in hand, listening to the Black Hawk approach. He'd thrown four green chem lights that would show her exactly where to place those two front wheels on the earth. Sarah was smart; she was coming in from the south, as far away from the wadi as she could get to protect her bird and crew from possible RPG attack.

His throat tightened as he watched the Black Hawk come in, flare, its belly up to quickly bleed off the forward air speed, the blades slicing heavily through the air. His mouth compressed into a hard line and his eyes narrowed as she set the bird's two front wheels down lightly on that knoll. Christ, she was good. He bowed his head, feeling the blasts from the rotors nearly knocking him over backward. Sarah had to come in hot, had to keep the power up to takeoff speed and she knew there was no place to put down the rear wheel.

The door slid open on the Black Hawk. He recognized Pascal and the crew chief leaping out onto the rocky ground, NVGs on. Instantly, Ethan waved, getting their attention to where he had the wounded SEALs. Slipping the M4 over his shoulder, he got ready to carry the most critical SEAL, Dylan, the one with the head wound who was unconscious. It would require all of them to carry the SEAL to the hovering Black Hawk.

"This one first," Ethan yelled to them, pointing down at Dylan. "Head wound."

Pascal nodded, his face unreadable. The medic and crew chief each took Dylan's shoulders and Ethan took his friend's feet. They started carrying him as fast as they could toward the helicopter. Bullets started snapping and popping around them. Ethan crouched, cursing. Where the hell were those bullets coming from? His eyes were riveted on the helo. The rotor wash slapped them brutally, tearing at their clothes, making it hard to move forward or see where they were putting their feet. Ethan helped ease Dylan up and into the deck of the helo.

Pascal and Potter quickly hauled him over to the other side and placed him in the top litter.

"Stay there!" Ethan yelled. "I'll get the other SEAL!" He turned, nearly losing his footing on the bumpy ground and rocks. Bullets were flying into the Black Hawk. He could hear them hitting the metal skin, ripping it open. Just as he crouched and lunged down the knoll, he heard the Plexiglas on the left side of the helo crack as four bullets smashed into it. The hardened plastic shattered, raining down around him like snow.

It was on Sarah's side of the helo, dammit! Ethan couldn't stop to look to see if she was all right or not. He raced down the knoll, heading for the second SEAL, Bristol, who was wounded in the thigh. The bullets spit up geysers around his boots as he raced toward the safety of the rocks.

Ethan grabbed his friend, sliding his arm around his waist, hauling his arm around his shoulder. Bristol had a tourniquet on his upper thigh, but he was weak from loss of blood. The SEAL was semiconscious, trying to get his legs under him as Ethan hauled him up to his feet. Gasping for breath, his lungs burning like fire because of the high altitude, Ethan knew he had to hurry. The longer that Black Hawk was on the ground, the bigger and better target it was for the Taliban.

Ethan made sure he was on the mountainside where the bullets originated. It had to be a new group swinging around to try and attack the SEAL force from the rear. The Taliban in the wadi were silenced by the continued fire suppression laid down by the SEALs.

Sonofabitch! He tripped and scrambled, lunging forward with Bristol, practically dragging him along. Climbing, slipping and nearly falling several times, Ethan managed to haul the heavier SEAL up to the lip of the helo. Pascal was there, hands outstretched to receive the wounded man. Ethan pushed Bristol up into the helo. Gasps of air exploded out of his mouth from the monumental rescue effort.

As Ethan turned to leave, he took a bullet to his Kevlar. It spun him around, knocking and lifting him off his feet, throwing him backward. He slammed into the ground, rolling.

Damn! Ethan felt the red-hot pain, the fire blossoming hotly across his chest, spreading, burning deeply. Grunting, he rolled to his knees, jerking the M4 off his shoulder. Through the Night Force scope he could see four Taliban running up, firing wildly toward the helo. He kneeled and shouldered the M4 with the rotor wash battering him from behind. He fired slowly, accurately, brushing the trigger each time. Just as the helo lifted into the air, he killed the last Taliban soldier, then watched his body fly backward, his AK-47 cartwheeling through the air. Satisfaction thrummed through Ethan. He crouched and risked a look upward.

The belly of the Black Hawk was sliding down the mountain, picking up air, picking up speed and banking to the south, getting the hell out of Dodge.

Ethan wiped his mouth, sweat stinging his eyes. As he turned, he ignored the burning pain in his chest. The chest ceramic plate in his Kevlar vest had just taken a bullet meant to kill him. He'd have one hell of a bruise, but he was alive and that was all that counted. Ethan raced back toward his team, his mission accomplished. He was on the radio as he ran, talking to two Apache helicopters that were now speeding toward them from Camp Bravo.

As he raced over the uneven ground, lunging to the ground, landing next to Tolleson, Ethan knew the tide would turn shortly. No one survived the lethal power of an Apache. No one. And he felt good being able to call them in, sending a red laser beam into that wadi to show them where to focus their massive, obliterating firepower.

Tolleson ordered the fire suppression to halt. For a moment, there was a lull. And then, suddenly, the Taliban were laying lead into the team again. Ethan remained near Tolleson, calling in the air wolves that were going to arrive any moment. His mind and heart touched briefly on Sarah. She'd flown in under withering fire, landed that bird perfectly on that small knoll and kept it steady, enabling him to get his two SEAL brothers on board. God, he loved her. And if he got out of this alive, he was damn well going to let her know it.

* * *

Sarah bit down hard on her lip as pain radiated outward in her upper right arm. She'd taken a shard of Plexiglas—again. Only this time, it was bad. Saying nothing, ignoring the pain flaring every time she moved her hand, she flew the Black Hawk. The bullet had blown out a quarter of the Plexiglas inward on her side, allowing the wind to roar into the bird, making it freezing cold within the cabin.

She'd sent Tait back to help Pascal and Potter, who had their hands full. They desperately needed more help. Tait could do little things to help the medic stabilize the SEALs on board. The copilot could help the SEALs' oxygen, hold a tourniquet in place or help prepare IVs for the wounded in their care. Tait was good with medical stuff, and Sarah felt positive about ordering him back to help. Just his help could save a life.

Stiffening, Sarah felt blood running down her arm. Sonofabitch, it hurt. She kept her focus on redlining the Black Hawk, sending it hurtling at top speed through the black night toward Bagram. The hospital was standing by to receive the SEALs. A neurology team was already preparing a surgery theater for the SEAL with the head wound. She felt hopeful, knowing that everything humanly possible was being done to save their lives.

Her mind went back to Ethan. She'd recognize his form anywhere. He'd been the one helping to get his SEAL friends to the helo with Pascal's and Potter's help. She'd nearly cried out as she happened to glance back toward the door for just a second and see him get struck by a bullet. Pascal had yelled that he'd been hit in the Kevlar vest and was all right. Otherwise, Sarah would have stayed and picked him up also. She knew Kevlar hits were a bastard and hurt like hell, but the person would survive. As she'd lifted her Black Hawk off that knoll, she'd glanced at Ethan kneeling and firing at some unseen enemy down the slope of the mountain. She knew he was all right, but that ridge was teeming with Taliban.

Within thirty minutes of Bagram, Sarah felt relief soar through her as she listened in on radio traffic with the women Apache pilots flying toward the SEAL position on that cold ridge. It took ten minutes. She listened to Ethan calmly guide the pilots to eradicate every last Taliban hidden in the wadi. Sarah closed her eyes for a moment, feeling her heart pound, knowing that he and his team were saved. All that would remain was for them to be picked up by Army Night Stalker pilots flying in a Chinook. Safe. Ethan and his men were safe. *Thank God.*

Sarah brought in her Black Hawk, flaring it out at the last second, the wheels kissing the painted concrete circle just outside the doors of Bagram's E.R. doors. It was 0300, and the night was black as two gurneys pushed by orderlies along with nurses and two doctors headed toward them. She turned, pain making her grimace. Tait was sliding open the door. The first gurney arrived, and the SEAL with the head injury was put on it and swiftly wheeled away. She watched as Pascal and Tait carefully moved the SEAL with the thigh wound. He was gently placed on the gurney. Pascal hopped out, holding the IV above the SEAL's head. He was already yelling above the moving blades of the helo, telling the surgeon trotting at his side what his stats were.

Turning, Sarah pushed up her NVGs, feeling light-headed. "Tait," she whispered. "Get up here."

Tait climbed into the cockpit. He took one look at her and his face paled.

"You've got the controls, Tait," Sarah said, her voice sounding so faraway. "Call E.R. here. Tell them I've got a piece of Plexiglas in my upper right arm." She closed her eyes, feeling herself beginning to faint. Her last words were, "I've lost a lot of blood...."

Ethan walked into Bagram E.R. with Tolleson under his arm. It was 0400, and the first gray light of dawn was on the desert horizon around the huge air base. The bright lights of the E.R. hurt his eyes, and he winced.

"Hey!" he called out. "I've got a wounded SEAL here. I need help!" Ethan noticed a number of busy nurses halt, turn and run toward him. Tolleson had taken a bullet to the lower leg. Luckily, Ethan had been there, jerked out his blowout kit, found the tourniquet and slid it up above the bleeding wound. It had shut off most of the heavy bleeding.

Within seconds, Ethan was surrounded by orderlies helping him, taking Tolleson out of his arms. They placed the semiconscious SEAL on a gurney and rushed him into a cubicle. There was chaos everywhere Ethan looked. The curtained cubicles were open, and groups of medical staff frantically working over the wounded.

He wiped the sweat away from his eyes, standing there, feeling the effects of adrenaline still crashing through his bloodstream. The MH-47 Night Stalker helicopter had landed at Bagram, bringing Tolleson directly to the hospital. Ethan and the medic, Johnson, had cared for their semiconscious LPO.

Exhaustion began to encroach on his adrenaline high. They were safe. The word made him relax just a little. He was dying of thirst, and he headed for a water fountain located near the doors of the E.R. area. After drinking his fill, Ethan turned, wiping his mouth. And then his eyes widened.

Sarah!

Ethan's heart thundered with shock. He saw her lying unconscious on a gurney in the second cubicle, her face so damned white he thought she was dead. Mind reeling, his emotions scattering through him uncontrolled, he walked quickly toward her. As he drew near, he could see the dark blood down the right sleeve of her flight suit. What the hell had happened to her?

And then he remembered the Plexiglas exploding above him, simultaneous bullets striking it, shattering it inward into the cockpit, where Sarah was sitting.

Shaken, he moved in a daze toward the cubicle, his gaze locked on her slack face. The doctor, a woman in her forties, was cutting away the arm of her flight suit. The name on her white lab coat was Tisdale. When she pulled the fabric aside, Ethan nearly groaned out loud. There was a fist-size piece of Plexiglas embedded deeply in Sarah's upper arm. His entire world ruptured as he watched, unable to do anything but see the blood still leaking out around it.

"Sir," a nurse said in a rush, hurrying over to Ethan. "I'm sorry, but you have to leave."

Ethan's gaze turned hard as he swung toward her. "Like hell I will," he snarled, stepping farther into the cubicle, situating himself next to the doctor. He was damned if he was leaving Sarah's side.

"You aren't family, sir," the nurse said, scowling. "Now, please, leave."

"She's my fiancée. She's family, Nurse. I'm staying with Sarah." There was no way he was leaving. No matter if she'd pushed him away or not. A fierce feeling of protection for Sarah rose in him. He loved her. Ethan would never leave her alone at a time like this.

The nurse paled, her brown eyes widening over his snarling words. She gave a panicked look over at the physician.

Dr. Tisdale looked up. "He stays," she snapped. "Call E.R., get an operating theater ready for Chief Benson. Stat."

Ethan gave Tisdale a nod of thanks. He knew enough to stay out of the way, and he eased around her to stand near Sarah's left shoulder. "How bad is it, Doc?"

The woman grimaced. "Let's put it this way, Petty Officer, that piece of shrapnel has cut into her brachial artery. It's the most major artery in a person's arm. If we pull it out here, Chief Benson will bleed to death. She's got to have surgery in order to have it safely removed. The cut artery is going to have to be sewn back together."

Ethan nodded, forcing all his reactions into a box.

"You really her fiancé?" the doctor demanded, her

gaze moving to his as she finished her examination of Sarah.

"Damn straight." Ethan would lie to God himself in order to remain with Sarah. He'd take any punishment if the medical staff found out later he'd lied.

"Figures. You SEALs are all alike. You take care of your own."

"Always," Ethan ground out.

The doctor gave a number of swift orders to the two nurses and two orderlies standing by. Within minutes, they were transporting Sarah out of the cubicle and into the hall, heading for an elevator at the end that would take her up to the surgery floor.

Once there, Ethan reached out and gripped the doctor's arm as they swiftly moved the gurney toward the operating room doors. "Dr. Tisdale, take good care of her?" He drilled the doctor with a dark look. A silent warning she'd damn well better save Sarah's life.

The woman shook her head and pulled her arm loose from his grip. "There's no way I'm earning a SEAL's anger. I'll take good care of her for you."

Ethan stepped aside, watching Sarah being taken down the polished green hall toward an operating theater. He could go no farther, even though he wanted to.

He once again felt the adrenaline crash plummeting through him, and exhaustion slammed into him. His legs suddenly felt weak. He went to find the surgery waiting room. It was empty, and Ethan was grateful.

Knowing he had to check with Master Chief Hunter, he sat down and pulled out the radio, then punched in the channel that would link him with his team at Camp Bravo.

His heart, however, was with Sarah. She'd looked so pale. He couldn't lose her. Not like this. Somehow he'd repair the damage he'd done to their fragile relationship. Ethan didn't know how, but he'd figure it out. He felt a lump forming in his throat. Tears burned in his eyes as he felt all his carefully boxed emotions come roaring out of him. He wanted a chance with Sarah. She couldn't die on that damned surgery table, bleeding out. Those surgeons *had* to save her life!

Ethan felt overwhelmed. Three of his SEAL brothers were fighting for their lives, too. Making the call, reporting in, Ethan apprised the master chief of the status of his SEAL team, including the names of the three who were currently in surgery.

"I've been monitoring the medevac, Hawk. How's Chief Benson doing?" Ethan's voice grew hoarse as he told Hunter about her condition.

"And you're there at Bagram with her?"

"Yes."

"Contact that Night Stalker pilot that brought your team into Bagram. Tell him to send the rest of the team back here. You stay there with her."

The unexpected good news almost broke Ethan. Hot, burning tears in his eyes, his voice grew thick. "Thank you. I will."

Hunter didn't know they'd broken up. He only knew about the letter, and Ethan hadn't said much to the master chief. Only to give the letter to Sarah in case she came over to HQ. He didn't broach it now with Hunter. Later maybe.

"I just got a radio dispatch saying you took a hit to your vest?" the master chief continued.

"Yes," he managed. "I'm good." Ethan wasn't going to whine about some pain and a huge bruise across his chest.

"The LT is authorizing you to remain there and get it checked out by a doctor. We're not expecting you back here for forty-eight hours. Got it?"

Ethan felt an avalanche of emotions. The master chief knew he and Sarah had some kind of a relationship. Under ordinary circumstances, he would have ordered him back with the rest of the team at Camp Bravo. "I got it. Thank you, Master Chief."

"Let me know how the SEALs are doing when they get out of surgery. And I want to know about Chief Benson, as well. She's one ballsy broad. We were monitoring her all the way in."

Ethan almost smiled. "That she is, Master Chief. I'll give you updates on all of them."

A warmth stole over Sarah. And then, as she slowly became conscious, she was aware of a strong, cool hand wrapped around hers. It took most of her energy to lift her lashes. The anesthesia was still in her bloodstream, and her eyes wouldn't focus for a moment. Finally they did, and she saw Ethan standing next to her, holding her hand, his gaze intense on her. Even in her semiconscious state, her heart thudded. Ethan was there. With her.

"You're here at Bagram, Sarah," Ethan told her quietly. He smiled a little, relief in his low voice. "You're going to be okay." He leaned over, taking her mouth gently, giving her his warmth, his love, breathing his life into her.

Ethan's mouth felt wonderful on her lips—so warm. His trembling hand moved across her hair; the tender gesture brought tears to her closed eyes. As Ethan lifted his mouth from hers, she looked up into his face. He was wearing clean cammies, his face and hair clean, as well. Her heart expanded fiercely with that unnamed emotion that lifted her. Fed her hope.

His kiss heated her body. Tears pricked the backs of her eyes. She saw his worry for her reflected in his stormy gray eyes.

"Y-you're okay?" she managed, her throat dry and sore. So much of her wanted Ethan. When she had been losing consciousness, Sarah had understood that by running away from him, she'd made the worst decision of her life. But she'd been adamant. She'd seen Ethan die before her over her sharp words, her demands. Her heart ached unremittingly. The damage had been irrevocable.

"I'm good. How are you feeling?" Ethan anxiously looked at her face, at the purple shadows beneath her glorious blue eyes. He didn't care if Sarah had asked him to leave her and never return. He'd take the flak. Her anger. Anything. He just wasn't going to abandon her in her hour of need. Sarah had more color now. He could see the fine veins beneath her eyes. The taut skin across her cheekbones told him she was under stress.

"Thirsty," she muttered.

Ethan was grateful Dr. Tisdale had given Sarah a private room instead of putting her in a ward with six other wounded men. He slid his arm beneath her shoulders and lifted her just enough so that she could drink from the straw in the glass. Just getting to hold Sarah, to feel her in his arms, made his heart surge with joy.

They had washed her black hair, washed away the blood and sweat he'd seen on her in the E.R. The light blue gown did nothing but enhance the beauty of her cloudy-looking eyes. Ethan could tell she was fighting the anesthesia.

"More?" he asked.

"No, I'm fine...thanks," Sarah whispered, reveling in the strength of his arm around her shoulders. She wearily rested her head against him, feeling infinitely weak but happy. "You're okay. That's what I needed to know." She closed her eyes and sank back into the netherworld of anesthesia and sleep.

Ethan watched anxiously as Sarah drew out of her deep sleep. It was near noon, and the sun shone through the venetian blinds of the small, quiet room. After easing stiffly out of the chair where he'd slept off and on all night, he stood at her bedside. In her left arm was an IV giving her nutrients. He could see part of the white dressing, her right arm in a sling, keeping the injured area protected. He heard her moan, her lips parting, her brow wrinkling. Was she in pain? Ethan almost pushed the buzzer attached to the edge of her pillow to get a nurse in there to give her more medication. Something cautioned him to wait. He tried to brace himself because Sarah had made it abundantly clear she did not want him in her life. His emotions were raw and screaming to reclaim Sarah, to beg her for forgiveness, but he couldn't protect himself from whatever truth she might say to him. This time, she'd be wide-awake. Not in the netherworld of anesthesia.

When Sarah's blue eyes slowly opened, Ethan's breath jammed in his throat. Her gaze was no longer cloudy. The anesthesia was finally dissolving out of her system. Did Sarah see him? He wasn't sure until he lifted the fingers of her left hand and gently held them in his own. And then those glacier-blue eyes of hers moved slowly, meeting his gaze. He smiled a little, feeling soul-deep relief.

"You're home," he told her, his voice unsteady. "And you're going to be okay, Sarah." His throat ached with tears of relief. Ethan swallowed several times.

Ethan's voice was like a healing balm poured over her heart. Sarah felt his calloused fingers around her own, heard the barely veiled emotions in his voice, saw the anxiety deep in his eyes as he watched her closely. She managed a grimace. "Where am I?"

Ethan slowly went over a very abbreviated list of events that had gotten her to Bagram hospital. Every minute, he watched Sarah becoming more alert, her eyes cleaner and more sharply focused on him. By the time he was done, she sighed.

"I didn't think I was going to make it here. Pascal and Potter had their hands full with your brothers in the rear. He needed my copilot, Tait, back there to help stabilize them." Her mouth pursed with tension, and she closed her eyes. "I was bleeding out, and I knew it. I was praying like hell I could last until we landed." Sarah was grateful he was still there with her. She only vaguely remembered Ethan at her bedside the first time she'd become conscious.

Frowning, Ethan began to realize her quiet courage. "The two SEALs you picked up are going to make it," he told her, squeezing her fingers gently. "And Tolleson, who got wounded later, is in good shape. We took a lot of hits up on that ridge." He tried to keep the anger out of his tone.

Raising her lashes, Sarah muttered, "It's good to hear they are going to make it. I like happy news." And then she studied him. "You were hit in the Kevlar, Ethan. How are you?"

Ethan was struck by Sarah's care over his SEAL friends and himself. She wasn't asking about herself, but about the others she had saved. His heart expanded with an intense love for her. "I got hit here." He pointed to the left side of his chest. "I'm good."

"Thank God," Sarah whispered, "because I just happened to see you spin around and fall. It scared the hell out of me, Ethan." Tears came to her eyes, and her voice was hoarse and scratchy with emotion.

Leaning down, Ethan cupped her cheek, his face inches from her. "You are the bravest woman I've ever known, Sarah." His voice grew unsteady. "Out there on that ridge, you were magnificent. You sat that Black Hawk down like you owned the real estate, never a hesitation or a bauble." Ethan smiled tenderly down at her, and, God help him, he was driven to kiss her, to somehow let her know even now that he loved her. He could never tell Sarah that, but he felt raw and aching for what might have been. "But I know you do now." He took a huge risk and curved his mouth gently across hers, feeling her warmth, her life blossom beneath his in her returning kiss. She wasn't going to push him away. A tendril of hope spiraled through his chest.

Sarah felt Ethan's mouth lift from hers. Heat and joy flooded her as she looked up, drowning in his stormy gray gaze. She knew that look. He eased his trembling fingers through her clean, shining hair. "You told me last night. Don't you remember?"

Brows drawing down, Sarah said, "No…I don't remember much." Except his kiss. She remembered that, remembered how the heat of his kiss warmed her icy-cold body, warmed her heart, her soul. She had told him to walk out of her life. Yet, he was here. He'd come. He hadn't abandoned her. What had she done? Ethan smoothed out the wrinkles across her brow with his thumb.

The door opened, and Dr. Tisdale entered. She shut it and said, "Well, well, good to see you awake, Chief Benson." She walked over to her and gently eased the blue gown down off her right shoulder, checking the dressing over the wound. "So far, so good. How are you doing?"

Sarah liked the lean woman with the long, graceful hands. Tisdale had short gray-and-brown hair and caring hazel eyes. "I'm good, Dr. Tisdale."

"I kept that piece of Plexiglas that severed your brachial artery. Want it as a souvenir?"

Managing a sour grin, Sarah muttered, "No. I've seen enough Plexiglas to last me a lifetime."

The doctor eased the gown up on her shoulder. "What I want to know," Tisdale said, getting serious, "is how did you manage to fly that helo into Bagram? We put nearly two pints of blood back into you. By all rights, you should have passed out halfway here." She drilled a hard look down into Sarah's widening eyes.

"I—don't know," Sarah admitted, sobering over the news.

"I found this out from your copilot, Tait. He said he was in the back, helping your medics save those two SEALs." Tisdale wagged her finger into Sarah's face. "If this *ever* happens again, Chief Benson? You get your copilot up there to take over immediately. If you'd have passed out from blood loss, that bird would have gone down and all six of you wouldn't be here today. All right?"

Nodding, Sarah knew she had an ass-chewing coming. "Yes, ma'am. It won't happen again."

"Good." Tisdale snorted, reading over her chart. "Because you got very, very lucky, Chief Benson. That Plexiglas cut the main artery in your arm. Could have sliced through and cut some nerves that would have rendered your hand numb for the rest of your life." She closely observed Sarah's hand peeking out from the white sling. "Move your fingers for me?"

Sarah did.

"Your wrist? Slowly. You don't want to aggravate the

wound. I did a good job of sewing you up, and I don't want to see my fine work screwed up."

Almost smiling, Sarah did as she requested.

"You have full feeling in every finger?" Dr. Tisdale took each one and poked it with a somewhat dulled steel needle.

"I can feel every finger," Sarah said. Stunned, she realized that if she'd lost the use of any part of her hand, never mind her arm, she'd never be allowed to fly again, and that just couldn't happen.

"Hmm, good," Dr. Tisdale murmured, picking up her chart and writing notes on it. Looking up, she said, "Your fiancé was like a junkyard dog last night, snarling and snapping at my team when they brought you in."

"What?" Sarah looked over at Ethan, stunned. Her fiancé? He had an innocent look on his face, if it was possible for him to look innocent.

"Yes," Dr. Tisdale muttered. "I've been around this place for two years and learned early on you don't screw with a SEAL team member who's wounded. Or—" she gave Sarah a one-eyebrow-raised look "—with his fiancée." Dr. Tisdale smiled. "You're going to be going into rehab in about a week, Chief Benson. Now, just between you and me, I think you'd rather rehab here at Bagram, and we do have a fine physical therapy facility for it, rather than be sent stateside?"

Sarah did not want to leave Ethan. Her heart wrenched over the possibility they'd be separated. "I'd much rather rehab here, Doctor."

"Thought so." Dr. Tisdale grinned. "I'll get my nursing team to get a room assigned to you at the barracks officer's quarters here on base. You can spend time in our physical therapy unit, our gym and swimming pool getting well."

"When can I start flying again?" Sarah asked, giving Ethan a glance. There was amusement in his lowered eyes.

"That's what rehab is designed to do for you," Dr. Tisdale said. "As soon as you can prove you can work that cyclic and collective, I'll put you back on active duty and you can go back to your squadron at Camp Bravo. Maybe two or three weeks, depending."

"Thank you, ma'am. Really, I appreciate it."

Dr. Tisdale became serious. "I'm putting you in for a medal, Chief Benson. What you did was extraordinary. I'm sending the recommendation to Major Donaldson. I hope he approves it."

Shocked, Sarah didn't know what to say. She didn't live to get a medal. They were all political anyway. But she saw the woman's eyes, heard the grit in her voice and wasn't going to argue the point. "Thank you. All I want is to get well, Doctor."

"And so you shall, Chief Benson. You'll spend another night here and then we'll transfer you over to the BOQ and you can get a bus from there to our physical therapy department here at the hospital. I'll see you tomorrow morning."

Sarah turned after the doctor left and looked up at Ethan. "Fiancé? Is that what you told them?" Her heart pounded.

Having the good grace to look sheepish, Ethan murmured, "They weren't going to let me stay any other way." He saw the surprise in her expression, then understanding. "It was a lie, but I wasn't going to leave you alone without any support here at Bagram." His mouth tightened, and his voice became strained as he held her wavering gaze. "You've been abandoned before, Sarah, but I wasn't walking away from you even though I knew you told me to. I—I just couldn't do it." Sarah's eyes widened in surprise again. He wanted to tell her that she was in his blood. In his heart. Ethan couldn't think two thoughts without thinking of Sarah, her goodness, her beauty. And when he slept, he dreamed of her. Of loving her.

"I see…" Sarah whispered, feeling so many emotions flooding like a brightly colored rainbow through her. "I guess…" She grimaced. "I live so much in the hour, the day, Ethan." Overwhelmed, she whispered, "We live in chaos, Ethan." Why had he stayed, then? She was confused by him, by her own feelings. She'd just nearly died. Sarah knew she needed time to sort it all out.

"You need to rest, Sarah," Ethan said, his chest tightening as he saw exhaustion stalking her. "We'll talk again when you want," he soothed her, watching her long, thick black lashes come gently to rest against her pale cheeks. Ethan stood quietly, watching Sarah drift into sleep. His heart opened with love for her. Ethan understood where she was coming from. Sarah was afraid of commitment. Afraid the chaos of war would tear her away from him. It almost had tonight. And he couldn't stand there and argue differently. Dammit, he wasn't going to walk away from her. No matter how much Sarah wanted him to do it, he couldn't. It would be one hour, one day at a time between them and their fragile, growing love for one another.

Somehow, Ethan knew Sarah loved him. She'd never said it and would probably never say it. But he *knew*. And that gave him hope in a damned hopeless situation. He'd seen her needing him, felt it, felt so much around her. Ethan knew he had to try and beg Sarah to give him another chance. Would she?

Chapter 15

Sarah felt the ache in her shoulder after finishing her physical therapy exercises in the large room. Two weeks had flown by because of her intense desire to regain her health. Next door was an Olympic-size pool, where other wounded soldiers swam to strengthen their torn, healing bodies. Grimacing, she pressed against the pink scar on her right arm. She sat on a floor mat dressed in gray workout pants and a blue tank top. Sweat was rolling off her because the exercises triggered ongoing pain. The sun was just rising over the desert, the rays long and blinding through the window at the other end of the rectangular area.

Around her, men were lifting weights, exercising, grunting and groaning. She was in good company. Pushing the light film of perspiration off her brow,

Sarah slowly got to her feet. Every day, her arm improved. Got stronger.

She walked over to a wooden bar and picked up her towel. She missed Ethan so damn much the ache was far more painful than her healing limb. Sarah wanted to get back together with him, but she didn't know how. She had the courage to fly into hell, but she couldn't find it to tell Ethan she yearned to see him. If only she could see herself the way he saw her, she would feel brave enough to accept his love. Was there any way out of this ugliness that had always been within her? The need to talk to him was eating Sarah alive.

After she showered, Sarah climbed into a pair of jeans, a pink tank top and sneakers. She allowed her damp hair to fall loose and it curled slightly at the ends around her shoulders. In this hot desert environment, damp hair was cooling for her whole body.

Emma Trayhern-Shaheen had come over shortly after Ethan had said goodbye to her on the second day at the Bagram hospital. Her friend had been a huge help. That afternoon, Emma was sending her driver over to pick her up and she would have dinner with them. Sarah was looking forward to it.

As Sarah pushed the door open to go to the bus stop, she gasped. There, coming up the walk, was Ethan. She stopped in her tracks. He saw her and gave her a sheepish, almost apologetic grin of hello. He was wearing his uniform, his M4 in a harness across his chest, SIG in his drop holster on his right thigh and the knife in a sheath strapped to his left calf.

"Ethan! What are you doing here?" Sarah asked,

breathless with joy. She could see the dirt smudges on his face, the gleaming sweat.

"To see you. What else?" Ethan said, increasing his stride toward her. Would Sarah push him away? Two weeks he'd lived in a special hell. More than ever, he was determined to stop her from running away from him. Whatever was making her run, Ethan wanted to know what it was. They'd face it together. He loved her. He drowned in her shining blue eyes. God, he'd missed her. Glancing left and right, Ethan saw there were way too many people around. But he didn't give a damn. "Come here," he growled, gently taking her into his arms, mindful of her injury.

Sarah's eyes widened, and she stiffened. Public affection was prohibited in the military. Then she wholeheartedly gave in.

He slid his fingers through her damp hair, cradling her head, his other arm sliding around her waist, drawing her as close as he dared. His mouth swept down on hers, tasting her and inhaling that special fragrance that was only Sarah. He felt her stop resisting, and she moaned, the vibration filling him; then she melted into his embrace, trusting him fully.

He eased his mouth from hers and studied her, breathing hard. Sarah's cheeks were flushed, her eyes a drowsy blue color, telling him she wanted more. So did he.

Someone approached, and Ethan helped Sarah stand on her own, his hand resting protectively against the small of her back. Looking toward the sound, Ethan saw it was an Army captain in uniform. The man stared at them, reprisal in his eyes, ready to tell them that there was no affection showed in public. Ethan straightened and gave him a don't-screw-with-me glare of warning.

The captain noted his silent challenge and walked by without saying a word. Ethan saw Sarah's concern.

"Don't worry," Ethan urged huskily, touching her chin, giving her a warm look. "Nobody takes on a SEAL." He gave her a searching look. Would she tell him to leave?

Rattled, Sarah touched her hair, giving the departing officer a worried look. "I guess so," she murmured, meeting his dark gray eyes, which burned with desire. "You look whipped," Sarah said, worried. Ethan had told her they would be going out on a mission soon after he'd left her at the hospital.

He took off his baseball cap and rubbed the sweat off his brow with the back of his arm. "I am. We've been out in the Badlands for a week." He gave her a feral grin. "And we got even with those bastards who jumped us up on that mountain ridge where you rescued two of our SEALs. Mustafa Khogani, who gave us the intel, double-crossed us. I want that bastard. He's on our platoon's top five list to take down, and it will happen."

"That's good news. Did you take any more casualties?" Sarah hoped not, understanding as never before how tight the SEALs were with one another. They were a family of a different sort, but family nonetheless. One man being killed or injured powerfully affected the rest of his brothers. It distressed the whole team for days and weeks afterward.

Shaking his head, Ethan took her arm. "None. We

put the Taliban in the hurt locker. Hey, I'm starving. Have you had breakfast yet?" He held his breath, praying she'd say yes.

Sarah felt her heart spill open with joy as they walked toward one of the many chow halls. "Not yet. I'll go with you."

Ethan settled the cap on his head, walking close to her, their hands occasionally touching. "How's your arm?"

Sarah's cheeks were pink, and it only enhanced the beauty of her eyes. Ethan felt his entire lower body harden, hunger for her to be in his arms once more almost making him detour from food to find a place they could make love to one another. On a base this size, he knew of such places. But that was wishful thinking. Right now, he had to focus on getting Sarah to allow him back into her life. He could see that she was torn. Confused. So was he.

"Getting better every day," Sarah admitted softly, flexing her right hand and giving him a look of relief. "Dr. Tisdale did a great job. She says I'm progressing very well. Once I get her to sign me off flight waivers, I'll have to take a flight test here at Bagram to requalify for medevac pilot status. That won't be a problem. I'm ready to get back in the saddle. I miss the adrenaline rush."

"You're an adrenaline junkie." Ethan laughed. "Hell, so are SEALs. We wrote the book on it." He absorbed Sarah's breathy laughter, and it felt as if his flesh was being touched by her voice.

They made a turn and crossed a street. Ethan remained on the outside of Sarah as they walked down the block. "Do you like being here at Bagram?" he teased, catching her look of chagrin over the question. Ethan was counting the days when she would return to Bravo and to him.

"I think you know the answer to that. I'd much rather be at Camp Bravo." And then Sarah took a huge risk, her voice hesitant. "I miss those wonderful poems you gave me."

His heart squeezed with joy, but Ethan didn't let her admission rock his world. Everything was so tentative between them. Fragile glass. God, it could shatter in an instant. He rasped, "I've missed the hell out of you, Sarah." He watched her, admiring how her shoulder-length black hair fell like a shining cape over her proud shoulders.

Already, the sun was climbing into the sky, promising temperatures over a hundred degrees by noontime. Being in civilian clothes had its advantages, he thought as he appreciated her long legs. He enjoyed the sway of Sarah's hips, the way that tank top outlined her full breasts. Breasts that he had held in his hands, had felt tighten with need when he'd made love with her. Damn, Ethan needed her back in his life, his arms.

"I'm trying to…to understand myself right now, Ethan." Sarah couldn't force out, *I made a horrible mistake in pushing you away.* At least not yet. What an emotional coward she was.

"Let's just take this one step at a time?" He needed to hear what she was thinking, feeling. There was such anguish in her eyes. Ethan could feel her torn emotions, and she was so tentative in his presence.

"Yes." Sarah sighed, trading a quick, shy glance with him. She felt Ethan's protection, his possessiveness toward her. It wasn't a bad thing, rather Sarah was beginning to understand that a SEAL was like an alpha male wolf. And he had his alpha female mate: her. The look in his gleaming eyes confirmed that. Sarah would never tire of looking at Ethan. His profile was clean and strong, his skin burned dark by the sun. There was nothing soft about him, except maybe his poet's soul.

As they neared the busy chow hall, Sarah noticed how many would turn their heads and stare openly at him. Black ops kept a low profile on this base of twenty thousand people. SEALs were a very small unit compared to all the other military branches based there. And SEALs always stood out because of their distinctive walk, their in-your-face confidence and the way they wore their weapons. Everyone gave way to him as he walked through the crowds in front of the chow hall. SEALs were accorded a respectful place in the military world, Sarah was discovering firsthand, as she followed him into the large two-story building.

Inside the huge chow hall, there were at least four hundred people at tables. A line of about fifty people stretched around the wall, waiting to go through the chow line. The noise was high. Ethan touched her hand and pulled her down a hallway before they reached the long line.

"This way," he coaxed, releasing her hand.

"You know this place?"

"SEALs know all the stealth places," he promised, smiling over at her. "There's a smaller chow hall in the rear of this building. The cooks usually handle officers, warrants and us. We don't like eating out in the public."

"You're special," she teased.

"Yes, we are. No apologies for it, either. We've earned that status in blood and lives."

Curious because Bagram was so huge—it would take weeks to know it all—Sarah followed Ethan into a very small, secluded and much quieter chow hall. It was about three thousand square feet and felt intimate to Sarah. There were two Army cooks at the rear, waiting for customers to give them their orders. Only ten other men were in the place, and they all looked up when they entered. Ethan ignored their curious looks and zeroed in on the cooks. Sarah could feel the eyes of the officers checking out Ethan. He was the only black ops male in there that she could tell. Most of the men were Army officers.

As she halted and Ethan drew her in front of him to give the cooks her request, Sarah felt the eyes of the men checking her out. A woman in civilian clothes. This time, their stares didn't bother her half as much as they would normally. Maybe because Ethan was there, lending her his invisible SEAL protection, she didn't feel like the usual bug under the microscope.

As they sat at a table near the wall, away from the entrance, they enjoyed fresh eggs, bacon and toast. Sarah sighed when she was finished and pushed the tray aside. She picked up her coffee, absorbing Ethan's nearness at her elbow. He had ordered a dozen eggs, ate a pound of bacon and still had ten slices of toast stacked nearby on another plate. Sarah understood SEALs could burn calories like a training Olympic athlete. No wonder Ethan was wolfing down the hot food with relish.

"How's your Kevlar bruise?" she asked.

"It's good," he said between bites. "Just a big ugly yellow-green bruise is left. Nothing to write home about."

Dragging in a deep breath of air, Sarah forced herself to speak. To step up to the plate. "Emma and Khalid have invited me over for dinner tonight. Could you come with me?" She felt her heart cringe. And Sarah tried to prepare herself for him saying no. Ethan had every right to do that. She'd put him in that position.

Brows raising, Ethan wiped his mouth with the paper napkin. "Try and stop me."

Sarah hoped they would be able to stay overnight in their villa. That would be an opportunity to confess her mistakes to him. To apologize for what she'd done to Ethan. She felt heat sweep into her face. Sarah wasn't used to a man letting her know she was desirable and cherished at the same time. Even though she saw Ethan wanting her, she also saw his tenderness. In some ways, he wore his heart on his sleeve. That was a surprise, given he was a SEAL. Perhaps Ethan became vulnerable around her. It made her heart flutter with anticipation.

"Do you have duties here on base for your platoon?" Sarah hoped they had the entire day to themselves, which would be an unexpected godsend.

He slathered blueberry jam over six pieces of toast,

sat them in a row in front of his tray and picked up the first one. "Master Chief Hunter gave me some requisition orders to fill over at the Navy supply depot. I've got to get the order together, get it trucked out to the helo airstrip, get it strapped on a pallet and then make sure it comes to Bravo with me tomorrow morning."

"Can you get that all done before Emma's driver picks me up at 1600 today?"

"I'll make it happen," Ethan said. God, Sarah was giving him a chance. She didn't have to say a thing about dinner at Khalid's home. He felt a break between them. A whisper of possibility that they could repair what was torn. He'd never wanted anything more.

"I don't think SEALs take no for an answer," she said before sipping her coffee. Because it had been Ethan's determination to win her back that had given her the courage to approach him once again.

Ethan polished off three more pieces of toast in a row, licking his fingers where the jam had collected. "You're right. Words like *no* and *can't* don't exist in our world." He shared a smile with her, enjoying Sarah so close to him. His voice went low and gritty as he held her shimmering gaze. "I've got Khalid's sat phone number. I'll call him and let him know I'm coming for dinner tonight. I'll ask him if it's all right if we stay over if you want. I'm sure it will be, but they should know ahead of time."

Her body flamed with possibility. How badly Sarah wanted to apologize for her actions, but she couldn't do it here. It would have to wait until tonight. "Yes, let's stay overnight if we can." There, the words, the truth, was out. Sarah had never been so scared. It was a fear she had to walk through. Ethan deserved her courage, not her cowardice. All Ethan had to do was give her that hungry, hunterlike stare and Sarah could feel dampness collecting between her thighs. How was it possible that one look could make her so hot? He was utterly male in every sense of the word. An alpha male who feared nothing and no one. Ethan's gaze locked on hers.

"I want to talk with you tonight," he said quietly so no one else could overhear them.

"Yes," she whispered, her voice filled with regret. Sarah tried to send him a look of apology.

After they said good-night to Emma and Khalid, they remained in the living room. They sat on either end of the couch. Sarah felt her heart beating wildly in her heart. All day, she'd waited for this moment.

"Ethan? I—I need to apologize for what I did to you at Bravo." Her hands were cool and damp as she clasped them in her lap, forcing herself to hold his warming gaze. "I was scared. Everything was moving so fast. I have such a hard time thinking I'm beautiful because I don't feel that way inside myself." Sarah briefly touched her stomach. "I don't see how you can see me like that."

Ethan sat very still. He heard Sarah's soft, painful words and it made him want to cry for her. She looked like a young child right now, so wounded and hurt and so unaware of her own beauty. "Come here." He extended his hand toward her. "Please?"

His low timbre flowed through her tense body, touching her aching heart. Sarah stared at his hand, unable to believe Ethan wouldn't hold what she'd done to him against her. Hesitantly, she placed her hand into his, watched it be swallowed up, warm and strong. Scooting toward him, she held his hooded gaze. Felt how much Ethan wanted her. When she was close enough, their knees touching one another, he continued to hold her hand against his thigh, his gaze never leaving hers.

"I'm sorry for pushing you so fast, Sarah. I knew you were gun-shy of me…of a relationship with me." Ethan gently squeezed her hand. "I did this—you didn't. It was my fault." He swallowed around his closing throat. "I'm sorry, Sarah. God, I knew better. You had enough courage to tell me about your past. I should have slowed down. I should have given you time to get used to being around me."

Tears filled her eyes, and Sarah closed them, her lips compressing. "Oh, God, Ethan…" Her voice broke. She pulled her hand out of his, pressing it against her eyes, forcing herself not to cry. "I'm the one who did this. Not you." She sniffed and her hand fell away as she stared miserably into his anguished eyes. "It's me, Ethan. You called me beautiful. And I'm *not*. I'm not."

"What do you mean, Sarah?" he asked, pain in his voice as he searched her eyes. "I don't understand."

How could he? Sarah barely got out, "I'm ugly inside. I don't know why you don't see it."

Stunned, Ethan sat back, digesting her words. Frowning, his mind spinning, he said, "Who told you this?" Someone *had* to have told Sarah she was ugly inside and out. His hands slowly curled into fists, rage soaring through him because he saw the damage in her eyes, in her expression. The struggle in Sarah's vulnerable face ripped him apart.

"Someone…" she managed. "M-maybe later I can talk about it, Ethan." She gave him a pleading look. "Almost dying…I woke up knowing I'd run for all the wrong reasons from you, Ethan. But I'm still scared. I don't see how you see me but…it's so hard…I can't—"

To hell with it. Ethan pulled her gently into his arms, not knowing what to expect. He loved Sarah so damn much, wanted to protect her, give her that safe harbor to sort out the trauma she'd experienced as a young child. Ethan knew he could do this for Sarah, knew he had the strength, the love, to support and help her heal from those tragic wounds. She flowed into his opening arms, whispered his name, her arms sliding around his shoulders, face pressed against his neck. Her heart beat like a wild, trapped bird against his chest, and he pressed his face against her hair, dragging in her scent like a dying man just given a reprieve.

"Tell me what you want, Sarah. Just tell me," Ethan coaxed huskily, a catch in his throat. He tightened his grip around her, relief flooding him because despite her terror, her distorted belief she was ugly, she'd come to him. He felt her tremble. Felt her breath against the column of his neck. She had burrowed up against him like a frightened child, not a woman. He was her protection against an inner storm only she could feel. That lived within her.

"You, Ethan. I want you. You made such beautiful love to me…I want that again if you could forgive me for what I did to you." Sarah pulled out of his arms enough to lift her head and meet his stormy eyes. "I want to love you. I want you to love me. I've never felt so wonderful. So happy…"

Cupping her cheek, Ethan leaned down and brushed her lips. "There's nothing to forgive, Sarah. I'm as much at fault in this. It's not you. Just give me a chance to show you how beautiful you really are." He eased away, holding her blue gaze, noting the tears swimming in them. He held back telling her he loved her. Sarah couldn't be rushed. They would go at a pace that was right for her.

Her lower lip trembled and then his heart melted as she tried to smile but failed.

"I need you, Ethan…."

Ethan picked Sarah up into his arms and walked her down the hall to their suite. Sarah gave a soft sound of surprise, caught off guard.

"I'm sweeping you off your feet," Ethan rasped as he pushed the door open with the toe of his boot. Inside the suite, the darkness was chased away by the stained glass lamp on the dresser. After setting Sarah down onto the bed, Ethan walked over and shut and locked the door. Anyone looking at Sarah right now in the civilian world would think she was a college graduate, not the hell-bent-for-leather medevac pilot she was. Looks were so damned deceiving. And, regardless, she was his.

Sarah sat tensely on the edge of the bed, watching him, anticipation thrumming through her. All evening, her body ached, wanting Ethan. There was such incredible male grace about him she would never tire of watching Ethan move, dress or undress. He came over and eased her thighs apart, his hands remaining on each one as he knelt on one knee between them.

"I need a shower. Want to join me?"

Sarah hesitated marginally.

"What is it?" he coaxed, cupping her cheek.

Sarah drowned in his dark, searching look. "I've never taken a shower with a man, Ethan."

He framed her face, his voice gentle. "You're my woman." He held her soft gaze. "And I want to show you just how much. A shower is just another way to love one another. You don't have to take a shower with me if it doesn't feel right to you. You're in control here. And if you don't, I won't be upset about it. Okay?"

Sarah worried her lower lip. "No…it's not that, Ethan." She gave him a wry look. "I just don't know what you expect of me." Instantly, she saw Ethan's expression soften.

"I want you to enjoy it, Sarah. I'll teach you as we go along?"

The tender look, the patience in his eyes, swept away all her concerns. "Sort of like learning how to fly?" she ventured softly.

Ethan's mouth drew into a very male smile. "Yes, exactly like that." He released her.

Sarah moved her fingers through his very short, dark hair, allowing them to trail to his corded neck and come to rest across his broad shoulders. "I will go anywhere with you, anytime, Ethan."

Sarah met his hooded gaze, which was stormy with desire for her alone. Settling her mouth against his, she felt his arm move around her waist, drawing her forward, taking her without apology, his lips driving hers open, his tongue sliding commandingly into her mouth. It sent a sheet of instant fire arcing down through her, and she sighed, surrendering to his arms.

Tearing his mouth from hers, Ethan urged her. "Come on. Let's get undressed and get into the water."

Her lips throbbed with the power of his mouth. "SEALs love water," she teased, her voice a little breathless, husky with desire.

"Water is our home," he agreed with her. Ethan stood and quickly opened his shirt and discarded it. He grabbed the ends of his tan T-shirt and pulled it over his head, exposing his deep chest, the muscles flexing across his broad set of shoulders. He got rid of his boots and trousers. Off came the socks and his boxer shorts. "Come swim with me," Ethan teased, his eyes glinting with challenge. His heart would burst open, the joy so intense and powerful. He wanted to yell at the top of his voice that Sarah was giving him a second chance.

Sarah gave him a challenging look and took off her sneakers with shaky fingers. "If anyone is beautiful, it's you, Ethan." His body was ripped, tight and strong. She could see the vestiges of the huge yellow-and-green bruise on the left side of his chest. The light in the room accentuated the hard angles of his body.

Ethan stood naked before her. He eased his fingers through her silky hair. There was no guess about him wanting her. "Need some help undressing?"

Struggling out of her jeans, Sarah lifted her feet as she leaned back on the bed. He obliged her by pulling the jeans off. Sarah sat up and pulled off her tank top, revealing her white cotton bra. Before she could get to it, Ethan leaned over, sliding his hands around her back, his fingers quickly unfastening it. Her full breasts tumbled free, and she saw his eyes go feral as he slowly slid his hands around the curves. A soft gasp escaped her, and she closed her eyes, wanting even more of Ethan's touch. Sarah leaned forward into his large, calloused hands. Her skin ignited with blazing fire as he grazed her nipples with his thumbs. A soft, delicious sound slipped from her lips and she automatically gripped his powerful biceps.

Opening her eyes, she watched Ethan give her that stalking look of a hunter coming after his prey—her.

Chapter 16

"Come on," Ethan urged, his voice thick. "Let's get your panties off and we'll go get in that shower. Otherwise," he growled, "I'm taking you here. Right now." Sarah's knees felt incredibly shaky as they walked into the huge bathroom. Within minutes, the shower nozzles were like warm raindrops sliding softly across her hair, soaking the strands and then her. Ethan quickly washed himself, and the dirt and sweat slid off his hard, lean body. After he washed his hair and rinsed it, he turned to her.

"Your turn," Ethan said, sliding his hand around Sarah's waist, drawing her close so he could nibble her delicate earlobe. Ethan felt her respond and arch against him. He released Sarah and allowed her to lean against the warm, wet tiles of the shower. Smiling down into her half-closed eyes that were already drowsy with arousal, Ethan took the soap, lathered it between his large hands and gently moved the bubbles across her face. Sarah closed her eyes, her hands coming to rest on his narrow hips, leaning languidly against the tile wall.

A look of satisfaction flared in her expression, telling him she was enjoying his hands as they teased her brow and slid down across her high cheekbones. He ached so damn much, but he placed steel control over his own desire. Sarah came first. Always.

Sarah opened her eyes, beads of water catching on her lashes as Ethan began to lather the soap and follow the slender length of her neck. Then, his fingers kneaded her shoulders, erasing the tension. She moaned, feeling his fingers work magic against her tight muscles. Ethan's gaze moved to the reddened, puckered flesh of her arm where she'd had surgery. A flash of pain came into his eyes. His fingertips grazed the area as he carefully washed her skin. Neither of them would forget the night it had happened. Ethan leaned down, placing a soft kiss across the healing area after he rinsed it.

Sarah's breath hitched, and her eyes shuttered closed as Ethan kissed her injury. It was as if his love were strong enough to pull the experience of her almost bleeding to death before she landed at Bagram out of her memory. His hands then glided across her torso and gently cupped her shoulders. She felt incredibly cherished in that moment, the warm water falling around them, the steam beginning to gather like fog between their bodies.

Ethan lifted his head and took her parted lips, wanting to give back to Sarah. The water slid into the corners of their mouths, the heat inside them building like a wildfire, their breathing changing. He tunneled his fingers through her wet, glistening hair, watching her blue eyes open, seeing the feverish, smoky quality awaken in them. He realized once more that Sarah had almost died. His heart wrenched in his chest. She was such a damned courageous woman. Fearless. As Ethan held her melting gaze, he kissed her gently. Tenderly. With all the love he had inside him, trying to share it with her as their mouths met wetly in exploration. He silently promised her he would make her feel the beauty he saw and felt inside and outside herself.

Ethan's mouth possessed hers; his hands trailed splintering paths of fire around the curves of her aching breasts. Then Sarah felt him anchor her, his arm supporting her lower back, positioning her so that she could use the wall to lean against, as well as his body. His fingers followed the glistening curve of her thigh, and she shuddered in anticipation. A hungry gnawing began in her lower body. His fingers slid inside her thigh and she automatically opened to him, wanting him, wanting his incredible touch. Already she was trembling, barely able to stand.

Sarah's entire body melted around him as he teased her. He felt the wetness surrounding his fingers. She nearly collapsed against him as he explored her a little more deeply, barely inside her. A whimper tore from her lips as he pressed his fingers slowly within her. Her sweetness sent a shaft of rocketing need firing through him. The instant he slid more deeply into her depths, she cried out, her entire body convulsing with the orgasm. Her knees nearly gave way, and he anchored her with his arm. Humbled by her trust of him, Ethan silently promised Sarah he would always consider her sacred to him, to never give her pain, only pleasure.

Sarah's world flew apart; her knees were so damned weak. Ethan's strong, stabilizing arm stayed around her waist. And then he slowly eased out of her wetness. She gave him a desperate look, her breathing uneven.

He held her aroused look, her lips parted. "Trust me," he whispered against her lips. "It's only going to get better."

Ethan hooked his arm beneath her left knee, lifting her up, using the wall as support for her back. "Bring your legs around my waist," he told her. Moving his hands beneath her as her long legs slid around his hips, he smiled. "Now, relax against the wall. Put your hands around my shoulders, angel. I've got you."

Trusting him completely, Sarah wrapped her arms around his shoulders, trembling violently. She felt his erection barely graze her ravenous body. He teased her aching entrance. Her breath exploded in shallow gasps as she tipped her head against the wet tiles and Ethan pressed more firmly against her entrance.

The soft raindrops fell around them. As his lips captured one of her hardened nipples, Sarah arched, her fingers digging deeply into his shoulders, her hips thrusting against him. The electric bolts coursed wildly between her nipple and womb, making her sob out his name. She writhed against Ethan, wanting him inside her.

When he slid into her yielding body, Sarah's spine arched outward off the wall, head thrown back, a hoarse cry ripping out of her. She felt the hard muscling of his taut shoulders beneath her restless hands; her nipples were crazed with delicious, ongoing shocks. He held her easily, moving her hips slowly, allowing her time to accommodate him. He teased her nipples unmercifully, building her toward another wave of pleasure.

Ethan took her mouth, drawing Sarah deeper into the vortex of his body, his hands and lips. She quivered violently as he began to thrust rhythmically, more deeply into her with each stroke. The sensations made her mewl; the sound was absorbed by his mouth over hers. He deepened his kiss, sliding his tongue into her mouth, feeling her fiery reaction, wanting her in every possible way.

Their breaths unraveled and Sarah began to feel her flesh dissolve into his.

The warmth of the trickling water against her sensitized skin, his mouth suckling her hard nipple, moving her into a mounting rhythm, took her even deeper into the consuming fire racing through her. Sarah felt boneless in Ethan's arms, held captive between his hard, demanding body and the slick wall. The screaming pressure of an orgasm rose like a tsunami, and her entire lower body seized up. She jerked in a breath. As Ethan thrust hard and deep, she was consumed by the rippling implosion of an almost painful release competing alongside the most intense pleasure she had ever experienced.

The wild undulations of her body tightened repeatedly around him, and all Sarah could do was arch against him, hoarsely crying out Ethan's name. The intense fever pulsated through her mind, erasing it, connecting her only with the spasms of pleasure in their joined bodies.

And just when Sarah thought she could take no more pleasure, she heard Ethan's animal-like growl as he pulled her savagely against him, his face pressed between her glistening, wet breasts. A deep shudder worked its way through him. He rasped her name, clenched his teeth, eyes tightly shut as he rocked powerfully into her, taking her with him. Awed by her own body's response to his climax, Sarah felt fused into Ethan's flesh, into his soul as he held her tightly afterward, breathing in harsh gasps, his entire body quivering powerfully with release.

Barely opening her eyes, Sarah weakly leaned forward, kissing his wet hair, his temple, jaw and neck. She felt absolutely ravished in the best of ways. She rested her brow against his; the water like warm fingers soothed their trembling bodies. It was a delicious experience.

Sarah slid her hands up across his bearded jaw, drowning in his dark gray eyes. "I love you, Ethan." Sarah saw his face crumple with joy, saw a sudden glimmer in his eyes that could only be tears. And then Ethan gave her a smile that infused her heart with such happiness that she thought for a moment she would die from this heaven.

Ethan slowly lifted her off him and allowed her feet to gently touch the tiled floor. He held on to Sarah as her knees nearly buckled. Her blue eyes were lustrous, fulfilled. She stared up at him in wonder. Her mouth was soft, pouty and well kissed by him. Ethan leaned against her, aware of his weight pinning her gently against the drenched wall.

"Sarah, you are beautiful," he told her. His whole body was hotly collapsing in on itself. Glowing coals of desire burned his lower body with satisfaction. He eased wet strands of her hair away from her flushed cheeks and smiled into her eyes. "I love you, Sarah Benson. I see you, angel. And you are perfect and beautiful inside and out to me."

Sarah awoke slowly. She didn't know what had awakened her. Content and wrapped within Ethan's arms, their bodies pressed warmly against one another in the bed, Sarah sighed softly. Her head was nestled beneath Ethan's jaw, her cheek against the soft hair of his chest. Feeling the slow pound of his heart beneath her palm, she felt a wave of such intense love for this man. It literally made her want to weep for joy. How long had she waited for someone like Ethan? She never thought a man like him existed at all. And then she'd pushed him away because she felt so ugly inside.

Sarah blinked back tears, realizing how rare Ethan was. He'd forgiven her. How lucky she'd been, thinking that her life was doomed to men who were selfish and self-serving. Even now, her body glowed; Ethan was drawing out the fractured feminine part of her that had remained hidden until now. Sarah felt him stir. It was that SEAL alertness. She lifted her head, looking into his half-opened eyes.

"I didn't mean to wake you," she whispered, reaching up and kissing his mouth. What a mouth Ethan had. It was so sensual, strong and cherishing all at the same time. Sarah felt like she was a goddess being worshipped by him as he groaned, rolled onto his side and took her mouth more deeply. She could feel him growing hard against her belly, and heat skittered through her core, wanting him all over again.

Easing from her mouth, Ethan rasped, "Waking up anytime with you, angel, is a miracle to me." He kissed the tip of her nose. Ethan settled back, gathering her into his arms, drawing her one leg over his, holding her close.

Sarah slid her hand against his jaw. "I just woke up," she whispered. "And I was thinking, how did I ever manage to meet you? I've never met a man like you, Ethan. I'd always dreamed of someone like you existing, but after a while, after several forgettable relationships, I gave up." Sarah pressed a kiss to his chest, feeling his muscles flex beneath her lips. She trailed her fingers languidly through the soft strands of hair across his powerful chest. She felt Ethan's calloused hand move in a caressing gesture across her shoulder and down her good arm.

"And here I was thinking the same thing."

She laughed softly, hearing the thickness in his voice. "You can't tell me women don't fall all over you."

Ethan stirred, sifting strands of her dry, silky hair through his fingers. Her hair glinted like black diamonds in the soft moonlight peeking around the floor-to-ceiling drapes. "I never found the woman I was looking for," he admitted huskily, "until I met you. And I knew you were the one." One corner of his mouth pulled up in a wry smile. "And with your reputation as a man killer, I was trying to find some way to meet you without you nailing me with one of your karate black belt moves."

"Man killer. Really, Ethan, that's over the top." Sarah sniffed, her feelings hurt.

He heard her protest and lost his smile. Easing her head onto the pillow so he could look deeply into her slumberous eyes, he said, "I understand now why you closed up when you were around men at the canteen and at the chow hall." Seeing the pain he'd caused by his words, Ethan gently pressed his lips to her hair, inhaling her sweet, womanly scent. "You were protecting yourself, Sarah. And I can't blame you."

"I wish," she said, her throat tightening as she became lost in the tender look in his gray eyes, "that I could just forget those first twelve years of my life."

The anguished admittance caused his heart to contract with pain for her. "I wish I'd known you then. I'd have realized something was wrong. I might have been able to protect you." Ethan wondered how many times Sarah, as a young, scared little girl, had fallen through the cracks of the state child protection system. Hadn't the social worker seen a change in her behavior? Seen the frightened look he now saw deep in the recesses of her shadowed blue eyes? Why the hell hadn't some adult cared enough to see Sarah was being sexually abused by her foster father for all those years? He felt rage, and he wanted desperately to erase the painful beginning to her life, but he couldn't.

Sarah fought back the tears. Ethan's face was open and vulnerable, his words a balm for her wounded psyche, her fractured soul. Just the look burning in his eyes, the care he bestowed on her, the love he shared, had a healing effect on her whether he knew it or not.

"I tried running away so many times, Ethan. I was so scared. I tried to be a shadow, tried not to get Bill's attention. There were three of us girls there and…" She shut her eyes, her voice broken. "And he took turns with us. I knew when it was my turn. I could feel him hunting me. I ran. I always ran."

A sob caught in her throat. "Every time, he found me. Every time, he picked me up in his arms, say hello to the neighbors, as if out for an evening walk as he took me back into the house. After a while, I couldn't even cry. I just…left my body. I wanted to die." Sarah covered her face with her hand, feeling a huge upwell of grief surging through her.

Ethan cursed softly, pulling Sarah into his arms, rocking her, holding her. "That sick sonofabitch," he snarled. "I'm so sorry, Sarah…God…" His voice trembled with emotion. "It won't *ever* happen again, Sarah. Not ever."

The perfect evening with Ethan was once more

spoiled by her past, Sarah thought, as she cried unwillingly in his arms. For over a decade, she had sworn not to cry, not to give voice to her shadowed past, and she had not. There was just something about Ethan that dissolved her shields. Sarah was vulnerable once more. Ethan rocked her slowly in his arms, as if she were that hurt child, trying to soothe and calm her. There was such savage pain ripping through her heart. She sobbed, and her tears flowed across his chest and were absorbed in his dark hair. Sarah couldn't stop the convulsive sobs that tore out of her. She'd never cried like this in her life, never released the terror and hurt that still resided deep within her soul.

Ethan felt helpless rage. As a SEAL, he hadn't often felt that because there were always steps to be taken, actions to be initiated. How could he affect Sarah's haunting past, which even now threw a shadow over her life?

Ethan closed his eyes, pressing small kisses against her tangled hair, feeling anger he couldn't act on.

And what amazed him the most was Sarah's warrior side, which was solid, brazen and gutsy. But the woman side of her, the wounded, abandoned child living within her—there was a war going on for control of her soul.

Slowly, Ethan was beginning to grasp that he had forged more of Sarah's trust between them tonight. And it was probably the first time she'd ever given so much to a man. After all, a man had killed a part of her soul, taken something from her so precious and beautiful, without asking. God, he wanted to kill that bastard with his own two hands. Was that the ugliness she felt inside herself?

Ethan buried his feelings deep. "You know what?" he rasped softly against her temple, strands of her hair tickling his nose and mouth. "You are a treasure to me, Sarah. You are giving me your trust, your heart and your incredibly sensitive, beautiful body. You are an extraordinary being, angel. And if you don't know that, then I intend to show you over time just how beautiful a woman you are."

Ethan gave Sarah a long embrace, as if to imprint his emotional words on her heart. In the deepest recesses of himself, he wanted to help Sarah heal from what she had endured as a child. He was stunned to realize that he'd somehow slipped past those walls, her defensiveness, her distrust. Now he understood even more deeply his responsibility toward her, to treat Sarah as the woman he saw in her, not as how she felt inwardly about herself. Ethan could show her the way through his caresses, his loving her, his treating her as an equal so that she was allowed to discover herself.

It scared the hell out of Ethan when he looked at the larger picture, comprehending the depth of wounding Sarah had endured. Only love, his mother had told him over and over again, could ever heal a broken heart. And in Sarah's case, a broken soul. But even a broken soul could be put back together with love. And he had more than enough love in his heart to share it with her.

Sniffing, Sarah murmured apologetically, "I'm sorry, Ethan. I didn't mean to bawl like a baby."

"You never have to apologize to me, Sarah. You needed a good cry," Ethan assured her, reaching over to the nightstand to find her a tissue. "I'm glad I was the one you trusted enough to cry with."

Sarah sniffed, blotted her eyes and blew her nose. Ethan ached for her, seeing the terror deep in her grief-stricken blue eyes. No wonder she had appeared so sad when he'd first met her. His intuition had been right about how truly disconsolate she was. He held her tightly in his arms.

"I learned early on crying didn't help anything. It just got me into more trouble, not less." Sarah dabbed her eyes, content to be curled up and surrounded by Ethan's body. She felt safe in her always unsafe world. Sarah looked up into his shadowed, serious face. "I guess it's you," she said. "There's just something about you that if I fly apart and I know you'll catch all the ugly pieces of me."

"That's what a good relationship should be, don't you think? Taking care of one another?" Ethan took his thumb and brushed away the tear clinging to her cheek. He knew the brave woman medevac pilot. Hell, he'd seen her in action twice. And yet, when it came to personal relationships, she was a cowering child, so unsure of herself. He wanted to kill Caldwell. The force was so powerful within him that Ethan had to compress his lips and not say it out loud. It wouldn't help Sarah.

"You're different," Sarah finally said, her voice a little stronger. "I was watching you this morning coming up the sidewalk toward me. I saw other men around, but none of them walked like you did. There's such a rock-solid confidence in you, Ethan. The way you look at me makes me want to melt, not cringe. And when you smile at me, I swear I feel sunlight flooding my soul."

"Now who's the poet?" Ethan teased, kissing her cheek, her brow, inhaling her scent. Just breathing in Sarah's sweet, fragrant skin was an aphrodisiac to him in every way. Her lips curved into a partial smile.

"No, you're the poet." Sarah looked up at him. "How did you get the way you are? The way you see the world? How do you see through people so easily? Your words are incredible. You paint such beauty with them."

Ethan closed his eyes and laid his head back on the pillow, contentment flowing through him. "Blame my mom. She's written and published many books of poetry. She schooled all of us kids in words and their meanings. I remember she began teaching us Latin, as a root language, when I was nine years old. She was a teacher in school and a teacher to us in all kinds of good ways."

"Do you all write poetry?"

"No. It just rubbed off on me, I guess."

"Maybe that's why you're different," Sarah murmured, trying to find out what made him unique and, therefore, trustworthy with her heart.

Ethan laughed a little. "Well, don't tell my SEAL brothers I write poetry or I'd never live it down. They'd razz the hell out of me. I keep a journal with me and when I get time, I write in it about my feelings, what I saw, what touched me, what made me cry or laugh. Sometimes, when I'm inspired by something amazingly out of this world, I write poetry." Ethan opened his eyes and shared a tender smile with Sarah. "You caught my attention and inspired me the first time I saw you. I went back to my tent, and I couldn't write fast enough to put all the beautiful things about you down in words that I saw and wanted to capture."

Sarah absorbed his whispered words, feeling his emotions very close to the surface. This was Ethan's vulnerable side he was sharing with her. The one he never showed his fellow SEALs, but it was equally a part of him. "How do you reconcile these two very different sides of yourself?"

Ethan shrugged. "My journal. The guys just think I'm keeping a daily journal that I'll someday give to my kids, when I have them. And that's not a lie—that's what I let them think. Sometimes—" he rested his arm across his eyes "—the stuff I see, I can't wrap my mind, morals, values or beliefs around. The children starving, going barefoot, so thin and hungry. I use the journal more for a personal way to dump my feelings, good and bad, on white paper. It's better than turning into an alcoholic or trying to run away from the monsters I've seen up front and close. And it's better than pretending I'm tough and nothing can bother me. Because it does."

Ethan lifted his arm from across his eyes and sifted strands of her silky hair between his fingers. "And sometimes I cry, Sarah. There's more than a few pages in my journal that are crinkled with my tears because I let go. I never write in my journal around the guys. I go off somewhere alone where I can think and feel."

"Maybe that's why I trust you, Ethan. You're in touch with your emotions. You can cry when most men can't."

He tangled his long, scarred fingers between her own. Light against dark. Male entwined with female. And it felt so good. So wonderfully freeing to Sarah.

"Listen, the other SEALs will never admit this, but they cry, too. When one of us is wounded or, worse, killed, we're crying for days afterward. It's so gut-wrenching. It's like losing a brother you loved so much and he's torn out of your life so suddenly…forever."

Sarah watched as he closed his eyes, as if not wanting to remember those devastating times when he'd lost friends. She ached for him. "That's the problem with war," she said, frowning. And it was their problem, too. They were both risk takers in the unpredictable business of chaotic war that played no favorites.

Sarah loved the slow beat of his heart beneath her ear. A heart that loved her. "Ethan? Where are we going? I've got another six months here to fulfill before I get sent stateside with my squadron." She searched his gaze. "War makes realists out of everyone. The idealist in me wants to preserve what we have, but I'm so afraid. We live dangerous lives."

"I'm a dreamer, too, Sarah." Ethan continued to run his hands through her silky hair, feeling her relax beneath his ministrations. "Nothing can destroy love if it's held by both people. Not even a war." His mouth flattened. "We're always going to be in a gunfight as long as we're at Bravo. There's nothing either of us can do about it." He eased Sarah onto her back, propping up on one elbow, his other hand moving slowly across her belly. "I have one fix, though."

She saw the gleam in his eyes. "Uh-oh, when I see

that look, I know you're up to something." She grinned. His hard face was deeply shadowed. A stranger would find Ethan's look frightening. But she knew the warrior and the poet beneath that rugged sunburned, bearded face. She had experienced his love, his care and protection.

Ethan's mouth quirked. "It's a little fix," he amended, drowning in her soft blue gaze. "I can let it be known by my platoon that you're my woman, that we're serious about one another."

Sarah started to open her mouth to protest, and he pressed his finger to her lips. "Hear me out."

Sarah nodded and kissed his finger.

"SEALs look out for their own. They will protect you as quickly as they would me. No man on that forward operating base will ever dare make any kind of pass at you again, Sarah, if the word gets out you belong to a SEAL. And that will get out fast among a thousand guys. They know SEALs won't tolerate anyone bothering their woman." His voice dropped with controlled anger. "And that Army guy trying to rape you won't ever happen again. I could have killed him with the blow I gave him. We're taught how to kill very quickly and efficiently, but I pulled my punch on him and stunned him instead."

A hard glitter came to Ethan's eyes. She felt his rage for just a second before he hid it from her. The saying that if you scratched a civilized man, you'd find a savage just beneath the surface of his skin applied fully to Ethan. He was so gentle with her, sensitive, loving, but just as suddenly, in a different situation, he was a battle-hardened warrior who would fight to his last breath to protect her. She'd seen him in battle twice and knew.

"Yes, well, I tried to take out that guy first. I was walking near the building, just turned the corner and I heard someone coming up behind me. I turned just in time to see his fist coming down at me. I know he wanted to knock me out, but thank God for my karate training. I sidestepped and it was a glancing blow. When he thought he had me on the ground, I hit his nose and broke it. And then he got pissed. I hit him in the eye when he tried to drag me up to my feet. I knew he was trying to haul me around the other corner of that building where no one could see what he was going to do to me." Sarah shivered, remembering it all too clearly.

"My focus was on you," Ethan told her quietly. "All I wanted to do was disable the bastard because your nose was bleeding and you were hurt."

"You still have that interview to look forward to," she said with distaste. "Since I was here at Bagram, I went over one afternoon to the military police station and they took my testimony."

"That bastard is going to get court-martialed and thrown out of the military. And he'll get a helluva lot of brig time."

"I hope so," Sarah said.

"That's why I want you to give me permission to tell my platoon you're my woman." He tipped his head, seeing her thinking her way through it.

"Given what happened, I'm okay with it. If I ever

get attacked again and you're not around, maybe one of
your SEAL friends can step in and help me."

"That's the idea," Ethan said. "You got nearly a thousand horny men at Bravo. And you got maybe sev-
enty women, mostly pilots. And you're always going to
have some bastard like that Army guy who thought he
could take what he wanted and get away with it. Seeing women as weaklings, something he could control."

"Well, I wasn't a weakling. If you hadn't come along
when you did, I was going to fight until he killed me
because I was *not* going to give in to the bastard."

Ethan believed her. Sarah was a scrapper of the first
order. Flying that Black Hawk, she took no prisoners,
either. She expected the same courage of herself as she
did her crew. And he wondered if some of that courage
had been born in the fires of hardship and experiences
she'd had in her young life. What was the saying? What
didn't kill you made you stronger? Sarah was a case in
point. Nobody messed with her and got off lightly. He
smiled a little. "Well, you're going to have thirty-nine
of my brothers watching your back from now on," he
murmured.

Sarah closed her eyes, inhaling his wonderful male
scent of sun, desert and him. "I think I'm going to like
having thirty-nine big brothers," she agreed.

Ethan felt Sarah begin to fall asleep. He smiled and
gently caressed her hair, feeling her lush body fully
relax against him. God, was there any better feeling
than this? Just having her in his arms, her shallow
breath flowing softly across his chest, seemed like a

dream to Ethan. What were the odds? The last thought he had as he drifted off to sleep was how they could hold what they had and not lose it to the chaos of war.

Chapter 17

Ethan stood just inside Ops at Camp Bravo, watching Sarah land the Black Hawk medevac. She'd passed her requalification for medevac pilot status at Bagram yesterday. Sarah had brought two new and badly needed replacement medevac pilots back with her to the forward operating base that morning. He smiled, casually leaning against a column that faced the doors out to the tarmac. He hungered for Sarah. His heart felt lonely without her in his life. Now he was discovering what real love was about.

Ethan's mind revolved around to some of the married SEALs in his platoon. Those who had stable marriages and strong partners were solid operators. They could focus and carry out their parts of a mission. Other SEALs who had weaker marriages were preoccupied.

They were distracted a little or a lot and consequently made mistakes out in the field.

Ethan was now appreciating what love and commitment meant in the world of black ops. It was a fine balancing on the edge of the sword. He watched Sarah leave the Black Hawk and walk with the two pilots who would bring their medevac squadron up to the needed personnel once again. That would mean Sarah would get time off. With him. He watched with quiet pride as she brought the two male pilots into Major Donaldson's office.

Sarah caught Ethan's eye. She smiled warmly in silent welcome to him and lifted her hand in his direction as she escorted the relief pilots into Donaldson's office. Her heart picked up in beat and her body began to glow inwardly. *Just a look.* One look from Ethan's hooded gray eyes and she was melting. It was a wonderful sensation, and Sarah welcomed it into her life. He loved her. She loved him. For the first time, she knew what love was, what it felt like, how much it could lift her and start taking the stains of the past and dissolving them forever. Sarah loved Ethan with a fierceness she couldn't put in words.

Ethan watched the other men in Ops. When Sarah arrived, all eyes gravitated to her. She oozed sensuality. And she was completely unaware of it. When she left Donaldson's office, the pilots taken care of, he eased from his position against the column. Now he was going to make damn sure the thirty or so males in Ops knew that Sarah was his woman. As he walked toward her,

Ethan gave her an intense look. Her mouth widened into a soft smile of hello.

Sarah was caught off guard as Ethan took her into his arms and kissed her long and deep. The expression in his eyes as he finished the powerful kiss was one of him possessing her. Claiming her heart. Her soul. Sarah's eyes widened in shock. She hadn't expected any contact with him out in a public place. Ethan merely gave her the confident smile of a male proclaiming what was his. Shaken, she quickly looked around Ops. Every man was staring openmouthed at them. And then Sarah wondered if Donaldson had seen it. She turned. His door was closed. He was busy with the two newly assigned pilots coming into his squadron.

"Ethan," she whispered, pressing her hand against her pounding heart.

"Come on," he urged her quietly, placing his arm beneath her elbow and guiding her toward the other doors that opened up into the tent city of Bravo.

Outside, Sarah gave him a distressed look. "Why did you do that?"

"Didn't you like it?"

"Of course I did. It was—unexpected. We're not supposed to show affection to one another in public."

And then, as they walked toward the SEAL HQ area, Sarah got it. Her mouth tingled in the wake of Ethan's branding kiss. She liked it. A lot. A week without Ethan was excruciatingly painful to her. "Okay, I know why you kissed me in Ops."

He chuckled and slid her a sidelong glance. "Yeah?"

What a male alpha wolf Ethan really was.

"You're lucky Major Donaldson didn't see it. I could be in trouble with him."

"I waited until the door closed, angel. I'm not going to put your career in jeopardy." Ethan gave her a burning look. "He's going to hear about it through the gossip mill, anyway, which is faster than the internet. And I don't think he's going to say anything to you about it. So relax."

Feeling flushed, Sarah muttered, "This is your way of telling the men here at Bravo to back off, isn't it?" Kiss her in public, a not-so-subtle warning to the males, that she was Ethan Quinn's woman. And everyone knew about the SEALs protecting their own, and it wouldn't be lost on any of them.

Ethan's mouth pulled into a slight grin. "I wanted to send a very clear message to everyone that you're my lady."

Groaning, Sarah said, "All I want to do now is hide."

"No," he said, meeting her worried gaze. "No more hiding, Sarah. You've done that all your life. This is a chance to change and break that pattern. You have nothing to be apologetic or embarrassed about. You're allowed to love me. And these guys around here know it."

There was such a pleased expression on his face. The gleam in his gray eyes reflected a savage male satisfaction. Okay, maybe Ethan was right. She had been running all her life. But now he was in her life, a part of it in a way she'd never had any experience with. And his confidence in himself was like a beacon to Sarah. Ethan didn't care who saw them, that he'd just pulled her into his arms and kissed her breathless. Men were just…dif-

ferent that way. It wasn't Sarah's way, but maybe she
was getting a taste of a man who cared enough, loved
her enough, to defend and protect her. And he'd sent the
warning out to everyone. It couldn't be misinterpreted.
It was just such a strange sensation to Sarah, having
never been afforded that kind of sanctuary before.

"Let's go in," Ethan coaxed, opening the door to
SEAL HQ.

Sarah saw the gleam in Ethan's eyes. He wasn't taking no for an answer. "You had this all planned out,
didn't you?" she accused him.

"Guilty on all counts, angel." Ethan waited patiently,
holding the door open for her. "It's time you meet *my*
family. They're going to love you."

Sarah wanted to run. She hadn't met any of the other
SEALs at Bravo except for Ethan, the master chief and
the wounded in the medevac. In a way, she felt like she
was entering a wolf's lair. Ethan placed his hand against
the small of her back, gently easing her forward. Un-
easy, Sarah trusted him enough to step into the narrow hall. Her heart was pounding with fear. It was a
throwback to another time and place. Being in a crowd
of strange men frightened her and Sarah felt panic eating at the edges of her composure. As if sensing her
distress, he placed his arm around her shoulder and
walked her down the hall toward a room at the end of it.

"Relax," he whispered against her ear, placing a
quick kiss to her hair. "These are my friends, Sarah.
They have my back." And then his gaze held hers. "And
now, they're going to have your back, too."

Sarah put on her game face as Ethan directed her

into a large room. There were long tables with maps strewn across them. In one corner was a coffee machine. She was amazed to see it was an espresso machine. Against another wall were bleachers, three deep. And on another wall was a big whiteboard. She noticed red, blue and green markings on it, and she assumed it was for a patrol mission. She saw several SEALs sitting and gabbing with one another at a few tables, coffee in hand. Other SEALs were playing with their Game Boy devices.

They all looked up when Ethan entered.

Sarah had no expectation except to be stared at like a piece of meat on a hook. SEALs had such a reputation with women. Instead, Ethan guided her down a side hall. He halted outside a small room and knocked politely.

"Master Chief Hunter?"

"C'mon in, Hawk."

Sarah eyed Ethan worriedly.

"Relax—he likes you," he whispered, kissing her wrinkled brow.

Sarah's heart pounded anyway as Ethan led her into the platoon's master chief's office. The room was small, and Gil Hunter sat behind his desk. Sarah met his green eyes. He had a black beard and was darkly tanned, and she instantly sensed the power he held in the SEAL platoon as she had when she'd met him before.

"Ah, Chief Benson," he murmured, rising and thrusting his hand across the desk toward her. "It's about time. Come in—take a seat."

Stunned by his warmth and sincerity, Sarah took one

of the two chairs in front of his desk. "It's nice to meet you again, Master Chief Hunter." At least her voice sounded cool and calm even if her heart and stomach were doing flip-flops.

"You can call me Gil. Do you mind if I call you Sarah?"

"Er, no, I don't mind," she stammered. She'd always heard military formality wasn't a SEAL strength.

Ethan sat down. "Gil asked me to bring you over here for a reason, Sarah," he told her.

"Oh?" Was she in trouble? That was the only reason one got hauled up in front of the head sheds, the officers or the chiefs who ran a platoon. She pushed her damp palms against the thighs of her flight suit, watching as Hunter sat down.

"Would you like some real coffee, Sarah?" he asked her warmly.

"Uh…no, sir." She was too tense and worried to even drink espresso.

Nodding, Hunter smiled at her as he leaned back in his creaky red leather chair, his hand on the desk. "Relax. We don't bite. And you don't need to call me sir."

She managed an unsure smile. "Yes, sir… I mean—"

"Call me Gil. Sir is left for the head sheds I work under, okay?"

Hunter's voice was low and filled with natural authority. His voice, like Ethan's, could calm a person. His eyes were wide-spaced, intelligent and hard-looking as he met her less than confident gaze.

Hunter held some sheaves of paper toward her.

"These are two reports written up by Hawk here on the two medevac flights that you flew to rescue Marines and then our SEALs who had been badly injured."

Sarah took them, wondering where he was going with this conversation. "Yes, Master Chief? I mean—sorry—Gil."

Hunter rubbed his well-trimmed beard. "Our OIC reads them after I read them. We put notes, maybe questions or suggestions, on the last page. Hawk then has to answer them or elaborate further on anything that he's written up in his original report."

"Okay," Sarah murmured, giving him a confused look. "That's SOP with any squadron." She saw a glint in the man's eyes and felt as if he was subtly maneuvering her. But to where? And for what reason? Sarah felt uncomfortable. Ethan, who sat next to her, was grinning.

"My point," Hunter said, gesturing toward the reports in her hands, "is that myself and the OIC came to the same conclusion about your rescue of wounded men."

Great. So what did this mean? Sarah scowled. "Okay," she said warily.

Hunter sat up and handed her another piece of paper. "On the flight you flew involving some trapped Marines and SEALs, you went in hot. I found out through the transom that your CO, Major Donaldson, was pissed off at you for doing it."

"Wait a minute," Sarah said, rising anger in her tone. "I was given approval by the Marines HQ and SEAL HQ to go into that firefight and pick up those injured

Marines. Major Donaldson had originally given his approval on me doing so." Her nostrils flared, and she thought she was in hot water again because of that mission. Only this time, it was coming from the SEAL community. *Damn!* "When I flew back into Bravo, I had it out with my CO the next morning about his switching approvals on me. I was in the right, and he dropped the charge against me for disobeying his direct order."

"At ease, Sarah," Hunter soothed, holding up his hands. "This isn't a witch hunt aimed at you. It's supporting you and your bravery under fire to pick up those Marines who would have died if you hadn't had the balls to fly into that lead curtain. Okay?" He leaned across his desk and handed her another paper.

Startled, Sarah frowned and took it.

"Will you look at the paper I just handed you?" Hunter urged quietly, studying her beneath his thick brows.

Heart pounding, her anger and defenses well in place to protect herself, Sarah forced herself to read the paper in her hands. Her mouth fell open. She snapped a look across the desk at Gil Hunter, who had amusement in his eyes.

"This…this is a recommendation that I receive a Bronze Star and a V for valor?" Shock rolled through Sarah and she blinked once. In all her years as a medevac pilot, she had never been considered for any medals, except for the standard ones everyone received. She didn't live to collect medals like some of the other pilots in her squadron. They simply weren't part of her reality.

Hunter nodded. "Indeed, it is. My OIC has signed off on it and the paperwork has gone forward through SEAL Command Team Three in Coronado and is now sitting on the desk of Admiral Thompson, who is in command of all SEALs. I spoke to him yesterday by sat phone and he's going to authorize the medal for you, Sarah."

Ethan grinned a little more. "You earned that medal, Sarah. I was there. I saw what you did."

Heat flushed up her neck and to her face. Sarah felt as if she were pomegranate red, staring at the master chief, at Ethan and then down at the medal recommendation in her hand. "My crew and I were just doing our job, Master Chief. Nothing more."

Hunter shrugged and gave her a slight smile. "SEALs take the fight to the enemy. We've had instances in the past where medevac pilots were ordered to stop and not fly in to come pick up wounded. You—" his voice lowered "—have a special kind of courage, Sarah. And in our community we like to recognize someone who's going to come in and rescue wounded men, even if it's hot." His voice turned amused. "And after reading Hawk's two reports on your two mission rescues, I've just got a very dirty feeling that if you had to, you *would* go against orders and fly in and rescue wounded men. We owe you and your crew the lives of two of our SEAL operators in that second flight. This is our way of thanking you for your courage under fire."

Shaken, Sarah closed her eyes for a moment, tears burning in them. She choked down her tears and opened her eyes. "With all due respect, Master Chief Hunter—"

she handed the paper back to him "—my CO probably won't approve of it. I'm very touched you would do this for me. I didn't expect it. All I want to do is my job." And then her voice shook with emotion. "All I want to be able to do is protect wounded men and women out there. They deserve our best effort."

Ethan knew where that comment was coming from. He loved Sarah passionately, her flushed face, her emotional voice. Glancing at Hunter, who seemed equally affected by her low, ferocious words, Ethan knew the master chief would have her back. No question.

"Well," Gil murmured, smiling a little, "your CO can't stop this even if he wanted to. It's a Navy commendation. There's not anything the Army can do to stop it or protest it. Understood?"

"I didn't know that, sir. Yes, sir. I mean…yes, Master Chief Hunter."

Gil eased up in his chair, folding his large hands on the desk in front of him. "I think you know Dr. Tisdale at Bagram put you in for a medal when you saved our SEALs?"

"Yes, she told me she was going to do it. She said my CO would have to sign off on it." Sarah saw the master chief's eyes go from warm to hard.

Gil said, "My camp spies have informed me that Major Donaldson circular-filed her recommendation that you receive a Bronze Star. He denied it and refused to approve it."

Sarah heard the growl in the SEAL's tone; he was clearly upset with her CO's action. "I'm not surprised," she said quietly. "I'm not exactly his favorite pilot in his squadron." Again, she saw carefully banked anger deep in the master chief's eyes.

"We take a different attitude toward you, Sarah. Courage isn't predicated on gender. Hawk here has written in his reports that you're not only a fine pilot, but you take fire and stand your ground. That's the kind of people the Navy *wants* to support. You're a lifeline to us, and we know it. What makes you stand out is your coolness under fire and your flight skills." Then he said, "You're a SEAL by proxy in that area, Sarah. SEALs run toward a fight, not away from it, and you have the same heart as we do. It should be celebrated and you should be rewarded and supported for it."

Sarah didn't know what to say. She leaned back in the chair, her folded hands resting in her lap. "All I want to do is save lives, Master Chief. That's my reward. It's all I'll ever need."

"Understood." Hunter stood, took the reports and said, "Now, I think we're wanted out in the big room."

Confused, Sarah stood with Ethan. She shot him a questioning look. Ethan gave her a reassuring smile, his hand resting on her back, guiding her out of the door to follow the master chief down the hall.

When Sarah entered the large room, there were thirty-nine SEALs standing around a table that had a huge cake placed in the center of it. They snapped to attention when Sarah appeared. She saw Master Chief Hunter turn, and he held out his hand to her.

"Sarah, would you come over here and stand with me?"

She left Ethan's side and moved to where Gil Hunter

stood on the opposite side of the table. The SEAL platoon was facing them. Three SEAL officers stood with
their men, as well. She came to a halt next to Hunter.
She was completely confused.

"Men, let's give Chief Warrant Sarah Benson a big
welcome, shall we?" he called out.

Instantly, a huge *"Hooyah"* boomed out of the
SEALs and echoed around the room. Sarah was
stunned. Every man's gaze was on her. A fierce look.
A look of pride. A look of thank-you for what she'd done
for their brothers. And more than anything else, a sense
of overwhelming protection toward her.

"At ease, you animals," Master Chief Hunter
drawled, grinning.

The men broke into laughter.

Sarah watched as the SEALs relaxed. Shaken to her
core, she realized she'd been set up. Ethan, who joined
her, was smiling the most, pride gleaming in his eyes
for her alone.

"Would you do us the honors, Sarah?" the master chief
asked, handing her a large, vicious-looking KA-BAR
knife. "I think these guys are looking for a pretty big
piece of your medal cake."

Sarah looked down and saw a bronze medal with
a *V* for valor carefully designed in the enormous cake
covered with white frosting.

Her eyes filled with tears. Pursing her lips, she
nodded, unable to speak because her throat was tight.
Ethan's hand gently came to rest on her shoulder, and
she was glad for his unspoken support in that moment.
It gave her the strength to not cry as she stepped for-

ward with the knife carried by many of the SEAL operators. The cake was their way of thanking her. No one had ever celebrated her in this way before.

She turned to Hunter. "Master Chief, do you think this is a big enough knife to cut this cake?"

Snickers rippled through the SEAL platoon, who eagerly waited for her to cut up the cake.

Hunter grinned and chuckled. "SEALs are kinda Texas-size, Sarah. We do everything big or we don't do it at all. Go big or go home."

Sarah looked over at the platoon and became solemn. Her voice choked up as she whispered, "You are all heroes in my eyes." She shyly looked away, focused on the cake and began to cut it into big pieces. Someone took an official picture with a camera and many cell phones flashed as Sarah cut the cake.

Ethan saw every man's face go soft for a moment over her emotional words. What Sarah didn't understand was that she was *their* hero. His love for her moved powerfully through him. Stepping forward, he took the paper plates filled with cake and began to pass them out to his brothers.

The officers came over and shook her hand and thanked her. Sarah was then thanked by every man in the platoon, one at a time. They were sincere. Sometimes, their voices were strained with controlled emotion. In a few cases the men's eyes were suspiciously bright because Sarah had saved their closest friends from dying. She was getting an up-front and close understanding of just how tight the SEAL community was. And how much she was now a part of it. Ethan knew no other military unit on the face of the earth had the unparalleled team power of SEAL camaraderie. They took care of one another. They took care of their own. And now, she was going to realize that they would take care of her here at Bravo.

As he watched her expression as she shook each SEAL's hand and listened closely to what each had to say, he saw a remarkable change in her demeanor. Ethan sensed it with his highly attuned intuition. Sarah was now, for the first time in her life, experiencing the positive side of male respect. And he knew that it would help heal her fear of men in general, over time. SEAL protectiveness wasn't just a word or a concept. It was practiced 24/7/365. And to feel the care and sincerity from these men, who were unquestionably grateful that she'd saved their brothers' lives, was a powerful lesson in humanity between the genders and vividly poignant for Sarah. Someday, she might save one of them. He saw Sarah struggle not to cry.

"And just to be clear about Chief Sarah Benson," Gil Hunter said as the last SEAL shook her hand and thanked her. "We want her to know that she's now a part of our platoon. She isn't a SEAL, but she belongs to a SEAL, and that makes her an extended part of *our* family." Gil turned toward her, his eyes showing his emotions for the first time. "You're family now, Sarah. Hawk is a part of us, and now you've got a whole bunch of big brothers who will do anything they can to help you. You know so little about us, but you need to also know that if you need anything, you come and ask me. If there's something bothering you, see me. If I can fix it or make it happen, I'll do it. When Hawk is out on a patrol, you can always come over here and stay with us if you're worried or concerned about him. We've created a little room here at HQ with a locker and bed for you, just in case. This is your second home here at Camp Bravo if you want it. And, frankly, we'd rather have you staying with us than in that Army tent."

Tears ran down her cheeks, and there was nothing Sarah could do about it. Ethan stepped over, moving his hand across her shoulders, comforting Sarah.

Sarah struggled to stop the tears. She wiped her cheeks and whispered brokenly, "Master Chief, I'm more than grateful to all of you. T-thank you."

Ethan felt his chest tighten. He gazed over at his SEAL brothers. "This means a lot to Sarah that you have her back." He felt a lot of deep emotions well up in him, making his voice husky. "What you guys don't know is that Sarah has never had a positive male figure in her life. She didn't have any brothers. I know all of you will treat her like a little sister and be there for her when I can't be."

When she looked up through her blurred vision, Sarah noticed how vulnerable the men seemed, no longer hard or unreadable. There was moisture in some of their eyes, too. She felt Ethan's hand smooth gently across her shoulders, consoling her. "I just want to thank all of you for this—" Her voice cracked. Sarah wiped the tears from her eyes with trembling fingers. She looked to the right, where Gil Hunter stood. His expression was kind, not hard. "You remind me of the father I wish I'd had." She reached out, taking his hand

and squeezing it. "This is just the most mind-blowing day of my life, Master Chief."

"I'm the father of this platoon," Hunter told her, gently releasing her fingers. "And I have a lot of sons here, but now, I have a daughter here, too." He gave his SEALs a stern look. They all nodded in agreement. A master chief ran the platoon, not the officers. They were regarded as a god to the rock bed of the SEAL community. When they spoke, everyone listened, including the officers.

Sarah felt warmth open her heart. "I like being adopted by all of you, Master Chief. Thank you."

Gil smiled a little. "Why don't you go check out your new digs, Sarah? The guys here have been working on it for a couple of weeks. We hope you like it. We know you have a ready room at your squadron headquarters, but when you're not on standby status and you get lonely or want some brotherly company with these animals, come on down and stay with us. We can guarantee you the finest espresso coffee on this base." He grinned broadly.

"Hoooyyahhhh!" the SEALs roared, laughing and slapping each other on the back.

Sarah sat with Ethan in the room the SEALs had all had a hand in building, painting and decorating for her. There was a small wooden table, a chair and a lamp. The bed was a twin with a new thick mattress. She had no idea how they'd gotten one; it was such a rarity. There was a small TV with a recliner in another part of the room. They'd painted the walls a pale pink color for her benefit. Best of all, there was an air-conditioning unit in the room. No tent at Bravo had one, and everyone sweated through the summer nights. Just having cooling air was such an amazing gift to her. Deeply touched, Sarah didn't know how to begin to thank these men who were so far away from their own homes, their loved ones.

"I'm overwhelmed," she admitted hoarsely, sitting at the desk, looking at Ethan, who sat on the bed. "I just never thought…" Sarah swallowed hard, her chest tightening once more with emotion.

"I understand," he whispered, resting his elbows on his thighs, his hands clasped between them. Ethan saw the shock still rolling through her over their surprises for her. "It was the master chief's idea," he confided. "He read my reports on those two missions you flew on. Later, he made a call over to Major Donaldson after sending copies of the reports over to him. He asked your CO if he was going to put you up for a medal. When Donaldson said no, Master Chief took things into his own hands. He has ears all over this base and he found out how much the other pilots in your squadron were continually hazing you. It pissed him off. And when you piss off a master chief, you'd better run for cover. He decided you needed another kind of ready room over here, with us. We might be animals, but we don't eat our own kind."

"Then he knew about you and me?"

"Nothing escapes the attention of a master chief," Ethan said, chuckling. "Nothing. They know the military system, how it works, where it can be bent or redirected. And Gil was really pissed off at how you were being treated by your own squadron. He set about rectifying it."

Rubbing her face, Sarah muttered, "God. Now I hope it doesn't piss off Major Donaldson."

"Oh," Ethan said, raising a brow, "I don't think the major is going to do anything to you. Master Chief went over and had a closed-door chat with him a week ago. It didn't go well for your CO," Ethan said, grinning.

Eyes widening, Sarah whispered, "Oh, no…what happened? Do you know?" She knew Donaldson, who barely tolerated her, could screw her royally on this one. He could get even in so many ways and make her life even more miserable than it was already. Worse, he could subtly end her Army career of flying medevac over time. Her heart began to pound in earnest.

"No worries," Ethan assured her. He straightened, rubbing his hands on his trousers. "This goes no further than the three of us," he warned her. "No one knows the power a master chief has in the Navy or among the other military branches. It just so happens that Hunter has lines and favors into all of them. He told Donaldson to sit on the men who were constantly harassing and hazing you. And that if he didn't stop it, he was going to talk to the Army colonel who runs this medevac squadron, who is a longtime friend of his. Donaldson got the message loud and clear."

"You went to Gil, then? Told him about it?"

"Yes. I didn't want you coming off being wounded and coming back into your squadron to get hazed by those guys again, Sarah. Master Chief said he'd take care of it." Smiling a little, Ethan rubbed his hands together. "Donaldson was told by him that you're being awarded that medal. He said he wouldn't protest or try to stop it. In fact, I'd say that in the coming weeks, Sarah, you'll find the pilots in your squadron being very nice toward you." Satisfaction in the form of a low growl came out of him.

Sarah shook her head, in shock over all the events.

"Master Chief warned the major that if any pilot gave you crap from this day forward, he'd send one of his SEALs over to talk to that guy behind closed doors. And that it would be the last time that pilot ever played a mean joke on you, harassed you or didn't treat you with respect and as an equal."

"My God," she whispered.

"SEAL power, angel. You don't screw with our women, pure and simple." Ethan gave her a wolfish grin, his eyes glittering with love for her. "Donaldson will ensure you will be respected and that the hazing stops immediately. No one likes a SEAL in stealth mode coming over to visit them in the middle of the night."

Sarah drew in a ragged breath. "I'm just in shock, Ethan. It's going to take me a while to get used to all of this." She gestured around the room. Someone had found some silk flowers and thoughtfully put them in a vase for her. SEALs were so much more than she'd ever realized. Incredible men. A tight, fierce group of warriors who really did look out for one another. "I feel—" she held his warm gaze "—I really feel, well…wanted."

Ethan rose from the bed, walked over and pulled Sarah into his arms. She came willingly, sliding her hands across his shoulders. "Angel, you *are* wanted. You risk your life for so many. Frankly, it scares the hell out of me, but you're a warrior in your own right and I respect that." He eased strands of silky black hair behind her delicate ear. "You're just as much in harm's way as any SEAL is." Ethan's voice fell, and he became serious. "You're a part of us now, Sarah. You're mine. And now you've just joined the rest of my big, crazy family. From this day forward, you aren't going to have to hide any longer. You can go have a beer over at the canteen without feeling like a stripped piece of meat on display. You got thirty-nine other brothers here at Bravo who will make sure you're safe and protected when I'm not around."

Murmuring Ethan's name, Sarah leaned against him, resting her head against his chest. "I'm just reeling…." Her heart opened to him, to his breath against her temple, his lips pressed against her hair. "Thank you, Ethan."

"I love you, Sarah. Never doubt that." Ethan eased her away. "Remember that letter that Master Chief gave to you from me?"

"Yes. I carry it in my flight suit like you asked me to."

"Did you ever read it?"

She saw his eyes warm with love for her. "No. He told me not to open it, just to carry it on me when I flew. Why?"

"Are you carrying it now?"

She pulled out of his arms and bent down and opened

the large flight pocket on the right thigh. "Yes." Sarah pulled it out and handed it to him.

"Come here," Ethan rasped, pulling her over to the bed and sitting down beside her. He handed her back the badly crinkled, soiled white envelope. It was smudged with dust, wrinkled by her sweat. "Open it, Sarah. This is for you...how I see you."

Carefully, Sarah pulled out the paper and opened it.

A Love Poem to Sarah
By Ethan

Sarah, my precious and astounding beauty,
When puzzling pieces of a life
Conspire to carry its righteousness,
Then fortune and fame take steady flight
To locate a key in a once reluctant heart
Should make any man become truly fortunate.

And when this one man
Is blessed in simple seasons
To lift his heart beyond paths of sight
He loves one woman beyond all reason
And seeks to curry capricious circumstance
To harvest his love and to make it right.

I know the hardships committed in battle, Sarah,
The brave growth required to engage in a fight
I understand strength to save fellow SEALs
Timely reactions and the disciplined will
But I hardly understand the drive and discipline

You bring within me from the depth of what I feel.

I could not choose to live without you
I could not stand to step aside
From the wellspring of feelings
I champion to be able
To love you till the bookends of time
With absolutely no regret and nothing to hide.

You are my enduring beloved
And journeying through life
There is nothing left to show
Save to have you next to my side
That's all of eternity I require to know.

Wherever you go, I protect you from harm
No matter where you are securely hidden,
I am pledged to connect with you, to adore you
To find your aura bidden to merge with mine,
Love lifts you like a heat-seeking laser to my
arms.

I am devoted to shelter and take care of you
I am earnest to comfort you and to keep you real
I feel that our souls create one perfect shining
Like an ancient dowser, I'm yours and I'm divining:
We merge deeply as one, our fates intertwining.

You are my immortal beloved
And even if I should have to journey
To the gates of hell, I could never abandon you

No matter how harrowing, I will keep you well
I am your staff and your rod and I will nurture you
As your wellspring for gladness and your uncom-
promising future.

I will become your heritage and you will become
mine
We're each other's playmates till the last breaches
of time
You bless me with your touch, it's almost too
much
That I feel both elated and endlessly refined
Pulled into a perfect orbit when you artfully recline.

I've seen you bloom under my constant care
Just as your presence makes me want to linger
And you can trust I will be your extended family
As you see that I have only goodness to share
To lay at your lotus feet to make us both more
aware.

When you touch my soul
When you caress my lips with a finger
When you cause my heart to implode
I am certain there cannot be another
We are destined for happiness with each other.

We will have a glorious lifetime together
Through snow or sleet or inclement weather
And I sense that when you have my heartstrings
There is little I could withhold from you my darling

You are mine and I am yours
Through the gracious and radiantly eternal
sunshine.

* * * * *

Don't miss Sarah and Ethan's next adventure
in DEGREE OF RISK, available March 2014
from Harlequin Romantic Suspense!

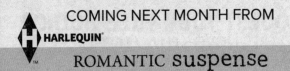

COMING NEXT MONTH FROM

HARLEQUIN®

ROMANTIC suspense

Available March 4, 2014

#1791 DEGREE OF RISK
Shadow Warriors • by Lindsay McKenna
After finding love in a war zone, medevac pilot Sarah Benson is taken hostage. Her last and only hope for rescue is her lover, Ethan Quinn. This SEAL will break every rule in the book to save the woman he loves!

#1792 DEADLY HUNTER
Conard County: The Next Generation
by Rachel Lee
When his sweet and stubborn neighbor receives death threats, veteran Jerrod Marquette steps in to protect her. But the closer they get to the truth, the more he falls for Allison, only to discover too late who the real threat is....

#1793 THE ROME AFFAIR
House of Steele • by Addison Fox
Rivals Jack and Kensington find their professional relationship heating up as the two strong-willed security experts go undercover in the Italian wine country to catch a diamond smuggler.

#1794 THE BURDEN OF DESIRE
by Natalie Charles
When a murder victim turns up alive, prosecutor Sally Dawson's career is on the line. She has no choice but to team with her ex Ben McNamara. But is it her error, or a criminal who just may have committed the perfect murder—and won't hesitate to kill again?

REQUEST YOUR FREE BOOKS!
2 FREE NOVELS PLUS 2 FREE GIFTS!

ROMANTIC suspense

Sparked by danger, fueled by passion

YES! Please send me 2 FREE Harlequin® Romantic Suspense novels and my 2 FREE gifts (gifts are worth about $10). After receiving them, if I don't wish to receive any more books, I can return the shipping statement marked "cancel." If I don't cancel, I will receive 4 brand-new novels every month and be billed just $4.74 per book in the U.S. or $5.24 per book in Canada. That's a savings of at least 14% off the cover price! It's quite a bargain! Shipping and handling is just 50¢ per book in the U.S. and 75¢ per book in Canada.* I understand that accepting the 2 free books and gifts places me under no obligation to buy anything. I can always return a shipment and cancel at any time. Even if I never buy another book, the two free books and gifts are mine to keep forever.

240/340 HDN F45N

Name _____ (PLEASE PRINT) _____

Address _____ Apt. # _____

City _____ State/Prov. _____ Zip/Postal Code _____

Signature (if under 18, a parent or guardian must sign) _____

Mail to the **Harlequin® Reader Service:**
IN U.S.A.: P.O. Box 1867, Buffalo, NY 14240-1867
IN CANADA: P.O. Box 609, Fort Erie, Ontario L2A 5X3

Want to try two free books from another line?
Call 1-800-873-8635 or visit www.ReaderService.com.

* Terms and prices subject to change without notice. Prices do not include applicable taxes. Sales tax applicable in N.Y. Canadian residents will be charged applicable taxes. Offer not valid in Quebec. This offer is limited to one order per household. Not valid for current subscribers to Harlequin Romantic Suspense books. All orders subject to credit approval. Credit or debit balances in a customer's account(s) may be offset by any other outstanding balance owed by or to the customer. Please allow 4 to 6 weeks for delivery. Offer available while quantities last.

Your Privacy—The Harlequin® Reader Service is committed to protecting your privacy. Our Privacy Policy is available online at www.ReaderService.com or upon request from the Harlequin Reader Service.

We make a portion of our mailing list available to reputable third parties that offer products we believe may interest you. If you prefer that we not exchange your name with third parties, or if you wish to clarify or modify your communication preferences, please visit us at www.ReaderService.com/consumerschoice or write to us at Harlequin Reader Service Preference Service, P.O. Box 9062, Buffalo, NY 14269. Include your complete name and address.

HRS13R

"What if someone is still using that poison?" she said as soon
as she saw him.

He leaned back against the counter, folding his arms. For
the first time she noticed he was armed with both knife and
pistol. "My God," she whispered.

He looked down, then looked at her. "I wasn't going out
there without protection. Want me to ditch this stuff?"

"Ditch it where?"

"I can put it by the front door with my jacket, or take it
home."

She met his inky gaze almost reluctantly. He really did come
from a different world. Well, not totally. Plenty of people
hereabouts had guns, and some wore them. But somehow this
felt different. Maybe because she hardly knew this man and
he was in her house?

Still, why this reaction?

Because there was only one reason he would have carried those weapons today. And it explained why he'd eaten lunch with his parka still on.

"I'll go home," he said.

"No." The word was out almost before she knew it was coming. "I'm just surprised." That was certainly true. "I don't have any guns. Well, except for the shotgun in the attic. It was my dad's."

"A moral objection?"

"No. This is gun country. I'd have to object to most of my neighbors if I felt that way. I'm just not used to seeing weapons inside my house."

"Then I'll get rid of them."

"It's okay. Really. This is you, right?"

Something in his eyes narrowed. "Yeah," he said, his voice rough. "This is me. This is me on high alert. I don't need to be on alert in your kitchen."

"I hope not."

Without another word, he unbuckled his belt and removed both holsters from it. The sound of leather slipping against denim, the sight of him tugging at his belt, caused a sensual shiver in her despite the situation. She repressed it swiftly.

**Don't miss
DEADLY HUNTER by *New York Times*
bestselling author Rachel Lee,
available March 2014 from
Harlequin® Romantic Suspense.**

ROMANTIC suspense

THE ROME AFFAIR
Addison Fox

A Risky Collaboration

It's bad enough that Jack Andrews had once again snatched a plum job away from House of Steele. But now that the assignment has gotten complicated, he wants Kensington Steele to partner him. Danger didn't faze the cool, controlled security expert, but working closely with her mind-numbingly attractive competitor completely unnerves her.

The assignment led them to the Italian vineyard of a diplomat suspected of diamond smuggling. Kensington was determined to keep things professional. But working undercover as a team fanned the flames of their mutual desire. And with a murderer stalking them, the threat to their lives only intensifies the risk to their hearts.

Look for *THE ROME AFFAIR* wherever books and ebooks are sold, available March 4, 2014.

Heart-racing romance, high-stakes suspense!

HARLEQUIN®

A *Romance* FOR EVERY MOOD™

**Stay up-to-date on all your
romance-reading news with the
Harlequin Shopping Guide,
featuring bestselling authors, exciting new
miniseries, books to watch and more!**

The newest issue will be delivered right to you
with our compliments! There are 4 each year.

Signing up is easy.

EMAIL

ShoppingGuide@Harlequin.ca

WRITE TO US

HARLEQUIN BOOKS
Attention: Customer Service Department
P.O. Box 9057, Buffalo, NY 14269-9057

OR PHONE

1-800-873-8635 in the United States
1-888-343-9777 in Canada

Please allow 4-6 weeks for delivery of the first issue by mail.